Chasing Red

Chasing Red

LAUREN WINDER FARNSWORTH

AN IMPRINT OF CEDAR FORT, INC.
SPRINGVILLE, UTAH

ISBN 13: 978-1-4621-2003-1

Published by Bonneville Books, an imprint of Cedar Fort, Inc.
2373 W. 700 S., Springville, UT 84663
Distributed by Cedar Fort, Inc., www.cedarfort.com

LIBRARY OF CONGRESS CATALOGING-IN-PUBLICATION DATA

Names: Farnsworth, Lauren Winder, 1986- author.
Title: Chasing Red / Lauren Winder Farnsworth.
Description: Springville, Utah : Bonneville Books, An Imprint of CFI, Inc., [2017]
Identifiers: LCCN 2016058706| ISBN 9781462120031 (perfect bound : alk. paper) | ISBN 9781462127627 (ebook)
Subjects: | GSAFD: Love stories.
Classification: LCC PS3606.A7262 C47 2017 | DDC 813/.6--dc23
LC record available at https://lccn.loc.gov/2016058706

Cover design by Priscilla Chaves

Edited by Hali Bird and Jennifer Johnson
Typeset by Jennifer Johnson

Printed in the United States of America

10 9 8 7 6 5 4 3 2 1

Printed on acid-free paper

To the amazing examples of loving and selfless motherhood
surrounding me—sisters, sisters-in-law, aunts, grandmothers,
cousins, friends . . . you all inspire me. But specifically to my own
angel mother, Carie, and my mother-in-law, Alice—it
is impossible for me to describe to you how much you
mean to me. Your examples have had a more
profound impact on me than you know.
I love you both so much.

Also by Lauren Winder Farnsworth

Catching Lucas Riley
Keeping Kate

One

"You know, Ryder, most people would feel some semblance of gratitude to the friend who had been there to punch Grey Marshall in the teeth after he managed to fly every single pair of bikini briefs they owned from the high school flagpole," Kara said, offhandedly chomping on her gum and shrugging. "Just sayin'."

I grinned at my best friend as I shoved my last folded T-shirt into my suitcase and tucked a lock of my dark red A-line bob behind my ear. "I'm still not convinced that it wasn't you who gave him the contents of my underwear drawer," I pointed out. "Your attempt to keep me here, while valiant, is ineffectual."

"Okay, fine," Kara drawled, pushing herself up from her lounging position on my bed and flipping her long blonde hair over her shoulder. "Who needs you? I'll go find myself another best friend. Preferably someone stupid and lazy who won't get a rockstar job in the big city and decide to desert me in my most formative years."

I barked out a laugh. "Formative years? Kara, I'm fairly certain you've left those far behind you."

"You know I'm mentally stuck in high school," Kara pointed out. "But if you feel you can still sleep at night knowing you've left your bosom friend socially floundering in the suburbs of Salt Lake, feel free to carry on." She heaved an exaggerated sigh and collapsed back on the bed, her five-foot-seven frame draped dramatically across it. When this elicited no reaction from me, she sat up again quickly. "Can you at least *try* to fit me in your suitcase?"

"No can do, jellybean," I replied, zipping up my suitcase with a flourish. "I am officially all packed with not an inch to spare."

"That was quick," came the voice of my mom from the doorway behind me. "In fact, it was so quick that I'm thinking you're leaving a whole host of things behind that I told you to take with you." She raised a dark eyebrow at me as she began opening drawers and closets.

"Mom, I can't drag everything I own to New York with me," I whined, heaving my suitcase off the bed and rolling it to stand next to my other bags. "I have to take the essentials only. You know, clothing, books, shoes, that kind of stuff."

"This room is not yours anymore," Mom pointed out, hands on her hips. "You can't just leave it all here. It's in the way. This is exactly why I told you to get a storage unit weeks ago."

"It makes no sense to get a storage unit when you have a half-empty storage room downstairs," I reminded her. "Seriously, Mom, no offense, but this is literally the last thing on my mind right now. I'm about to move to the other side of the country. This is a huge deal for me. It would be nice to feel like you cared about more than just turning my room into a craft space."

Welcome to my relationship with my mother. I know most girls leave the bickering behind in their teenage years, but I admit, I didn't manage to succeed at that feat. It's not that I like fighting with her. I really, really don't. But my mother is the Supreme Chancellor of the Guilt Trip. She typically doesn't come right out and tell me what I should do; she hints and implies and insinuates until I'm ready to scream for mercy. And then she offers sighs, head shakes, and mournful looks until I comply. And I hate it.

You might say my mother was a deciding factor in my decision to take a job in New York after I graduated from BYU with my master's degree in accounting. The two might have been related. You know, a bit. The problem is, she knows it. She is fully aware that I decided to move half a world away from my own family because I just can't take it anymore. The *gentle guidance*. The "well, that's not what I would do" looks. The expressions that imply that I have a distinct lack of answers for all questions directly related to my life path.

You might wonder on which topics my mother is so eager to guide me. The answer: all of them. She's had silent but resolute input into every decision I've made since I elected to wear the pink My Little Pony shirt to my first day of preschool.

Don't get me wrong. My mother is a wonderful woman. She's good and kind and unselfish. She's one of those people who is always first to volunteer to bring a Jell-O salad to the ward potluck and to shovel off widow so-and-so's driveway when it snows. She's been the president of nearly every church auxiliary group available to her in our South Jordan, Utah, LDS ward, and she's even paid those presidencies return visits as a counselor several times over. My mother amazes me.

So maybe I should rephrase. If I'm being completely honest with myself, maybe the reason my mother played such a large part in my decision to hoof it two thousand miles away was because I failed miserably at being her. She was the Ultimate. The Mother Theresa of the South Lake Fourth Ward. And I was the daughter who was nothing like her.

"Emma!" I heard my dad's voice call from below. "Pizza's here!"

Mom sighed and shuffled toward the door. She disapproves heartily of pizza. Perhaps that's why I had requested it as my last meal before heading off to the Big Apple. Where, by the way, I hear they have great pizza.

Before she left the room, she turned back to me and pointed to the closet. "If that stuff isn't in boxes in the basement before you leave, I'm Fed-Ex-ing it to you." She gave me one last threatening look and closed the door behind her.

"So back to my dilemma," Kara grumbled, turning to glare at me. "How exactly am I supposed to enjoy the rest of my twenties with my best friend across the country?"

"Well, there is a solution, you know," I pointed out as I began pulling things out of my closet to stuff in cardboard boxes. "You could always come visit."

Kara sat up straight. "Do you mean it? You actually want me to come stay with you?"

I suspected all the dramatic sighs and grumbling I'd endured from Kara today were calculated to get us to this moment.

"Of course I want you to come stay with me," I replied, smiling. "One of the primary reasons I decided to take this job was so I could provide you with cheap accommodations when you feel like hitting up New York." I winked at her.

"You really do care!" Kara cried, throwing her arms around me.

I laughed and hugged her back. "I really do, Kare-Bear."

- - - - -

"Sure you have everything?" my dad asked as he piled suitcases on the airport luggage cart. "Check now or forever hold your peace."

"I can think of about a dozen things she's missing," my mom muttered from behind me. I bit my lip to keep from smiling. To be perfectly honest, she was right. I had been fairly sneaky in what I had managed to spirit into the basement storage room the night before.

"Pretty sure," I answered my dad. I squeezed my hands into fists in the pockets of my skinny jeans and bounced up and down on my toes. Nervousness was warring with excitement inside me as I thought about the adventure I was about to begin.

My dad slung the last suitcase on the cart and turned to me, running a hand through his sandy brown hair contemplatively. "Are you sure you don't want us to come in with you? You might need help getting all of this to baggage check."

"No, I got it," I assured him. I wanted to avoid the airport good-bye scene. I absolutely detested good-byes. I was one of those people who would quietly sneak out the back door with her box of stuff on the last day of a job or skip graduation day just to avoid the awkwardness of tearful farewells. This was no different.

Don't misunderstand me—I would definitely miss my parents. But I figured the expressiveness of my leave-taking would likely have no effect on how well we were all able to cope with the separation, so I might as well make it as painless as possible for everyone involved.

"Well, see ya," I said, reaching out to begin pushing my luggage cart toward the terminal doors.

"Not so fast," my dad said, grabbing me by the neck of my shirt. "You don't get to just skip away this time. This is a little more permanent than your first day of kindergarten."

"Aw, Dad," I moaned. "But—"

"Tough beans, kid," he interrupted, pulling me against his chest. I felt his lips press into my hair. His arms tightened around me, and I could feel all of his worry in that single embrace. For a moment, I managed to feel a slight twinge of guilt at what I was putting him through. As his only daughter—heck, his only *child*—I knew there was little in the world he worried about more than me. To watch me move across the country on my own was probably the scariest thing he'd ever experienced. I allowed him to squeeze me tight, and I even managed to return the embrace.

"Be good, Red," he said, clearing his throat. His nickname for me, while unoriginal, was also his way of showing me how special I was to him. My dad hated nicknames, an attitude borne of being referred to as "Georgie Porgie" from birth through his senior year of college. My nickname was the only one he used—his way of telling me he loved me.

"Always," I grinned at him, feeling another twinge of guilt at the sheen of tears I saw in his eyes. Not wanting to develop a sheen of my own, I quickly turned to face my mom.

"Bye, Mom," I said, stepping forward to hug her. She took me by the shoulders and stopped my advance. Her bright green eyes stared fixedly into mine, and I knew I was about to receive her parting advice. I should have known.

"Ryder Alice Redmond," she began, her voice fierce, "We raised you to know exactly who you are. You know what is expected of you. Don't leave the path."

This advice may seem cryptic. It wasn't. I knew exactly what she was talking about. My mother's favorite teaching tool was the "straight and narrow" analogy. I had spent half my life hearing remonstrances to "stay the course" and "follow the path." Honestly, with my mother looking over my shoulder, I wouldn't have dared step a toe off of it. Not that I was planning to do so with her no longer breathing down my neck. But at least now I could skip calmly and voluntarily along my way, no longer frog-marched by the matriarch. Needless to say, I was about as surprised that she had chosen to make this her parting message as I was that the sky above me was blue and cloudless in mid-July.

"I know," I assured her, refraining from rolling my eyes with great effort. "I got it."

She didn't seem reassured by my response. "I mean it, Ryder. You have no idea how sheltered you've been."

Wanna bet? I thought silently. Nobody knew better than me how sheltered I'd been.

"The world is a darker and scarier place than you realize," she continued. "Stick to what you know. Stay on the path."

"I know, Mother," I almost whined, my voice reverting back to my pre-teenager tone. "I promise I'm not moving away so I can live a secret life of crime."

"Not a joking matter, Ryder," my mom chastised. "Just . . . remember what you've been taught."

"Trust me, forgetting it is an impossibility at this point," I assured her, attempting to sound sincere instead of sarcastic. I stepped forward again and gave her a quick squeeze. "I'll call when I land in New York."

Pushing the luggage cart quickly across the street toward the terminal, I could feel my parents' eyes on my back. I stopped at the door and turned to wave one last time. Ten feet to freedom. I could almost taste it.

Two

I stood staring at the mass of people in front of me. So. Many. People. And I was only twelve inches inside the JFK terminal.

"Seriously? You're going to stop *right there*?" came an irritated voice from behind me. I glanced over my shoulder to see a girl about my age glaring at me. She had beautiful milk chocolate brown skin and hair standing out from her head in tight, dark ringlets, gold highlights woven throughout.

"Sorry," I murmured, jumping out of her way, yanking my duffle bag and carry-on with me.

She eyed me with contempt and huffed, walking quickly past me with a canvas bag swinging from her shoulder and her carry-on bag rolling behind. I watched her walk away, envying her confidence. Now that I had officially made it to the big city, the sudden assault of so much of the unfamiliar made me want to turn right back around and camp out on the plane until it happened to make it back to Salt Lake.

The thought of myself huddled in the back corner of an airplane, pining for my hometown was enough to snap me out of it. Straightening my shoulders, I followed the ringlets bouncing thirty feet in front of me down the concourse.

I found the baggage claim relatively easily thanks to the abundant signage, but realized I had a problem as soon as I had all my bags pulled off the carousel. I had two large suitcases, a massive duffle, and my carry-on. How on earth was I supposed to get all this stuff to my hotel?

"Girl, did nobody ever teach you how to pack light?"

I turned to see the same girl I had been following eyeing my bags with incredulity.

"You some kind of diva or something?" she asked, her dark brown eyes transferring to my sweaty, flushed face.

"No," I said defensively, rubbing an arm across my forehead. "I'm just moving out here, so this is all my stuff."

"You realize that most sane people just sell their stuff before they move to city like New York and buy new stuff when they get there, right?" she asked pointedly. "They don't just haul it all along with them."

"Tell that to my mother," I said with considerable sarcasm.

She studied me for a second before speaking again. "What's your name?" she asked.

"Ryder," I answered. "Ryder Redmond."

"Did your parents give you a cheesy superhero name on purpose?" the girl asked, a skeptical eyebrow raised.

"A what?" I asked, confused.

"You know, Pepper Potts, Peter Parker, Bruce Banner . . ." she looked at me expectantly, waiting for me to catch on.

"Yes, my first and last name start with the same letter," I said, drawing the only conclusion I could from her words. "But I have no idea who any of those people are."

"So do you not like movies or something?" she asked, chomping her gum. "Because those names have been all over Hollywood for the past ten years."

"I'm a movie purist," I claimed. "I watch the old classics. You know, *Casablanca*, *It's a Wonderful Life*, *Sunset Boulevard*, *Charade*, the Rodgers and Hammerstein musicals, that kind of stuff."

The girl just shook her head at me. "Whatever," she said, obviously deciding the topic wasn't worth pursuing. "I'm Lily. I need to take off, but do you know what you're doing? Where you're going? I'd feel bad just leaving you here like this."

"You would?" I asked, surprised. She didn't seem like the overly empathetic type to me.

"Well, for about thirty seconds, anyway," Lily conceded. "Look, the taxi station is over there. You ever taken a cab before?"

"Um, not really," I admitted sheepishly. "We have probably five of them in Salt Lake. You know, total."

"Okay, well just tell the driver where you want to go and that's about it. Make sure to tip him. They take cards, but they prefer cash. Or you could Uber; that works too."

"Oh, right, Uber. I've heard of them. So is there a number I call or something?" I asked brightly.

Lily stared at me. "Just take a cab," she said. Her voice was a notch above contempt. A very small notch.

"Right," I said, trying to gather up my belongings and drag two suitcases with one hand. Lily watched me struggle for a few seconds before rolling her eyes and grabbing the handle of one of my suitcases.

"Come on," she said in disgust, dragging the bag toward the door of the baggage claim. "You are never going to survive in this city."

- - - - -

Once in the taxi with the address of my hotel given to the driver, I thanked Lily and watched as she strode away. I would have liked to talk to her more, despite her sassy attitude, if only to feel like something in New York was semi-familiar.

As the taxi made slow progress toward my hotel, I pulled out my phone and reviewed my schedule for the next couple of days. My first day with Durham & Tucker, a large international accounting firm, was roughly a week away. The company was paying for my stay in a hotel for a while until I was able to locate an apartment. I had started apartment hunting almost immediately after I had accepted the job, and I had appointments to visit a few in the next couple of days. There was a distinct lack of choice in my price range, which I had heard was pretty common in the New York real estate market, so I was really just glad to have any options at all.

My three options were all in Midtown, relatively close to the firm's location in Rockefeller Plaza, and all three required that I take on an immediate roommate. Meaning that I was being brought in as a candidate for that position, as all three apartments already had at least one resident. And despite the fact that living with a total stranger in a foreign city made me slightly nervous, I was grateful to know that I wouldn't be footing a massive monthly rent payment all by myself.

My first apartment viewing/interview took place the next day, and it did not set a positive tone for the others. Turns out the name "Sasha" may not actually be exclusively female. In fact, that name can also belong to a very burly, blond, Russian, male ballet dancer. Despite my initial shock at his gender, he was very nice, and proceeded to introduce me to the apartment and to his live-in girlfriend, Galina. The apartment had two bedrooms, the only apartment option on my list with that many, and Sasha and Galina were more than fair, offering me one of the bedrooms with only a third of the rent, but I could practically feel my mother's horror at finding out I had a male roommate. And somehow, I didn't think that the idea that the male roommate had a live-in girlfriend would assuage her worry. I thanked the frankly gorgeous pair for their offer, but politely declined.

The next apartment visit fared slightly better, as my potential roommate was at least a female. But that's about where the improvement ended. My "room" was actually the wide-open living room, and my "bed" was actually the couch. Which I was expected to share with her three mewing cats. All this I could enjoy for the low, low price of $2,000 a month (which I happened to know was significantly more than half of the total rent). No thanks.

I was silently praying by the time I reached the third apartment. If this didn't work out, I was back to the drawing board, with only five days before my new employers kicked me out of my hotel room. This apartment, as far as I could tell by my googling, was the swankiest on my list. It was in the Hell's Kitchen neighborhood, which I'd been told had been "gentrified" in the past several years, whatever that meant. I found when I arrived that the building was nicer than any I'd visited thus far. Which I had to admit, I liked. I was fairly certain that the apartment belonged to a female, given the name listed as my contact was "Lillian Thompson," so that was a definite step in the right direction. My heart brimmed with hope. But when the door opened, my mouth fell open too.

"You!" said the owner of the dark corkscrew curls as she stared dumbfounded at me. I stared right back, my eyes fixed on my beautiful, chocolate-skinned airport savior.

"Lily!" I exclaimed. "This is your apartment?"

"No, I routinely break into other people's apartments just to answer the door," she replied sarcastically. "What are you doing here? Did you stalk me or something?"

I shook my head, blinking silently. "I'm here about the room," I finally stuttered.

Her eyes narrowed. "Really? You're my three o'clock appointment?" She studied me carefully for a moment. "So what's with giving me a false name? That *really* makes me want to let you into my place."

"What false name?" I asked, confused. "I didn't give you a false name."

"Didn't you say your name was Red Rider or something weird like that at the airport?" she asked pointedly. "The girl who called to take a look at my place said her name was Kara." She raised an eyebrow at me.

"Oh!" I replied, recollecting. "That was my best friend from back home. She helped me find different apartment options and make appointments."

"Uh-huh . . ." Lily said, looking skeptical.

"Look, I'll prove it," I said, pulling out my cell phone and dialing Kara's number.

"Did you make it?" Kara's eager voice answered almost immediately without greeting. "Or are you calling to say you're dead in a New York gutter somewhere and I should call the police and notify your parents?" Her voice was so loud that Lily eyed the phone warily.

"Nope, still living," I replied. "I'm at my last apartment appointment and it's one that you set up. Since you oh-so-wisely used your name instead of mine, I need to establish that I'm not some kind of psycho attempting to gain entrance under false pretenses."

"Oh, well, sure," Kara answered as though she understood perfectly. "Who do I have to convince?"

"Her name is Lily," I said. "Can you just tell her that you're Kara and that it was you that called to make the appointment for me? I'm handing you over now."

I handed my phone to Lily, stopping to tap distinctly on the screen where Kara's name was showing.

"Hello?" Lily said in a lifeless voice.

"I'm Kara and I made the appointment for Ryder," I heard Kara say loudly. "She's totally normal and you should definitely let her into your apartment. Understood?"

Lily didn't bother to answer, but handed the phone back to me and opened the door wider so I could walk in.

"All good, Kara," I chirped into the phone. "Thanks for your help!" She started to ask questions about my flight and my initial reactions to New York, but I cut her off. "Hey, I'll have to fill you in on all that stuff later, okay? I'll call you tonight."

She sighed but agreed, and I hung up.

Stowing my phone back in my bag, I walked past Lily into the apartment. Immediately I knew this was where I wanted to live. It was larger than either of the apartments I had already seen, and had big, bright windows along one whole wall. The apartment was ablaze with afternoon sunshine. It was only a one-bedroom place, but thin, temporary walls of something that looked almost like poster board had been put up around the living room space to create a second bedroom. A blanket was strung across the improvised doorway of the room for privacy, but was draped back so I could see the large window making up nearly the entire back wall of the makeshift bedroom. Furniture was jam-packed into almost all the free spaces of the apartment, creating a cramped, yet funky feel, thanks to Lily's decorating prowess.

"I love it!" I said, looking around.

"Well, don't wet yourself. I haven't even shown it to you yet," Lily grumbled, closing the door and walking past me. "Okay, over here is the kitchen," she started, gesturing to our immediate left as she shuffled around a circular table and four chairs crowding the space between us and the kitchen. "The floor is a perpetual ice block, only one of us can actually fit in there at a time, and the microwave is broken. Although I guess that's my fault since I haven't actually called maintenance about it."

She walked toward the area behind the kitchen, her steps creaking on the wooden floor. "In this back corner is the living room. It was supposed to be the dining room, but since we needed the living space for the second bedroom, my last roommate and I had to make do," she explained. The room held a squashy, comfy-looking couch and loveseat with a small circular table holding a dying plant crammed between them. A scratched but expensive-looking coffee table sat in the middle of the room, close enough to the couches to double as an ottoman, and a flat screen TV was mounted to the wall. Cozy.

Lily moved back toward the front door, sliding again through the tight space between the kitchen table and the temporary wall of the second bedroom. She gestured to the bedroom as she passed it, allowing me to take a quick look inside. "This would be your room, should I decide you don't freak me out," she said warily, eyeing me. "Like I said, it used to be the living room, so that's why you have the wood floor instead of carpet. It creaks like you wouldn't believe, so I am extremely strict about what hours of the morning you're allowed to, you know, walk around."

I laughed, but stopped suddenly when she didn't join me. Okay . . . that would be an interesting dynamic to play around with. I scanned the room quickly, noting the absence of a closet and furniture. Just a bare, white-walled room with a huge, sunny window. I adored it.

"This is the bathroom," Lily continued, moving off to the right of the front door and down a narrow hallway. The hallway was more of an alcove, with the tiny bathroom (no counter space whatsoever) to the left, and a shallow, empty closet to the right.

"This would be your closet," she indicated to her right as she walked into the alcove. "There's not much space in there, but it's the same size as my closet and I manage to make it work, so I don't want to hear any complaints." I stared bleakly at the three-foot square space. I couldn't imagine such a small space successfully holding all my clothing. I might have to resort to storing things under my bed.

"And this is my bedroom," Lily declared, opening the door at the far end of the alcove. Her bedroom was easily one-and-a-half times the size of mine and carpeted, but I didn't mind. The carpet looked a little like a potential biohazard anyway. She had a queen-size bed with a colorful comforter, a purple plush chair in the corner, a turquoise dresser against the far wall, and a huge plant in the corner by the wall of windows. The room was a riot of bright colors, which told me a lot about Lily's personality. Just by looking at her room, I knew we would mesh well.

"And that's about it," Lily finished. "I'm asking $1,500 per month for rent plus half of the utilities. Total rent is about $3,800, but I'd cut you a bit of break, since your room would be so much smaller than mine."

Moment of truth. I considered clasping my hands in front of me to make myself look more pitiful, but decided against it.

"So . . . what do you think?" I asked her, hoping she had made up her mind within the last thirty seconds. "Do I freak you out? Think you can handle me as a roomie? I promise I'm totally normal."

Lily studied me silently for a second, but finally sighed. "Well, I'll probably regret it, but I'm desperate. So, yes, the room is yours."

"Thank you!" I cried in relief, throwing my arms around the girl. She stiffened, but didn't push me away or anything. For some reason, that made me feel even better about the arrangement.

"So . . . you can pay for it, right?" Lily asked me as I backed away. "You have a job and everything?"

"Of course," I replied, looking at her strangely. "The whole reason I moved out here was for a job. I start next Monday with Durham & Tucker."

"What's that? Some kind of uppity law firm?" she asked.

"Accounting firm," I corrected. "Not far from here, actually. Rockefeller Plaza."

"That's only about a ten-minute walk away," Lily nodded. "Straight shot down 50th. At least your commute won't be too bad."

"So when can I move in?" I asked excitedly. "I have my hotel room through Sunday, but I'd like to get my stuff here sooner rather than later. Plus, I'll need to buy furniture."

"Whenever," Lily shrugged. "I'm pretty busy during the day, and I work most nights 'til at least midnight, so I hope you're not going to ask me to help you move or anything."

"No, I can figure it out," I assured her. "So if you work nights, why are you so busy during the day?"

"I have auditions pretty much every day, along with a few classes during the week."

"Auditions?" I asked. "Are you an actress?" I tried to keep the awe out of my voice, but it came through loud and clear anyway.

"Well, I'm trying," Lily responded with a sour look. "Unfortunately, making it big on Broadway is a pipe dream for most of us."

"Broadway?" I cried, even more starstruck. "So those classes you take are like—"

"Singing, acting, dancing. Yeah," Lily interrupted, nodding. "Not sure how much they're helping though."

"Why do you say that?"

"Well, I play the dazzling role of a waitress and bartender for six hours every night, so that's how good this whole Broadway scheme is working out for me."

"You'll make it!" I encouraged. "This all sounds like it's straight out of a movie! The young actress moves to New York, determined to make it big! Working nights and weekends to make her dreams come true! Struggling, suffering, pinching pennies, all while her family tells her it's not worth it and to come home . . . "

I stifled my romantic sigh.

Lily just stared at me, her look an almost comical mix of amusement and disgust. "Well, unfortunately, I don't fit very well into that scenario," she said. "I'm originally from Brooklyn, my parents have more money than they know what to do with, and they pay for all my acting classes, although if my dad really wanted to be helpful, he could pay for my apartment." Lily's sour look returned to her face. "Anyway, my mom wants me to make it big even more than I do, and when I ran into you in the airport, I was coming back from two weeks at my parents' vacation home in Maui. So, sorry to ruin your romantic rags-to-riches fantasy."

"Oh, that's okay," I relented. "I can just pretend."

Lily's mouth twitched, and I suspected that she was working hard to conceal her smile. This was the beginning of a beautiful friendship. I could just feel it.

- - - - -

I winced as the suitcase crashed unceremoniously to the pavement and the cabbie slammed the trunk. "So do you think you can—" I started to ask him, but he was already climbing into his car, and the squeal of his tires let me know just what he thought of my half-raised plea for aid. "—help me get this upstairs?" I muttered under my breath, watching him go.

Four days in, and so far New York was just as friendly as I'd always heard it was.

Groaning, I bent down and yanked the heavy bag upright and over the curb, where I set it next to the three other pieces of luggage. How on earth was I supposed to get this up to Lily's apartment by myself? I could do it piecemeal, but that would require leaving one of my bags sitting by itself on the curb while I took the others inside. I wasn't sure if I was okay with that. I could try to get the attention of the doorman I supposed, but I couldn't see him anywhere, so I assumed he'd stepped away for something. I looked helplessly from my bags up to fifteenth floor and back. And again.

Just as I was about to pull out my cell and plead with an unsympathetic Lily to come down and help me get my stuff up to the apartment, I heard an unfamiliar voice behind me.

"Need a hand?" I turned, and the noise of the street all around me seemed to fade to a muffled hum.

He was, without a doubt, the most beautiful male specimen I had ever seen.

He was probably just under six feet tall, with a head of thick, wavy, dark hair. His piercingly blue eyes were spaced ideally on a chiseled, lightly tanned face with a shadow of dark stubble around his strong jaw. He wore a tailored, pinstriped, navy suit and a striped red and blue tie. As I stood there staring at him, unabashed, he smiled crookedly, his lips parting to reveal a mouthful of absolutely perfect teeth. My knees weakened. I'd always been a sucker for nice teeth.

Realizing that he was staring at me quizzically, one eyebrow raised, I figured I'd better give speaking a shot. "Wha—I me—you kn—I . . ."

This was obviously going very well for me.

He chuckled, the sound rising from deep in his (undoubtedly) chiseled and brawny chest. "Everything all right?"

I attempted a cool, nonchalant smile and an airy wave and ended up smacking my hand on the raised handle of my oversized suitcase. Hard.

"Ow," I muttered, hoping he hadn't noticed. Although I would have seriously marveled at his lack of observational skills if he hadn't.

"Oh, are you okay?" He quickly reached out and took my hand in his, examining the red mark carefully. "That's going to bruise."

He was touching my hand. The gorgeous man with the perfect teeth was *touching my hand*. And his quizzical glance at my face let me know that he still expected me to speak—probably coherently. But I couldn't focus on anything but the warmth of his hand holding mine and the sight of his thick, wavy hair rustling in the breeze, and his crystal clear blue eyes watching mine. Intently. Expectantly. Erm . . .

"Yo! Ryder!"

The lovely man and I turned to see Lily marching toward us, the door of the building swinging closed behind her. "You called me ages ago to open the door for you. Ages," she emphasized moodily. Technically it had only been about ten minutes, but to a New Yorker, time appeared to move more quickly. "I've just been chilling up there, waiting for you to grace me with your presence. As if I haven't got better things to do. Who the crap is this?" She turned to glare at the beautiful man. I had no idea how she managed to maintain such an unpleasant expression when confronted with such magnificence.

"Damian Wolfe," the man replied, surprised at the sudden assault. He released my hand and held his out to Lily in a friendly way. She ignored it.

"Look, if you want her number, get her number. But I'm late for class, and I have to let her into the apartment. So chop chop," she clapped her hands smartly in his face. Damian's mouth twitched violently and he pressed his lips together to keep from laughing. He nodded seriously at Lily and turned back to me, studying me silently for a moment. I just continued to stare at his perfect features like an idiot.

"Well, maybe next time," he teased, tantalizing me with his long, thick lashes and amazing dentistry. "It was nice to meet you . . . Ryder." He winked, gave me one last dazzling smile, and then nodded at Lily before continuing on down the sidewalk.

I felt the air leave my lungs slowly as I watched him walk away, until they felt like wrung-out rags. Then, suddenly recalling my ability to communicate, I inhaled dramatically and turned to grasp Lily around the shoulders. "Lily!" I gasped. "Did you *see* him? Have you ever seen a more gorgeous face?"

Lily extricated herself from my grasp. "You're a lunatic," she stated unequivocally, looking into my face. "You don't even know who he is. He could be a serial rapist, for all you know. For crying out loud, get a *grip*." She grabbed the handles of two of my suitcases and began dragging them toward the door to the building. I grabbed the other two and followed, straining my neck to catch sight of the loveliest man in New York before he turned the corner.

Three

Not being the overly adventurous type, I decided that instead of attempting to drag a mattress, box springs, and bed frame through the streets of New York, I would opt for the easier, if slightly more expensive option. I visited a furniture store on 38th Street, quickly picked out everything I needed, and gladly paid extra for the delivery service.

I wasn't in need of much furniture, as I would have roughly two feet of clearance around my twin-sized bed in my tiny new room. I purchased two miniscule nightstands as well and arranged for them to be delivered with the bed. My room wouldn't hold anything else. So, with that chore taken care of, I went exploring.

I had done a rudimentary amount of New York googling before I had left Utah, but nothing can prepare you for the sheer size of Manhattan except experiencing the sheer size of Manhattan. I walked until my feet were numb, my neck craned to see the tops of each of the skyscrapers I walked past. I kept my hand clenched tightly on my purse, as I was aware that I was exhibiting all the classic signs of a New York first-timer. The last thing I needed was to have my purse snatched by the savvy New York underbelly.

As I walked away from the furniture store, I noticed all the shops I passed, most of them proclaiming "fabrics" and "thread" in their titles or descriptions. I pulled out my phone and ran a quick Google search. Just as I suspected, I was currently walking through New York's famous Garment District. Like a true tourist, I immediately began craning my head, looking for familiar names like "Oscar de la Renta" and "Donna Karan." To my great disappointment, nothing cutting edge and fabulous caught my eye.

As I continued east, I moved into the southern part of Midtown, stopping for a few minutes to stare up at the Empire State Building and dream of old cinematic favorites like *An Affair to Remember* and *Sleepless in Seattle*. I would have gone inside, but I figured, now that I lived there, there was no hurry. Instead, I kept strolling east, finally entering the Murray Hill neighborhood. This was the neighborhood that Lily had informed me held much of the "young professional" crowd. I thought she sounded as though she were hinting that I might be happier there than in her apartment, but I chose to ignore that. I was determined to turn Lily into a bosom buddy, with or without her permission. She and I lived only about ten blocks north and five blocks west of where I stood, so I wasn't that far away if I ever craved immersion in the pool of professionalism. Besides, as I strolled through the neighborhood, I doubted I would have fit in—it felt so much more sophisticated than I was.

Eventually, I headed northwest again, back up into Midtown and past Rockefeller Plaza. I tried to imagine myself going to work there as I walked by. It didn't quite feel real yet. I stared around at all the towering buildings, a very nondescript, corporate gray color, and felt my stomach clench unpleasantly. I was just a sheltered girl from suburban Utah. Suddenly the "small-town girl heads to the big city to start a new life" storyline felt oh-so-cliché. And most of those stories began with the small-town girl making a complete idiot of herself. Continuing on toward my new apartment, I really hoped that wasn't what I was in for.

- - - - -

The day before I was to start at Durham & Tucker, I stood in my teensy bedroom, staring at myself in the full-length mirror leaning against the wall. I was about to embark on my first religious experience in New York, and given that my LDS singles ward was likely to provide most of my eligible dating options, I wanted to look my very best. I wore a short-sleeved, sheer emerald green shirt with a matching tank top beneath it and a light gray pencil skirt with matching gray pumps. I loved this outfit, as the green of the shirt almost exactly matched my eyes and really set off my pale skin and dark red hair. It was an ensemble that made a statement, and that statement was, "I am an intelligent, powerful woman who also happens to be beautiful, desirable, and yes, available." Obviously.

I felt a pang of guilt as I studied myself, knowing that every time I had worn the sheer top at home, I had paired it with a short-sleeved undershirt to conform to my mother's ideals of modesty. She had considered the tank top inappropriate for church. But she wasn't here now. And it wasn't as though my shoulders being visible beneath the sheer top was worthy of eternal damnation. They were just shoulders, after all. Girls wore shirts like this to church all the time. The thought of my mom's disapproving glare, far from tempting me to change my shirt, made me even more determined to wear whatever I wanted. The freedom was exhilarating, and despite the triviality of the decision at hand, felt even the slightest bit devious. I nearly shivered with my own daring . . . I was clearly a girl living on the edge.

Church began at nine a.m., and I was determined to get there on my own, and without the use of a taxi. I figured that meant that I would need plenty of time, as this was to be my first test of the New York subway system. At 8:15, I tiptoed (attempting to keep the floor from creaking, per Lily's threats) toward the door, my purse in hand. Lily's bedroom door suddenly opened, and my very groggy roommate appeared, heading toward the bathroom. She froze when she saw me.

"Where do you think you're going?" Lily asked, her expression suspicious. "Do you have any idea what time it is?"

"It's only quarter after eight," I answered, abandoning my attempts at stealth. "It's not that early."

"Spoken like a true outsider," Lily commented, shaking her head. "Just for future reference, anything before 9 a.m., especially on a Sunday, is considered 'early' in these parts." She emphasized the word with her fingers and leaned against her doorframe. "But I repeat, where are you going? You looked all shifty when I opened the door."

"I was trying not to wake you," I defended myself. "You threatened bodily harm if my movements ever disturbed you, remember? And to answer your question, I'm going to church."

"Church?" Lily repeated, as though I had spoken in a foreign tongue. "Do people actually still do that these days?"

"Well, apparently," I said, reaching for the doorknob. "I'll be back about one, probably."

Lily looked scandalized. "You're going to church for nearly *five hours*?" she screeched. "What crazy religion do you belong to, anyway?"

"It's only three hours," I replied, wincing at her high-pitched tone. "But I'm planning for travel time, since I'll probably get lost . . . you know, once or twice."

"Do you know where you're going?" Lily asked, not quite able to completely hide the sliver of humanity she possessed. "Do you need directions?"

"Nah, I've got my phone, and I know the address of the building," I answered, one foot out the door.

"Are you walking?" Lily called after me. I turned back to face her.

"No, I'm taking the subway," I replied. "Why?"

"Do you know how to take the subway?" Lily pressed. "Do you have a metro card? Do you know where the nearest station is? Do you know where to get off? Do you know how to conduct yourself on the train?"

I stared at her. "It can't possibly be that complicated," I said, my voice uncertain. "I got my metro card yesterday, and I know where the nearest station is. I figured that was all I needed."

"Oh, Ryder," Lily said, shaking her head slowly. "You have so much to learn." From there she launched into a long-winded explanation of the New York subway system, including in-depth descriptions of signage, the operation of turnstiles, the difference between express trains and local trains, and appropriate decorum whilst riding the train.

"Don't look anyone in the eye . . . at least not for longer than a second," she warned. "And don't try to talk to anyone unless it's to say something like 'sorry' or 'excuse me.' Trust me, they won't appreciate it."

"Should I be taking notes?" I asked, struggling to keep the sarcasm from my voice.

"You laugh now, but you're the one that told me you don't want to look like a tourist. Trust me, you'll thank me later."

"Okay, I think I got it," I said. "And now I've only got twenty minutes to get there. Am I free to go, Yoda?"

Lily waved me off, already having lost interest in me as she headed into the bathroom. I smiled to myself as I walked out the door, locking it behind me. Despite my complaints at Lily's instructions, I found myself very grateful that she had provided them as I looked for the appropriate train at the 50th Street station. Eventually I located the 1 train that took me to the Lincoln Center station uptown. Emerging on the street, I found myself right where I needed to be, and just in time.

The Manhattan New York LDS temple was directly in front of me, and the same building also housed my ward. I headed inside, walking confidently, but my stomach fluttered a bit with my nerves. Once I found the chapel, I seated myself quickly, noticing that a tall, well-dressed man had just approached the pulpit to begin the meeting. I allowed myself a quick look around to take stock of my competition, ah, fellow ward members. The ward appeared to be a bit on the older side compared to my singles ward back in Utah, which didn't surprise me. Being only twenty-three myself, I figured I was probably one of the younger ones in attendance.

"Welcome, brothers and sisters," said the man at the pulpit. "We're so glad that you've chosen to be here. I am Bishop Elias, and these are my counselors, Brother Holmes and Brother Checketts. We welcome you to our services today."

Bishop Elias was a handsome man, probably about fifty or so, with tanned skin, dark eyes, and salt-and-pepper hair. His smile was wide and engaging, and it surprised me how at home it made me feel. It truly was nice to know that no matter where I traveled, and how different this place was from Utah, that the Church remained the same. As he announced the opening hymn and opening prayer, I felt a sense of peace settle over me. I sighed as relief I hadn't known I needed washed over me, and I began to sing with the congregation.

- - - - -

After providing my information to the bishopric after sacrament meeting, I headed to the Gospel Doctrine classroom. Not wanting to draw attention to myself, I snuck stealthily in the back of the room and quickly took a seat, pretending I had been there all along. I immediately fixed my eyes upon the teacher and didn't move a muscle for several minutes, despite being pressed rather closely to the individual on my left.

After a few minutes, I began to notice the strange sensation of someone very subtly yet repeatedly stepping on my left foot. I imagined that it was just the by-product of so many people being pressed so closely into a small room, so I inconspicuously moved my foot slightly to the right and refocused my attention on the sister teaching the lesson. Almost immediately, I again felt the foot pressing softly down on my own.

What was this? Some kind of deranged game of footsies?

Finally unable to overcome my curiosity, I glanced down at my foot, noting that the black Italian loafer covering it did indeed belong to the presumptuous male to my left. He had to realize he was doing it, right? This couldn't possibly be unintentional.

Discreetly, I turned my head marginally to the left and peeked around my hair. *Well, he may be presumptuous, but at least he makes it look good*, I thought, noting his wide shoulders, muscular chest, and trim torso. He wore a tailored dark gray suit and bright blue tie, both of which looked expensive, but as my eyes flicked upward to his face, I forgot everything else. I felt my heart stutter.

It was him.

Damian Wolfe. Forgetting all about my attempt at sneakiness, I pushed my hair out of my face and fully stared at him. He didn't look back at me, but kept those glorious blue eyes focused on the instructor. However, his lips twitched suggestively, and as I watched, the eye closest to me closed momentarily in what was most certainly a wink. His foot pressed down on mine one more time, as if to assure me that it had all indeed been deliberate, and then returned to its rightful place in front of its owner.

I turned, facing forward again, my thoughts muddled. I had roughly twenty minutes before the end of class. Twenty minutes to decide what on earth to say to this magnificent man—because, even if I wanted to, I knew I couldn't avoid speaking to him this time. There was no Lily here to save me.

But I couldn't manage to focus on possible conversation topics. My head was reeling—what were the chances that I would not only encounter my own personal fairy tale prince twice within the span of a single week in a city the size of New York, but that he would share my religious beliefs as well? What kind of cosmic interference accounted for this? It had to mean something, right? That kind of coincidence pretty much guaranteed that he and I belonged together. It was, quite obviously, written in the stars.

The twenty minutes I had to calm my heartbeat and attempt to restore some sense of reason to my thoughts proved enough to guarantee at least thirty seconds of coherency from me. When the benediction to the meeting had been said and the room buzzed with activity, Damian turned to me with his brilliant toothpaste commercial smile.

"Well, hi," he said smoothly. The combination of his thick, wavy hair, bright blue eyes, and incredible teeth almost overwhelmed my determination to be lucid, but I managed to hang on.

"Hi," I responded, and I was thrilled that I didn't sound as close to breathless as I was. "Fancy meeting you here." The fact that I managed a pithy saying in my current frame of mind was nothing short of miraculous.

Damian chuckled. "I knew sitting in the back would someday serve me well. After years and years of teachers telling me that only slackers sit in the back, I finally have the last laugh. Today, the back row allowed me to sit next to you."

My mouth nearly fell open. He was flirting with me. The Adonis was flirting with me. Was this reality? I mean, don't get me wrong. I am self-aware enough to know that I am not a troll. Some people might even consider me to be quite attractive, but let me just tell you right now, I am not, and have never been, anywhere near Damian Wolfe's league.

"Lucky you," I said, my voice taking on a bit more of a breathless quality. *Keep it together, Ryder, keep it together*, I lectured myself. "I just can't believe I'm running into you again . . . here," I continued, gesturing at the walls surrounding us. "What are the odds?"

Damian chuckled again. "Well, it's an answer to my prayers," he said, winking at me again.

This was getting easier. The longer I looked at his face, the more used to it I became, kind of like acclimating to the sunlight after being indoors for, you know, a lifetime. My thoughts were beginning to calm down and move at somewhat regular speeds. In fact, I even managed to groan at his bad joke.

He laughed at my response to his horrifically cheesy humor. "Well, I thought it was cute, given our surroundings." He shrugged.

I smiled at him, rising to my feet. Sitting was not allowing me to funnel my excess energy anywhere, and I was beginning to fidget. "I don't believe we were ever properly introduced," I said, holding out my hand. "I'm Ryder."

"I remember," Damian said, also rising and taking my hand. "But it's nice to officially meet you. I'm Damian."

I nodded. As if I could ever forget that name and the splendid face that went along with it. "Are you originally from New York?" I asked, not wanting the conversation to end, even though the room was filling up for the next class. I began walking toward the door, hoping he would follow. Providentially, he did.

"I am," he answered. "I grew up over on the Upper East Side."

"Isn't the Upper East Side supposed to be kind of a ritzy location?" I asked tentatively, not sure if such a question was considered kosher. But I was intensely curious about his background, up to and including how such a tasty morsel could still be single.

Damian laughed. "Usually," he replied. "Let's just say my mom did all right for herself." He winked at me. He appeared to do that a lot . . . I decided I didn't mind.

"What did she do?" I asked, curious.

"Well, she married rich, first of all," he teased with a grin. "But no, actually she was quite high up in the publishing world for most of my childhood. I really didn't see her much. I was raised mostly by nannies and other household staff. But she's retired now, so we see more of each other."

"Oh," I said. It made me sad to think of Damian as a lonely child, not often seeing his own mother. But I didn't know how to appropriately respond to this unhappy familial revelation, so I decided to change the subject. "So what do you do?"

"I work for an investment bank," he replied. He propped himself casually against the wall and stuck his hands into his pockets.

"Oh really?" I asked, attempting to sound interested and/or impressed. Investment banking, while so thoroughly "New York" it was almost passé, was not something I was terribly fascinated by. "Wall Street, huh?"

"Yep," Damian replied. "I'm a vice president over at Collins Weiss. Tough grind, but it pays the bills. But enough about me. I'd rather talk about you. I imagine you're new to the city?"

I attempted to keep my expression neutral, despite this bombshell. He had just casually informed me that he was a VP of an investment bank. I may not have particularly enjoyed investment banking, but I was an accountant (we like numbers), and I knew roughly what an investment bank VP would stand to make in New York. Hint: it's a lot.

"Oh, um, what gave it away?" I asked, pulling my attention back to his question.

"Well, despite the fact that the last time I saw you you were buried in suitcases, you don't exactly have 'New Yorker' written all over you." He grinned.

I laughed self-consciously, feeling my face go red. How embarrassing. So far I was following the "small-town girl moves to a big city" formula to the letter. Fabulous. "I moved here from Utah just this past week. As of tomorrow, I'm an associate at Durham & Tucker."

"CPA?" Damian asked, eyebrow raised. I nodded. "Well, you don't look like an accountant . . . that's a compliment," he clarified when I raised an eyebrow right back at him.

"Thanks," I said sarcastically. "Well, look, I'd better get to Relief Society. It was nice to run into you again. Nice to run into anything somewhat familiar, really." I was hesitant to leave him behind, but the truth was, I was running out of conversation. His very presence seemed to be sapping my strength and mental capacity.

"Okay," Damian agreed, and he even managed to look disappointed. Either he was a first-rate actor or I was the luckiest girl in the known universe and had actually managed to intrigue him. "Hey, why don't you let me take you out to dinner this week? You know, as a 'welcome to the city' gesture. I can impart my lifetime of New York wisdom—it's a service I offer, really. Free of charge. You just have to be a knockout redhead to qualify."

The breathlessness was starting to return. A voice that sounded remarkably like Lily's was echoing in my head with warnings such as "reckless" and "serial rapist" and "don't even know the guy," but honestly, I had run into him in Sunday School! How much safer could you get? And after the absolute miracle of encountering him a second time, how could I *not* go? Really, I owed it to the angels that were obviously trying so hard to bring the two of us together. Why not make their job a little easier?

I was taking too long to mull this over in my head, and my lack of response was causing his confident smile to slip a little. "Sorry, am I too old for you?" Damian asked, surprising me with the question. "I guess I should have cleared that up first. It's totally okay if you feel that way."

Too old for me? Huh. Maybe. I'd never actually thought about his age—his beautiful face was enough to make me forget all about silly things like that.

"I actually have no idea," I responded with a smile. "How old are you, anyway?"

"Thirty."

"Dinner sounds nice," I replied instantly. Yes, seven years was pushing it. But not enough to keep me away, that was for sure.

Damian laughed. "Well, okay then." He handed me his cell phone, silently requesting my number. I provided it without comment and handed his phone back to him. Then, with one last smile in his direction, I headed toward the Relief Society room, my head somewhere above the clouds.

- - - - -

"I'm telling you, Lily, it was a miracle!"

Lily looked at me skeptically, her feet propped up on the coffee table, a bowl of cereal in her hand. I was pacing in front of the mounted TV, waving my hands wildly around as I told my story.

"I don't know, seems more creepy than miraculous to me," she replied, eyebrow raised. "How do you know he didn't just follow you in there?"

"How would he have known which classroom to be in so I would run into him?" I pointed out. "And you are vastly overestimating my power to attract stalkers. Trust me, I'm not worth that kind of effort."

"Well, it's your funeral," Lily said as she shoveled cereal into her mouth. "And just so you know, me forewarning you like this constitutes me being excused from attending the services when you turn up dismembered in a dumpster somewhere."

I rolled my eyes and collapsed into the loveseat, exhausted by my energetic storytelling. "Oh, I hope he calls. How depressing would it be if after all that, he never called?" I raised my fist to my mouth, tempted to start gnawing on my fingernails in angst.

Lily rose to her feet and headed toward the kitchen. "He'll call," she assured me, surprising me with hitherto unsuspected optimism. But then she said, "He has to see you again. It's very difficult to kill someone remotely."

I sighed at her persistent raining on my parade. I decided to change the subject. "So what about you? Do you have a boyfriend?"

Lily snorted, running her bowl under the kitchen faucet to rinse out the leftover cereal. "Who has time for men? I'm too busy trying to get a struggling Broadway career off the ground."

"But don't you have anybody you're interested in? What about in school? There's got to be some potential there, right?"

"Let me put it this way," Lily replied. "I take three types of classes. Singing, dancing, and acting. My vocal classes are individual, and my teacher is female. My dancing classes do not contain a single straight male, as far as I am aware. And let's just say that acting classes do not lend themselves to low-drama romantic attachments, if you get my drift. My best bet is to captivate some unsuspecting sucker while I'm serving his drinks."

"That works." I shrugged. "No such luck thus far, huh?"

"Not so much," Lily said sarcastically. "That's not to say that I don't frequently see something I like, but I can't exactly proposition some guy while I'm on the clock. The boss seems to frown on that for some reason."

"Speaking from experience?"

"You know it."

I laughed. "Well, I'll keep my eyes open. Maybe I'll find some good prospects for you at my work, and I can set you up."

"By all means, I'm all about the hard-core professionals," Lily agreed, rummaging in the refrigerator. "They make more money than I do and tend to keep the same hours outside of work."

"Oh, you mean the hours of one a.m. to two a.m. on weekdays and ten p.m. to five a.m. on weekends?" I teased her. I had been absolutely floored at what time she had finally stumbled through the door that morning, returning from her "Saturday night." The knowledge that she had only had three hours of sleep was the main motivation behind my attempt to sneak out silently for church.

"Hey, I watch people party all night every night during the week. I've earned the right to do some partying of my own on the weekends," she defended, her lips turning up slightly.

"Far be it from me to bad-mouth anybody else's partying habits," I held up my hands in mock self-defense. "But I honestly have no idea how you are standing upright right now. I hope you got some more sleep after I left this morning."

"A little," Lily answered, returning to the couch, this time with a bottle of Gatorade. "I may have had one too many drinks last night," she conceded, and I noticed that she did appear to be very conscious of how much she moved her head. It must have been questioning the wisdom of her partying habits as well. "I spent some quality time with the toilet."

"See, it's times like these when I become even more grateful that I do not drink," I declared, wrinkling my nose.

Lily stared at me. "You don't drink. Like, at all?"

"Nope." I shook my head at her. "My judgment is sketchy enough without 'help' from a bottle." I emphasized the word with my fingers.

Lily studied me wordlessly for a second before closing her eyes and wincing slightly. "Well, you don't criticize my partying habits, I guess I won't criticize yours."

"Sounds like a good compromise," I agreed. "Hey, do you need an aspirin or something? You look miserable. Can I get you anything?"

Lily opened her eyes and smiled momentarily at me. It was amazing how it transformed her face. "Thanks," she replied.

Four

The walk to Rockefeller Plaza the next morning went by way too fast. I stood in front of the building, staring up at gray stone that never actually seemed to end. The longer I looked, the taller the building looked. I was getting smaller and smaller. For a moment, I longed to be back in my bedroom in Salt Lake. The place where all things were safe and familiar and everything seemed to make sense. Until my bedroom door crashed open and my mother started lecturing at me.

Yep. Spell broken. Pulling myself back together, I took a deep breath, smoothed the jacket of my fabulous dark gray pantsuit, and pointed my black stilettos toward the door. Showtime.

My new hire packet from the Durham & Tucker recruiting team had included very specific instructions for my first day. I was to obtain a special access badge from the security desk in the lobby of the building, which would get me through the security turnstiles, up the elevator, and into the Durham & Tucker suite. From there, I was to stop at the front desk to pick up my welcome packet and a name tag for the day. Then I was to continue into the conference room directly past the front desk, where I would begin my new employee orientation.

I got as far as the elevators without incident.

See, I'm an elevator traditionalist. Typically, in my world, in the normal world, you push the elevator call button. It's quite simple really. Then, once you've boarded the contraption, your next task is to select the appropriate floor. No biggie. I'm generally up to the challenge. So after exiting the security turnstile and heading for the elevator bank, I figured I was home free. After all, who doesn't know how to operate an elevator?

But these were no ordinary elevators. I entered the first elevator bank, as it didn't look particularly crowded. I searched for the "up" button, figuring that was the only direction I could possibly go. But there was no button. I looked around at the other five people in the elevator bank. They all stood, waiting patiently, watching the digital numbers above each elevator flick by steadily. But I noticed something odd. These people weren't all crowded around one elevator, the one most likely to be next available, awaiting its arrival. No, indeed. A few well-dressed businessmen stood chatting in front of one, a lone dark-haired woman in front of another. Yet another woman stood alone in front of another. Were people so averse to sharing elevators in New York? But they all seemed to know where they were going. They all had a sense of purpose that I lacked.

Making a split-second decision, I stood next to one of the lone women, acting like I knew what I was doing. When the elevator arrived, I boarded it with her. As soon as we were aboard, I looked desperately for the buttons, knowing I needed to get to the thirty-eighth floor. But there were none! How in heaven's name did you operate an elevator with no buttons?! How did it know where you wanted to get off? Was it voice activated? Could it read minds? Had technology progressed that far in the posh office buildings of New York? Feeling slightly panicky, I waited to see what would happen.

The elevator stopped at the eleventh floor and the woman in the elevator with me politely waited for me to exit ahead of her. Why couldn't she just conform to New York stereotypes and stop being so obliging? Knowing that I didn't actually *want* to get off the elevator, and knowing that if I did, I'd have to figure out how to call it back again without the existence of a call button, I just stood and smiled inanely at her. She stared. Finally, I gestured to her to "go ahead" and after giving me a look that was half confusion, half contempt, she exited.

Relieved to be alone in the perplexing metal box, I looked frantically around, trying to see if I'd missed anything key to the elevator's operation. No buttons had magically appeared in the past ten seconds. However, there was a screen on the wall that indicated to me that the elevator was headed back down to the lobby.

Wait a minute, hadn't I seen a screen at the mouth of the elevator bank in the lobby? A screen that several people had been gathered around? Once back on the ground floor, I headed toward the screen I'd barely noticed on my way in. I watched a yawning girl in a fabulous pair of bright red Jimmy Choos scan her security badge and select a floor number from a displayed list. The screen then flashed an elevator number at her.

Ohhhhhh . . .

Feeling like a first-rate idiot, I waited in line, finally scanning my security badge and searching for the thirty-eighth floor on the provided list. It wasn't there. Criminy, was I in the wrong *building* or something? I knew I had entered the building that corresponded with my new hire instructions. They couldn't have given me the wrong address, could they? Typically you could trust these hoity-toity firms to at least know their own location. There was a line starting to form behind me, but I had no idea what to do.

"You have to select your floor," the man behind me supplied helpfully, eying the "visitor" security badge clipped to my waistband. He sounded irritated. I couldn't blame him. It was Monday morning after all, and a redheaded ditz was standing between him and his coffee.

"Right, I know," I said, looking apologetically at him. "But it doesn't, um, seem to be showing the thirty-eighth floor here. I could swear there were more than twenty floors in this building, but, um, the computer is disagreeing with me." I gave him a self-conscious smile, but he just eyed me disbelievingly and pointed to something behind me on the wall. There, in silver letters were the words "FLOORS 2–20."

"You're at the wrong elevator bank," he explained. "You want the next one over."

"Oh," I said, my cheeks darkening with a blush. "Um, so sorry. Thanks so much for the help."

I immediately headed for the screen at the next elevator bank, trying to keep my head high and my walk confident, despite my red face. I managed to make it up to the Durham & Tucker suite without further calamity, but I couldn't help feeling that my first day wasn't off to a particularly good start.

- - - - -

"Can I help you?" asked the sweet-looking, youngish Asian girl behind the front desk.

"Yes, I'm Ryder Redmond," I replied, hoping the sense of fatigue I was already feeling wasn't evident in my voice. "It's my first day."

"Oh, well, welcome to Durham & Tucker!" she exclaimed, her face breaking into a smile. "Now, let me just find your welcome packet . . ." she started rummaging through a pile of sturdy looking folders on her desk in the signature Durham & Tucker blue and yellow color scheme.

"Here we are!" she cried happily. She was far too perky for a Monday morning. "Your name tag is right in front. Go ahead and stick that on, and then head into the conference room." She pointed to a large room to her left, encased in glass, with a long, darkly wooded table situated in the middle, surrounded by expensive-looking office chairs. The table appeared to be covered with Durham & Tucker paraphernalia—the signature coffee mugs, pens, notepads, mini staplers, etc. all situated at each place.

"Once you find your seat, feel free to grab some breakfast, coffee, whatever from the buffet," the girl continued, pointing to a food spread in the back of the room. "Oh, and I'm Amy. You just let me know if you need anything."

"Thanks, Amy," I replied, sticking my name tag to my suit lapel and heading for the conference room. The first thing that struck me as I entered was that I was almost the first one there. Checking my watch, I noticed that I was a full ten minutes early. The only other person in the room was a pale girl with short, curly brown hair, wearing a business suit about ten years out of date. She sat halfway down the table, looking very nervous and jumpy.

The second thing I noticed was that there appeared to be assigned seating. I walked around the table, searching for my name. Finally, locating it directly across from the nervous girl, I gave her a kind smile, attempting to calm her as much as myself, and took a seat.

"Hi," said the girl, in a voice that almost exactly matched her appearance. It was small and squeaky, but not annoyingly so. It was how I imagined a squirrel would sound if it could talk.

"Hi," I replied, smiling at her again. "I'm Ryder Redmond. What's your name?"

"Melinda," she answered, with a smile of her own. "Melinda Simmons. I just moved here from Wisconsin. Are you from New York originally?"

It was gratifying to think that at least to other New York outsiders, I might look like a native. "No," I answered. "I'm from Utah." I looked around to make sure we were still the only ones in the room. "Do you find New York as overwhelming as I do?"

Melinda giggled and nodded. "I wanted to curl up and cry when I first got here, but I think I'm getting used to it. I had a chance to work in the Milwaukee office, but I didn't want to stay in Wisconsin for the rest of my life. I liked the idea of starting over in a big city."

"Likewise," I said, already starting to like this girl. "Don't get me wrong, I love my hometown, but when a job offer came through from the New York office, I didn't feel like I could pass up a chance like that."

"It's so different, though!" Melinda exclaimed. "For some reason, everything feels more complicated here. Transportation, shopping, socializing. And we haven't even started working yet! I'm hoping I don't regret this."

Secretly I agreed, but I didn't want to display so much vulnerability so quickly to someone I barely knew. I'd heard that business in New York was cutthroat, and I didn't want to risk putting myself at a disadvantage. Granted, Melinda seemed harmless enough, but maybe she was just a really good actress.

"I'm sure you'll be fine," was all I said, as several more people entered the room. A tall black woman who looked to be in her thirties, two Asian men who appeared to be about my age, and a blonde girl who looked even younger than me were chatting as they walked through the glass door.

Just behind the blonde was another girl. She had long, lank, mousy brown hair parted in the middle and wire-rimmed glasses. She wore a conservative brown suit and carried a briefcase. I couldn't really discern her age, because her presentation conflicted so strongly with her appearance. She had a young face, but her clothes and the way she carried herself hinted that she could be much older than she appeared. More people streamed in after her, but I was too intrigued by her to notice. Unsmiling, she walked down the table, looking for her name card. She stopped right next to me, at the spot assigned to "Amelia Applewhite."

"Amelia?" I asked, attempting to be friendly. I held out my hand to her. "I'm Ryder Redmond."

She studied me for a moment down her rather short, stubby nose. She took my hand, barely touching it, and almost immediately pulled away. She sat down stiffly in the chair next to mine and opened her welcome packet as though I weren't sitting right there, staring at her.

"So, Amelia, where are you from?" I asked her. She didn't reply. I watched her silently as she ignored both me and my question.

Finally looking up at Melinda with a bemused look on my face, I raised my eyebrows at her. Melinda put a hand to her mouth and giggled. "Strong and silent type, huh?" I addressed Amelia again, determined to get a reaction. "No, I totally get it. People tend to talk too much these days anyway. Why encourage it? Why pollute the air with worthless babbling? A sound philosophy, Amelia. I'm right there with you."

"And yet you continue to prattle on, directly in my ear," Amelia finally responded, still not looking up from her perusing. "If you're so fond of silence, perhaps you could give it a try." Apparently her standoffish demeanor was truly representative of her personality. What fun.

"Absolutely," I said, keeping my voice bright and sincere. "That's a good idea. Forgive my politeness. In the future I'll do my best to follow your example and disregard even the most basic of good manners." Melinda giggled again, but stopped quickly when Amelia finally looked up, eyes narrowed and expression frosty.

"Look, Pollyanna," she began, her voice crackling with a profound negative energy as she turned to me. "I'm not here to make friends. I'm not here to get to know you. You are my competition. Got it? There are only so many spots at the top, and I intend to score one, whatever it takes. So how's about you bother someone else with your inane, small-town charm?"

I stared at her, eyebrows raised. Turning back to Melinda, who appeared genuinely shocked, I mock-whispered across the table to her. "I don't think Amelia wants to be part of our club."

Melinda smiled back at me, but pinched her lips together quickly at the look on Amelia's face. Giving me one last glare for good measure, the unpleasant woman went back to studying her packet.

Our exchange had gotten the attention of several other individuals around the table, nearly all of which were either smiling at me or looking incredulously at Amelia. I was pleased to see that the majority of my Durham & Tucker starting class appeared to be reasonable individuals.

"Welcome, everybody!" came a voice from the front of the room. I looked up and saw the thirty-something black woman standing at the head of the table. "I'm Deirdre Sinclair, the head of recruiting for the New York office. We're so happy to have you all here with us at Durham & Tucker, which we've affectionately dubbed D&T."

I looked around the room quickly, sizing up the audience. There were about twenty of us, about half men and half women. Most looked at least a little uncertain of what awaited them in the unknown bowels of the D&T machine, but a few, including Amelia, looked supremely confident. I hoped I was one of the confident few, if less intensely so than my new "friend."

"We have a fantastic day planned for you—a chance for you to hear from our office managing partner, as well as from several other of your fellow employees within the various practices we have represented here in the New York office," Deirdre continued, smiling brightly. "Just to give you an idea of the mix of your starting class, about half of you are audit professionals, a quarter are advisory, and the other quarter are tax. You will have the opportunity to hear from some of our more seasoned audit, advisory, and tax professionals today, so you'll get a good view into your future here with the firm. But first, let's get the boring stuff out of the way."

From there, we launched into Human-Resources-mandated paperwork, tax forms, and getting our pictures taken for our permanent security ID badges.

"We'll have those badges ready for you by the end of the day," Deirdre told us as the HR manager left the room with her camera and our piles of paperwork. "Now, due to his busy schedule today, we had to push up one of our visitors ahead of our managing partner. Everybody, this is Hunter Payne."

She gestured to the back of the room, where a man I hadn't noticed was standing in a corner, a water bottle in hand. "Hunter is actually quite new to D&T as well," Deirdre informed the room. "He's a member of our legal team and came to us from a prominent law firm uptown about a month ago. We usually have Gerald Forrester, our general counsel, come in and speak to our new recruits, but he is unavailable today, so Hunter agreed to step in. Hunter, why don't you come on up and introduce yourself to everyone?"

Hunter Payne moved toward the front of the room, his face breaking into a friendly smile as he looked around the table. He certainly didn't strike me as a high-powered attorney. He wore the uniform (the signature suit and tie), but his face was wide open and honest. I wondered if that made his job in corporate law difficult for him. Or maybe I was just being snarky.

Hunter was tall, probably a few inches over six feet, with an athletic build. He was broad-shouldered and trim, and had thick, dark hair. As he walked by the window, the light from it reflected a reddish tinge through the abundant strands, and I smiled. A fellow ginger! His face was pleasant, fair-skinned, and freckled, but the freckles didn't make him look young—just approachable.

"Hi guys," he said in a casual tone. "As Deirdre said, my name is Hunter Payne. I'm an associate attorney here. Deirdre thought it would be a good idea for you to become familiar with someone from Legal, because it's likely that you will have at least some exposure to us during your tenure here at D&T. As an accounting firm, we tend to get a lot of lawsuits thrown at us, and nearly all of them involve our clients. Your clients. You are an integral part of any legal action we may need to take, but more than that, you're an integral part of the prevention of any legal action." His face took on an earnest look. "If you have any questions about the legality or appropriateness of something you see or encounter in your work, please give me a call. I'm always available for a consultation with any of you."

I was surprised that lawsuits were common enough with D&T that they felt it was important for the new hires to be familiar with the legal team. But I wasn't exactly up to speed on the inner workings of the firm, so I just accepted it along with everybody else. Hunter Payne smiled again at everyone in the room and wished us luck for our first week, then left without a backward glance.

After his departure, we were introduced to Claire Gomez, the New York office managing partner. She was short and slightly plump, with glistening black hair and full lips. She spoke about the greatness of D&T as a place to build our careers, the potential we all carried within ourselves, and all the usual lip service we were used to receiving from the executive management of accounting firms. She seemed nice enough, but I'd heard enough of this kind of stuff during my six months of recruiting visits, activities, and interviews that I really just wanted to get to work.

The rest of the day passed very slowly to me. After a lunch catered from an apparently famous New York deli, an endless parade of audit, tax, and advisory professionals began. They marched through the door of the conference room, proclaiming how marvelous it was to work at D&T and how lucky we were to be there. We were treated to some entertaining stories, a whole lot of not-so-entertaining stories, and we heard the same old platitudes again and again.

"Believe you can do anything!"

"Just do your best and everything will fall into place!"

"Be a rising star!"

Several times I wondered if I had been magically transported back in time to my high school graduation ceremony. My favorite comment of the day, probably because it was by far the most honest and the least patronizing, came from a shortish, curly-haired audit manager. "Honestly, people will tell you this job is hard. Sure, okay. It's hard," he said, shrugging. "But it's probably not as hard as they make it sound. You're obviously smart folks; you wouldn't be here if you weren't. So most likely, more than by your intelligence or your abilities, your success will be determined by what kind of effort you're willing to put in. Just make sure you can face yourself in the mirror at the end of every day, and nobody can ask more of you than that."

The last part of the day, we split into our separate practices. I was an audit professional, so I went with half the new hires to a separate conference room where we met specifically with audit personnel from the office. We were each assigned a "buddy" who was a more seasoned professional within our chosen practice. Our buddies gave us a quick tour of the office space and answered any of our more embarrassing questions (the ones we didn't want our fellow newbies to overhear) before dropping us off at the front desk to pick up our new security ID badges. After this, we were free to head home for the day.

My buddy was second-year associate about my height and build, but with honey-blonde hair and an olive complexion. Her name was Evangeline, and she was so beautiful that I felt almost physically diminished in her presence. She also spoke with a fabulous Australian accent that made her even more intimidating, and I was sure it increased her popularity around the office. I loved listening to her speak and I was tempted to try to repeat everything she said right after her in my own Australian accent. Don't worry—I managed to restrain myself.

"Well, it was wonderful to meet you, Ryder," Evangeline said as I put my new security badge into my bag and we walked toward the door to the suite. She pronounced my name "Roidah" . . . it was spectacular. "This office is huge and we have a few thousand employees, so I may not see you for a while, but make sure to ping me if you have any questions in the meantime, okay?"

"Absolutely," I agreed, smiling at her. "Thanks for showing me around the office."

Evangeline smiled and waved as she headed back toward the cubicles that made up the vast majority of the office space.

I sighed in relief as I headed toward the elevators. One day down.

Five

I sat, staring listlessly at my computer screen, scrolling through pages and pages of information on Durham & Tucker that I really, really didn't want to read. I needed something to do. Desperately. A girl could only google so many articles about New York and accounting firms therein before funny things started to happen in her head—I was reaching the breaking point.

It was day number three at D&T, and due to various administrative mix-ups and the firm's general short-handedness, I still had not been assigned to a client. My days thus far, instead of being dedicated to the audit of client financial statements, had consisted of wandering around the D&T office, setting up a voicemail it never seemed I would actually get to use, organizing email inboxes, and googling anything that happened to pop into my thoroughly uninterested brain.

Deciding another outing was in order, I jumped to my feet and headed for the break room. While I'd passed by several times, I still hadn't really explored it, and all the intense boredom had made me hungry. Evangeline had told me in our whirlwind tour of the office that most of the time, bagels and doughnuts could be found in that vicinity. If there was an apple fritter in that direction, it had my name written all over it.

I entered the cream and brown accented room and headed straight for the row of doughnut boxes along the far wall. Halfway there, I was distracted by a machine to my right. It was one of those fancy coffee machines, where you stuck a pouch in the machine and a cup under the spout, and magically, your coffee spurted out. Usually I ignored such things, not being a coffee drinker myself, but D&T had included in their repertoire of flavors a Milky Way hot chocolate flavor. Hello, gooey, caramely, chocolaty goodness.

I altered my course, heading for the machine. I'd never used one before, so I proceeded with caution. Loading the pouch seemed simple enough. I stuck a cup under the spout and pushed the big silver button. Proud of my instant mastering of the mysterious gadget, I folded my arms and waited for chocolate bliss to start pouring into my little cup.

Instead, within three seconds, scalding hot water tinged with brown I assume was either old coffee or new hot chocolate, was spraying all over my flowy white button-up and dry-clean-only gray slacks. I let out a cry of rage and leapt out of the way. Frantically punching the silver button, I attempted to initiate a cease-fire, but to no avail.

"What the?" The deeply male exclamation rang out from behind me and suddenly a powerful, freckled forearm in a rolled white shirt sleeve reached around to yank the machine's plug out of the wall.

"I didn't think of that," I panted, turning to face my savior. It was the dark-haired attorney from orientation. Hunter Payne.

"How did you manage to anger the coffee maker?" Hunter asked. He set the water bottle he'd been carrying on the counter and reached for paper towels to wipe the brownish, hot water from the floor.

"Who knows?" I asked, still traumatized from the attack. "Maybe it could tell that I was a first-timer and demanded some kind of ritual sacrifice."

Hunter chuckled as he knelt to wipe up the mess.

"Here, let me do that," I insisted, crouching next to him. "I'm the one polluting the break room—you shouldn't protect me from the consequences of my actions like that."

He smiled at me as he threw a wad of paper towels on the puddle and began soaking up the moisture. "No worries, I got this. I don't claim to be a maintenance man by any stretch of the imagination, but this, I can handle." He swiped at the last of the drops on the floor and then lobbed the wad into the garbage can as we both stood. "Are you okay? The water didn't burn you or anything, did it?" His eyebrows scrunched together, creating an adorable little crease atop his nose. I wondered if, as an attorney, it had occurred to him that I might sue the firm for damages or something.

"I'm fine," I assured him, but then frowned down at my once adorable outfit. "I'm not sure I'll be able to save the ensemble, though. Coffee and Calvin Klein aren't exactly the best of friends."

"Yeah . . ." Hunter winced at my splattered clothing. "Unfortunately my expertise does not extend to laundry. Sorry about that."

I sighed and shrugged. "Live and learn. I'm Ryder, by the way." I reached out my hand to him.

"Hunter," he replied, taking it and giving it a firm shake. "You're new right? I think I saw you in the new hire orientation the other day?"

I nodded. "Just moved out here from Salt Lake City. Ready to conquer the world and all that. Unfortunately I'm not doing a great job thus far. I haven't been assigned any clients yet. So I'm just ghosting around the office, trying to keep myself entertained until I'm given a client to harass."

"Well, I'm one of the few who comes into the office nearly every day," Hunter replied. "Most everyone else, at least on this floor, works at client sites. So if you ever need a distraction, feel free to pop into my office for a bit. Chances are, I'll need one too. I'm in the northeast corner, right by Gerald Forrester's office."

"Thanks for the offer," I said. "I'm actually just down the row from you in the cubicle by the window. So the proposition stands in reverse."

"Deal," Hunter said, nodding once. "Nice to meet you, Ryder. I'll talk to you later, okay?" Snagging the water bottle from the counter, he smiled and left.

- - - - -

"You're actually letting him pick you up here?" Lily screeched from the doorway of my bedroom. "It was bad enough when he just knew which building we were in, but now you've actually told him our apartment number? Why didn't you just cut off your own head and give it to him on a silver platter?" She crumpled onto my bed with a groan.

I rolled my eyes. An impressive feat, given that I was in the process of applying mascara. I sat cross-legged on the edge of the bed, the contents of my makeup bag spread around me, utilizing a tiny hand mirror as I attempted to make myself beautiful for Damian Wolfe. Tonight was our first date, although Lily was refusing to acknowledge it as such. To her, it was just a chance for Damian to scout out our location so he could sneak in later and murder us.

"You know, I have no idea why you're having such a hard time breaking into show business," I informed her, my tongue half sticking out of my mouth as I tried to keep from poking myself in the eye. "You were born for drama."

"I know, right?" Lily responded, not moving from her position of despair across my bed. "But in this case, I'm not even displaying my genius."

"Why are you so convinced that going out with Damian is a bad idea?" I asked, turning to look at her. "I mean, what is so unusual about him asking me out like this? Isn't this how most relationships start? You meet someone somewhere, your unspeakable beauty and mystique intrigue them, they ask to spend some time with you, which tends to include them picking you up at your apartment . . . ?" I trailed off, an inquisitive eyebrow raised at her. Lily looked up at me, her eyes calculating and, I was surprised to see it, concerned.

"I don't know," she finally admitted. "I know that there's nothing really weird about how this all went down, but this whole thing just seems . . . I don't know, too good to be true. That guy's just a little too handsome and too successful . . . stuff like that is usually a front for something much worse."

"You've spent roughly twenty-seven seconds in his company," I pointed out. "How on earth can you possibly form any idea of his character?"

"I have an uncanny knack for reading people," Lily defended, sitting up. "Really, I'm well-known for it. You should listen to me. Why do you think I was okay with you moving in after spending only three minutes with you?" She looked at me pointedly. "It's because I could *read* you. I knew that, while you may have some less desirable personality traits, you weren't some kind of dangerous psychopath. In fact, you struck me as a thoroughly safe option. Although I am tempted to reevaluate that opinion now." She narrowed her eyes at me.

I laughed. "Look, I appreciate your concern. Really, I do. But let me just see how this dinner goes. I promise I will be totally skeptical, and I won't jump into anything, and I'll keep one hand on my pepper spray all night. Okay? And if anything feels off, I won't go out with him again. How's that?"

"Better than nothing, I guess," she grunted. She pulled herself off my bed and glanced at me uneasily one more time before leaving the room.

I really was touched by her concern for me. But I couldn't share it. I was ecstatic. Never before had I gone out with so promising of a Prince Charming prospect as Damian Wolfe. I stood before my full-length mirror and studied myself. I wore a light, flowy red top tucked into the low waist of my dark skinny jeans and bright red stiletto heels. I'd managed to tease a little more volume into my chin-length bob, and I'd lined my light green eyes a bit to make them pop. Overall, the affect was quite encouraging. I heard a knock on the door as I reached for my purse. I rushed to answer it before Lily could terrify my date, but she was far ahead of me . . . as I knew had been her plan all along.

"Oh, it's you," Lily said to Damian, sounding for all the world as though she hadn't known he was expected. Trying out her acting prowess, it seemed. "What are you doing here?" She blocked Damian's view into the apartment, hand on her bony hip.

"He's here to pick me up," I said, walking toward her. "As you know full well," I muttered quietly to the back of her head. She finally moved slightly to allow him entrance into the apartment, her mistrustful gaze fixed resentfully on his handsome face.

"Hello, Lily," Damian said as he sauntered inside, his lips twitching at her glare. "Ryder, you look fantastic." He looked incredible. He wore a pair of dark gray designer slacks and a slim-fitting blue button-up shirt. The absence of a suit coat, which he'd been wearing both times I'd seen him before, emphasized his magnificent body. I did not deserve this. And I certainly didn't belong next to him, looking as he did.

"Am I underdressed?" I asked worriedly, eyeing his outfit.

"Nope," he assured me. "You're perfect. I just haven't had a chance to make it back to my apartment, so you get to hang with Damian Wolfe, investment banker, tonight." He grinned at me, looking me up and down again. "You know, I've heard that redheads aren't supposed to wear red, but judging from what I'm seeing, it would be a real shame if they didn't."

Lily shot us a look of the purest disgust. "Oh, get out of here," she grumbled, apparently unable to stomach the sight for a moment longer. I couldn't help smiling at her bad temper.

"See you later, Lil," I said, giving her a bright smile as I walked through the door after Damian. She mouthed the words "pepper spray" at me as I turned back to close it firmly behind me.

- - - - -

"So, how far do you estimate you can walk in those?" Damian asked, eyeing my stiletto-clad feet uncertainly. "I have a place in mind for dinner, but it's several blocks away."

"Oh, I'm fine," I assured him. "I wear heels just about every day so I'm used to the discomfort. Beauty is pain, you know," I winked, and he laughed. So far, the disorientation I was used to experiencing in his glorious presence hadn't materialized. Maybe I just needed a few days of preparation time in order to prevent it.

"Well, okay then," he said. "We're off."

He led me north up 8th Avenue toward Central Park, chatting all the way. He asked about my first week of work, and I told him about my lazy days just loafing around the office while the big bosses attempted to work out my client schedule. I had found out earlier that day that usually client schedules were worked out far in advance, but that a recent spate of nasty employee turnovers had prevented this for the current group of new hires. So, thus far, I had been thoroughly useless to my employer. But at least I'd been provided with my laptop, which gave me the opportunity to read through what felt like countless pages of dull history on the firm, educate myself on my new resident city, and, ahem, do a little Damian Wolfe research. I'd discovered that he was indeed a VP at Collins Weiss (I had been sure to communicate to Lily that so far—he wasn't a liar) as he had been quoted in a "Day in the Life of an Investment Banking VP" article in an online magazine I'd found.

"But they're nice offices, right?" Damian pressed after I'd communicated my itinerary of the last few days (leaving out my internet stalking of him, naturally). "You might be bored out of your mind, but you have a nice office, right? D&T is a huge firm. Tell me that they at least gave you a nice office."

"No such luck," I lamented. "I'm just a lowly first-year staff. I don't score an office. In fact, I won't score an office until I hit senior manager level, which is a good eight years away."

"Man . . ." he said, wincing in sympathy. "Although, now that I think about it, I guess I understand. I didn't have an office when I joined Collins Weiss as an associate, either. It wasn't until I hit VP two years ago that I managed one of those."

"What I don't understand," I said as I carefully avoided a mini trash heap on the sidewalk. "Is how you have time to take me to dinner at all. I was under the impression that in your line of business, you're at the office until midnight every night."

Damian chuckled. "A few years ago, I would agree with that viewpoint wholeheartedly. But since my promotion to VP, my hours have gotten a little more flexible." He stopped at a corner and looked quickly around before grabbing my hand and pulling me with him across the street. "I usually get out of the office around nine p.m. these days, but if I have a hot date," he winked at me, "then I'll take off a little early."

"Well, you'll be in good company," I informed him. "Once I actually get assigned to a client, my hours will be just as nightmarish as yours. Eighty-hour weeks are par for the course in the public accounting universe."

"So I've heard," Damian replied. "But I'll bet working for a company like Durham & Tucker opens all kinds of doors for you."

"One can only hope," I sighed. "I'm a little bit nervous, actually. I did an internship about a year ago with the D&T office in Salt Lake, but I imagine being an intern in Salt Lake and being a first-year staff in New York are pretty different experiences."

"Probably," Damian nodded. "But I'm sure you're up to the challenge. What made you decide to come all the way out here, anyway? Did the Salt Lake office not want you or something?" He nudged me, and I smiled.

"No, they gave me a full-time offer, but I was afraid of being pigeonholed," I admitted. "I've lived in Salt Lake my entire life. I didn't want to stay there forever, and taking that job felt like a lifetime sentence."

"What's so bad about Utah?" Damian asked curiously. "Typically for members of the Church, that place is Mecca."

"It is," I replied, shrugging. "I guess that's the problem. I've grown up so surrounded by all things safe and nicely Mormon that I felt like I needed to challenge myself a little. Get outside my comfort zone."

"Well you certainly did that," Damian laughed, gesturing around us at the bustling city. "Apparently you don't do things by halves."

"No," I agreed with him with a smile. We walked around Columbus Circle, heading toward what looked like a tall office building.

"Here we are," Damian said, gesturing toward the door to the skyscraper.

"We're going to dinner in an office building?" I asked. I looked up at the tall structure, confused.

Damian laughed. "It's actually a hotel, and the restaurant is on the ground floor," he informed me. "You'll find that's common in this city."

"Oh, okay," I said, feeling my face go red. "What's it called?"

"Jean-Marques," Damian answered, pulling me up the steps toward the door.

"Jean-Marques?" I asked. It just so happened that one of my coworkers had named this restaurant as one of the more exclusive places to dine in the city just the day before. And now I was actually supposed to be eating there? On a first date? On a first date with someone I wanted desperately to impress? I felt slightly panicky. I didn't know how to conduct myself in a restaurant frequented by celebrities and business tycoons. I was a fast food kind of girl. My feet stumbled on the stairs.

"You okay?" Damian asked solicitously, trying to keep me upright. His forehead crinkled at the look of alarm on my face. "What's the matter?"

"Isn't this place really fancy?" I asked, feeling a blush creep across my face. "I feel like I shouldn't go in there wearing jeans or something."

Damian laughed, his bright blue eyes lighting brilliantly. "Don't worry about that. We're actually going to be eating at Jean-Marques' more casual sister restaurant. They're right next to each other—they even share a wall, in fact. It's called Bistro at Jean-Marques. Come on." He pulled me once again toward the door.

As we approached the rather solemn but fabulously dressed girl at the hostess station, I felt horribly out of place. My surroundings were screaming their affluence at me, and I was not taking it well. This was definitely not my neck of the woods.

"Why, Mr. Wolfe," the hostess said, her formerly glum look exploding into one of absolute delight. She looked to be about my age, beautiful, olive-skinned, with a spectacular dark pixie cut. And apparently she was just as captivated by Damian Wolfe as I was. "What a pleasure to see you!" She purred. Suddenly she seemed to notice his hand encircling mine and her smile dimmed. She raised a slender hand up to play with the gold locket at her throat.

"Hey, Carmen," Damian responded familiarly. "How's your dad?"

"Oh, he's hanging in there," she said, dropping some of her formal hostess manner. "I keep telling him to slow down, but you know him. Work is life. Regular table?"

"Not tonight, thanks," he responded quickly. "I think we're going to go with Bistro tonight."

"Oh, really?" Carmen asked, surprised. Apparently he didn't do this often. It seemed his tastes ran to the more expensive most of the time.

"Yeah, we're thinking something a bit more relaxed," Damian said, smiling at her.

"Sure thing," she responded, masking her reaction. "I'll take you right back."

We followed Carmen's tall, graceful form to the right, entering a chic, cafe-looking restaurant with dim lighting, a bar extending along nearly one whole wall and small tables scattered around.

"How's this?" she asked, gesturing to a table in a relatively private corner of the restaurant.

"Perfect. Thanks, Carmen," Damian said, pulling my chair out for me. Carmen handed us our menus and eyed me one more time before heading back toward the hostess station.

I opened my menu and saw exactly what I had been expecting to see. A whole lot of fancy-sounding food for much higher prices than I would have ever even considered paying myself. I hated to think what the formal restaurant on the other side of the wall charged for their fare.

"So it seems you come here often," I said, glancing up from my menu. With so many unfamiliar words on the page, I wondered if I'd be able to determine what it was I was ordering. What exactly was an "emulsion" or a "coulis"? Would it be appropriate to pull out my phone at the table and google these foodie terms?

"I love good food," Damian responded, perusing the menu. "And this place is one of the best."

"It must be, if you come here often enough to be on first-name terms with the hostess," I teased. He looked up from his menu again, his eyes searching my face. Probably to see if I was really as jealous as I sounded. Better work on reining that in . . . this was just a first date, after all.

"Oh, that's just a coincidence," Damian assured me. "Carmen and I grew up in the same building over on the Upper East Side. I've known her family forever, and her father is, uh, a good friend of my mother's."

Something about his tone made me wonder about the meaning behind his stutter, but I decided to ignore it. We were interrupted by our server anyway, a dark-haired young man with a slight accent I couldn't place. He introduced himself as Stephen. After placing our drink orders—Diet Coke for me (it's a serious habit of mine . . . so sue me) and sparkling water for Damian—I turned back to him with a new topic.

"So what about your father?" I asked. "You've mentioned that your mother was successful in publishing, but you've never really told me anything about your dad."

Damian bit his lip. "My dad . . ." he began, then stopped, considering. "My dad is a thoroughly decent guy."

Again, something in his tone caught my attention. "But?" I prompted, knowing I was being unbelievably pushy, but he didn't seem to be taking offense to it.

"But," Damian continued, pushing a hand through his hair. "It didn't really help him much in the end."

"In the end?"

Damian chuckled mirthlessly. "My mom still ended up leaving him. Seems the old saying 'nice guys finish last' isn't entirely untrue."

I flinched a little, sorry I had asked. "I'm so sorry," I said, reaching out to cover his hand with my own.

Damian looked up at me, surprised. "Oh, it's okay," he said, and to my surprise, he truly sounded it. "It happened a long time ago. Even when they were married, we were never really what you'd call a happy family. I barely even remember what it was like to have us all together. And I'm sure my dad's much happier now than he was with my mom, anyway."

"Does he still live in New York?" I asked.

"No, he's in Houston now. He's in the oil business, so Texas is a much more convenient location for him than New York ever was."

"Do you get to see him often?" I couldn't imagine living in a different city than my dad. Then, suddenly, I realized that, as of a week and a half earlier, I did live in a different city than my dad. I actually lived on the opposite side of the country from my dad. I'd never really thought about it in those terms before. I suddenly felt so . . . adult.

"Not really," Damian answered. His look was regretful. "I try to fly down there at least a couple of times a year to see him, but I haven't had much chance lately. If any of my clients were oil and gas companies it would be a cinch, but I work mostly with tech clients. So I don't travel much to anywhere but California and sometimes Asia."

"Does he ever come up here?" I asked, trying to conceal the impact his offhand commentary was having on me. Damian's life, outside of his family situation, sounded so glamorous. Expensive restaurants, high-paying Wall Street career, trips to Silicon Valley and Asia. The more he told me about himself, the more certain I was that someone as thoroughly ordinary as myself would never be able to keep his interest. I decided that meant I'd better enjoy this date more than I'd ever enjoyed anything before. A good memory could sustain me for a long while.

"Not much," Damian answered, taking a drink from his water glass. "He doesn't like the city. I imagine it holds too many bad memories for him. But sometimes, when it's been a while since we've seen each other, he'll come up here and stay with me for a few days. Those are good times." He smiled down at his menu, his eyes resuming their perusing. "Got any idea what you're going to order?"

"Um, why don't you order for me?" I suggested. It seemed the safest option, given that my meal would be a total mystery to me either way and by this method, I'd at least get something that one of us liked. Besides, everything on this menu was so pricey, and I didn't want to run the risk of ordering something expensive enough that he would secretly resent me for it. Or think I was some kind of high maintenance diva. "You've been here before, so I'm sure you have great recommendations."

"Ooh, trust," he winked at me. "I like it."

As though the server had planted a bug in the flower arrangement at our table, he mysteriously materialized at that moment to take our orders. "What can I get you?" Stephen asked in a polished manner as he set my Diet Coke on the table and a bottle of Pellegrino in front of Damian.

"We'll both start with the kale and strawberry salad," Damian said, then turned to me to mock whisper, "I know, it sounds horrible, but trust me, you won't want to miss it. It's one of the best things on the menu." Then he turned back to the server. "And then the lady will have the duck confit, and I will have the lobster tartine."

"Excellent choices," Stephen complimented, taking the menus from Damian. "We'll have those out to you shortly." We thanked him and he walked away.

"So, your turn," Damian said, turning back to me, a killer smile splitting his face. "Tell me about your family."

For the next ten minutes, I told him all about my parents, focusing enough on my adoration for my dad that I hoped he wouldn't ask too much about my relationship with my mother. No such luck.

"So what about your mom?" he asked innocently. "What's she like?"

"Oh, she's . . . you know, amazing," I said, but I could hear the lack of enthusiasm in my voice. I renewed my efforts. "I mean, you should hear people talk about her. She has a very faithful following."

Damian laughed. "She sounds like a celebrity."

"She is, in some ways," I said with a smile. "Look, there's a part of me that's in awe of my mother, but I won't pretend that we have the best relationship. I should probably work on that."

"Well, at least you've got a good attitude about it," he said. "Knowing you need to do things differently is most of the battle." I detected something just below the surface of his words, as though he had personal experience as his authority.

"Well, I just think I'm a disappointment to her," I said wryly. "She's never said as much, but we can't seem to get on the same page with regard to my life choices. We'll work it out eventually."

"You have no siblings?" Damian asked. When I shook my head, he nodded in understanding. "So all her hopes and dreams for her offspring are centered on you."

I nodded with a mournful sigh. "Therein lies my constant struggle with the matriarch."

"I don't know," he said with a hesitant look on his face. "Think about how much worse it could be. Despite popular belief, the opposite of love is not hate; it's indifference. Take it from someone whose mother was always fairly indifferent. Sincere concern is definitely preferable."

I watched several emotions flit across his face. So much about this man intrigued me, and everything he said just fanned the flames. I had no idea where this whole thing was going but one thing was for sure, I really didn't want it to end any time soon.

- - - - -

"Ouch!" I cried, snapping my hand back from the metal filing cabinet that had just attempted to ingest it. So far my Monday morning was going just about as well as Mondays typically do. "Stupid thing," I muttered. I grabbed the next audit folder in the pile next to me and opened the applicable drawer to file it away.

"Well, hello," said a voice approaching from down the hall. I looked up to see Hunter Payne walking toward me, tossing a water bottle back and forth between his hands as he came.

"Hi," I responded, blowing a piece of hair out of my eyes in frustration as I jammed the audit file into the appropriate folder in the drawer. I closed it gently to preserve my fingers. "You might not want to linger over here. I may or may not be throwing a few profanities around, and I'd hate to offend any delicate ears in the vicinity."

Hunter laughed. "I'm not that delicate." He leaned against the wall and tucked a hand into his pocket. "So, are you just practicing? I imagine you've heard more colorful profanity since you arrived in New York than you are generally used to. Trying some of it out?"

"Not exactly." I held up my hands for him to see. "I've managed three paper cuts and two smashed fingertips already. This job is deadly."

"I didn't realize filing was such a dangerous sport."

"I didn't either, unfortunately. Otherwise I never would have agreed to this." I gave him a teasing smile.

"Who condemned you to filing duty anyway?" Hunter asked, raising an eyebrow. "Why aren't you at a client yet?"

"I still don't have my schedule," I said with a sigh. "My staff buddy Evangeline stopped by the office this morning and asked if I might be willing to file these for her so she could head back out to her client. Apparently she's busy or something." I shrugged as though I couldn't understand how that could possibly be.

"Would you like some help?" Hunter asked kindly. "I have ten minutes until my next meeting, and I file all my own paperwork. So, you know, I'm very qualified."

I grinned up at him, but shook my head. "Thanks, but I would never so carelessly risk the fingers of our legal counsel like that. You might lose one and sue me." I winked at him and picked up my next audit file. "Besides, I'm just about done."

Hunter chuckled again. "Well, let me know if you change your mind. I think you underestimate my talents." He continued down the hall, calling back to me, "I'll catch you later, okay?"

"Sure thing."

Six

"Okay, I really mean it this time," Deirdre said to me the following Thursday, her look sincere. "We really do have a client schedule worked out for you. Starting tomorrow."

"I'm starting a new client on a Friday?" I asked, eyebrow raised. "Unorthodox, but I'm so desperate to do something constructive, I'll take it." I grinned at her mischievously. I had been wandering the office for two weeks now and had pondered offering myself up to maintenance as a window washer, just to break the monotony.

"Beggars can't be choosers," Deirdre teased in response. "Anyway, we're putting you on Feldman Partners for the next couple of months. We typically have a team out there full time, so depending on how it goes for you, we may keep you on that client permanently."

"Investment banking?" I questioned, unable to keep the smile off my face. What a strange coincidence. Feldman's offices were on Broad Street downtown, very near the Collins Weiss offices. I'd seen them on the map I'd found when I was googling information on Damian's employer. The idea that the universe appeared determined to thrust me and Damian together struck me again momentarily before I managed to focus on what Deirdre was telling me about Feldman.

When she left, I sat and contemplated, wondering if I'd be out of my depth at an investment bank client. I didn't exactly have a rich history in the industry. Well, at least I'd have a very handsome someone to ask about the ins and outs, even if I couldn't discuss specific client matters with him. That wonderful little piece of news had just provided me with an ideal excuse to see my current fixation.

My date with Damian the week before had been nearly perfect. Since then, I found myself hoping and praying that he'd call or text me, just so I'd know this whole thing wasn't completely one-sided. But it had only been a first date, so I told myself I couldn't expect too much from him. I'd been looking forward to seeing him at church the following Sunday, but he hadn't been there. The level of disappointment I had felt had been almost embarrassing.

Just then, my phone vibrated. I nearly dislocated my shoulder trying to grab it out of my bag, which was hanging on a hook on the other side of my cubicle. It was a text from Damian . . . finally. My face split into a smile as wide as the Grand Canyon.

Hey you, the text said. *How's your week been?*

Despite the fact that the greeting was somewhat generic, my middle erupted in a spontaneous happy dance.

Not bad, I replied. *Finally got my client schedule today. Looks like I'm headed out your way, starting tomorrow.*

He answered almost instantly. *You're coming to Collins Weiss? I didn't think we were a client of D&T.*

You're not. But my first client is Feldman. I'll be down there for the next two months at least. Probably longer. I may be needing some extensive investment banking tutelage. I know virtually nothing about your world. Not particularly subtle, but it got my point across. I wanted to see him again. Like, right now.

I'm well-known for my investment banking tutelage. You've come to the right man, he said in return. My internal happy dance turned into an all-out rave.

This weekend? I asked. That might be pushing it, but I didn't seem to be capable of any semblance of self-respect or dignity when it came to Damian Wolfe. The rave raging in my middle was making me bold to a dangerous degree. In fact, it just might bold me right out of a miraculous relationship. I found myself holding my breath as I watched the three flashing dots in the text window, indicating that Damian was typing. Finally, after what felt like roughly six and a half years, his message appeared.

I'll pick you up Saturday at eight p.m. I might have floated out of my seat at that point. I beamed at my cell phone, certain I had never seen anything quite as beautiful as that little device before. It had just delivered the closest thing to poetry I'd ever received, and therefore, it was beloved.

"I'm pretty sure expressions like that should not be wasted on electronics," said a voice to my left.

I turned to see Hunter Payne leaning against the column just outside my cubicle, staring at me with a quizzical look on his face, the ever-present water bottle in his hand. Ever since the unfortunate Filing Cabinet of Death sequence the Monday before, he had been stopping by my desk at least a couple of times a day, just to chat. I had attempted to return the favor, but he was almost always either buried up to his eyeballs in paperwork or on the phone whenever I stopped by, so eventually I gave up. I thoroughly enjoyed his company, though. He was friendly and down-to-earth, and he had a fantastic sense of humor.

"You have no idea what this little beauty has just done for me," I cooed, stroking the smartphone gently and grinning at him.

"I'm pretty sure I don't want to know," he replied. He stared silently at me caressing my phone for several seconds before sighing and giving in. "Never mind, I want to know."

I giggled. "This gorgeous little gadget has just allowed me to cleverly secure a second date with a man that is as close to heaven as I am ever likely to get."

"You conned your way into a date with an angel?" Hunter asked, raising an eyebrow. "Haven't you read enough fairy tales to learn that that kind of thing will only get you into trouble?"

"Well now, conned is a harsh word," I said, returning my phone to my bag and folding my arms across my chest. "I prefer verbs like 'captivated' or 'charmed.' It's not easy being this irresistible, Hunter."

"My apologies," Hunter muttered, his lips twitching. He stuck his free hand casually into the pocket of his blue pinstripe slacks. "So, who is this angelic fellow?"

"His name is Damian Wolfe," I said, letting my head fall back dramatically. "And he's just about the most ama—,"

"Damian Wolfe?" Hunter interrupted. "The VP at Collins Weiss?"

I raised my head and stared at him. "How do you know that? Do you know him?"

"No," Hunter replied, shrugging and taking a sip from his water bottle. "I've heard of him, though. He's risen pretty quickly through the ranks. One of my friends was passed over for a VP role at Collins Weiss and he thinks it was Wolfe who got it instead."

"He certainly seems to be successful," I agreed with a nod. "It's kind of intimidating, actually. But still, he's been so nice to me, and he's a perfect gentleman. I'm excited he wants to go out again. I wasn't sure he would."

"I'm happy for you," Hunter replied, not looking wholly devoted to this conversation topic. "Well, I was just up to get the blood flowing, but I'd better head back. I have a conference call."

"Bye," I said airily, waving at him. "Let me know when you're taking off. I'll walk out with you."

"Will do, unless it's looking like it'll be a late one for me," Hunter called over his shoulder. "If it is, I'll let you know so you don't wait."

"Sounds good," I said and, smiling, went back to my client listing.

- - - - -

"Can I help you?" The slim blonde behind the front desk at Feldman asked in a harassed voice the next day. She tapped her pen frantically on the wood as if to emphasize just how much of her time I was wasting by standing there.

"Hi," I said, and her face seemed to tighten further. Apparently my niceties were only making her day that much harder. "My name is Ryder Redmond. I'm with Durham & Tucker."

"Oh," she said, her lip curling. "The auditors." The way she said the word *auditors* made it sound as though it were synonymous with *terrorists*.

"Yep," I said brightly, plastering a ridiculously enthusiastic smile on my face. "Can you tell me where in the building my team is sitting, and I'll get out of your hair?"

She all but rolled her eyes. "I can't just let you in," she said with a withering glare. "I'll call up to the audit room and someone will come down and get you. In the meantime, you can fill out this application form to start the process of getting an access card to the building. It takes several days." She handed me a sheet of paper.

Security protocols in New York were beyond belief. In my internship days in Salt Lake, when I showed up at a new client, I'd walk in the front door, tell them who I was and what I was there to do, and I'd be immediately shown back to a conference room, no questions asked. In New York, you needed to provide your name, company, title, phone number, address, birthplace, parental lineage, urine and blood samples, notarized references from five unrelated individuals, and a letter of recommendation from the President of the United States. What was worse, when you attempted to procure the required items for access into the chambers beyond, people treated you like you were some kind of shady character up to something nefarious.

I sat down on one of the chic-looking suede couches lining the floor-to-ceiling windows of the starkly decorated building lobby and began filling out the form. Within five minutes, a man who looked to be about thirty approached me from the direction of the elevators.

"Hi, Ryder?" he asked with a smile. He was tall and pale with neatly parted brown hair and a light blue shirt tucked into dark blue slacks. He held out his hand to me. "I'm Dave. Dave Parks. I'm one of the managers on the Feldman audit engagement. Welcome!"

"Thanks!" I smiled at him and took his hand, rising to my feet. "I'm excited to get started."

"That's what we like to hear," he replied. He motioned to the paper in my hand. "You can bring that with you. We'll turn it in later. We'll get you a temporary access badge in the meantime." He took me over to the front desk. "Hey Megan, can you get Ryder a temporary badge until her permanent one comes through?"

Megan offered a fake smile and handed me a plain, white plastic card with a number on it. She then handed me a sheet of paper and told me to write my name, company, and the card number down. When I handed it back, she faked another smile (I assumed this show of friendliness was all for Dave's benefit) and said, "Well, you're all set. Get that form back to me for a permanent badge as soon as you can."

I nodded at her and followed Dave toward the elevators. He waved his card in front of a flashing red light and pushed a floor number on a screen. "So where are you from?" he asked congenially.

"Salt Lake City," I answered. "I just moved here a few weeks ago. Are you a native New Yorker?"

"Nope," Dave replied, gesturing for me to board the elevator. "Few of us are. There are nearly fifty of us on this audit and only about ten are native New Yorkers. I'm from Virginia."

"Wow," I said with a blink. "Fifty? That's quite . . . sizeable." The largest audit team I'd been on in Salt Lake was a team of eight.

"Not even close to the biggest," Dave said, smiling at the dumbstruck look on my face. "We have a couple tech company audit teams with over a hundred, although they spend most of their time in California and not here."

I nodded, looking impressed. Honestly, I couldn't imagine a company's financial statements being so complex that it required that many people to analyze them.

"I'll introduce you to the team and get you started on your first assignment," Dave continued, leading me off the elevator on the fifty-second floor. "Don't worry about remembering everyone. Chances are, you'll only work with a small number of them for the next few months anyway. We've assigned you to the cash team."

I attempted to look like I understood what this meant. What was a cash team?

"Guys!" Dave called as he entered a large room down the hall and to the right. It looked like a massive classroom with rows of tables spread across the space. There were probably around thirty-five people in the room, most of whom looked up from their laptops or conversations to focus on Dave. "This is our newest staff member, Ryder. She's joining us from Salt Lake City and will spend the next couple months with us. Vijaya, I've got her assigned to your team." An Indian girl with long, silky black hair nodded and smiled at me. "I'm not going to bother introducing you to everyone now," Dave informed me, "given that there are so many of us. But feel free to get out and meet people on your downtime."

I saw a few people smirk at the phrase "downtime." Even I knew that free time wasn't something that came around much in public accounting.

"Here's the team you'll be working with," Dave continued, gesturing over to where Vijaya stood. "Vijaya is the lead senior assigned to the cash team." Dave stopped for a second, and studied me quickly. "Okay, maybe I should pause here for a second to explain the hierarchy of a public accounting firm. I'll make it quick."

I opened my mouth to explain that I actually was familiar with the hierarchy, as a former intern, but he didn't notice.

"The commander-in-chief of an audit team is the partner," Dave explained. "Our partner is Jim Rose, but he's currently out of the country. I'll introduce you to him when he returns." As he said this, he gestured over to a large desk in the corner of the room. I assumed that was where my new boss sat when he was present. "Next in line are the senior managers and then the managers. That's me. I, along with the other managers, coordinate the members of the team at a general level. Next come the seniors." At this point he gestured around to Vijaya, who was looking at him with an amused look on her face. I wondered if she'd noticed my attempt to interrupt his explanation. "Their primary job is managing the staff and interns. That's you." He pointed at me with his forefinger. "As you probably know, staff are those who have typically been with the company for less than two years. The number of people in each level of the hierarchy varies widely depending on the size of the client and audit engagement, but typically the team is pyramid-shaped. Meaning, of course, there are far less senior managers than there are staff. Got it?"

I nodded, smiling.

Dave turned back to the cash team. "So, as I said before, Vijaya is the lead senior for the cash team. He proceeded to introduce the rest of the team, each of whom waved to me in turn as Dave said their names. "Well, I'll let you get to it," he said at the conclusion of the introductions. "Let me know if you need anything." And he strode off.

Just then, I noticed that a pretty Asian girl was gesturing me over to a seat next to her. "Hi!" she said brightly. "I'm Soon Li. Welcome to the Feldman Audit cash team. It's a riot." She winked at me.

"So . . . at the risk of sounding completely uninformed, what exactly is a cash team?" I asked. I nearly winced at how ignorant the question made me sound. But Soon Li just smiled.

"We are in charge of auditing the cash portion of the company's balance sheet," she said.

I stared at her. "You need eight people to audit one line item on the balance sheet?" I had never heard of such a thing. I had audited the cash section of client balance sheets by myself in a matter of hours in Salt Lake. Such was the difference between small private companies in Utah and huge public ones in New York, I guessed.

Soon Li laughed. "It's a big job," she agreed. "Let's get you started."

I spent the rest of the morning looking through the audit workpapers and asking questions to Soon Li, who was unbelievably patient with me. Around lunchtime, we were interrupted.

"At a good stopping place?" I looked up to see a slight, brown-haired guy who looked to be about twenty-five standing above me. I knew he was on my team, but I'd already forgotten his name. "Dimitriy," he said, as if he had read my mind. "We want to take you to lunch for your first day. What do you think?"

"Sounds good to me!" I smiled at him and flexed my fingers. They were stiff from typing all my notes from the past few hours. Soon Li and I rose and headed toward the door where the rest of the team was waiting.

A young-looking blond kid stepped forward and held out his hand to me. "Hi, I'm Parker," he said with a grin. "Nice to meet you." He was the first-year senior, I remembered. Man, he looked young. Far too young to have been with the firm for more than two years.

"Parker is our resident prodigy," said lead senior Vijaya, and I wondered if my expression had been showing my curiosity. "He graduated NYU at eighteen. He's the only twenty-year-old senior in the entire firm."

"Wow," I said, shaking Parker's hand. "That's impressive."

"Meh," he said, waving a hand through the air as though it were no big deal. "I never really liked school so I just found ways to get it over with as soon as possible." I laughed and followed him and the other team members as they headed toward the elevators.

"How do you feel about sushi?" The question came from the other Asian girl I was pretty sure was a staff named Jie. "There's a really good place just down the street."

"Sounds perfect to me!" I replied. The restaurant was less than a five-minute walk from the bank, and while it was crowded, we were seated quickly. I sat next to a short, thickly built man named Manuel who I would have guessed to be about thirty-five. He reminded me that he was a second-year staff, which only put him a year ahead of me.

"I was a late bloomer," he joked when I asked him about his background. "I actually worked in my family's dry cleaning business until I was almost thirty, but decided I wanted to do more for my children than my parents had been able to do for me. So I went back to school and then came to work for D&T." He then asked me about my home and family back in Salt Lake. I was in the middle of explaining that the Great Salt Lake was not actually a hot resort spot but more like a smelly, salty, 1,500-square-mile puddle, when I saw him.

Sitting across the restaurant, surrounded by guys dressed as sharply as he was, sat Damian Wolfe. He appeared to be telling a story, his face animated and eyes shining with mirth. The men at the table were laughing raucously, apparently highly entertained.

Manuel noticed the direction of my attention and turned to see what I was so interested in. "See someone you know?" he asked curiously.

"Sort of," I replied, not really wanting to go into detail. I'd never seen Damian look so energetic. Granted, I'd only seen him in a few situations, so that wasn't surprising. He looked even handsomer than usual as he grinned in wholehearted amusement at something his colleague was saying.

Then, to my horror, one of the men sitting across the table from Damian caught me staring and made a comment to the group at large, nodding in my direction. In unison, they all turned to look at me. Face flaming, I turned quickly away. Darn my weakness for a pretty face! Why couldn't I just be dignified for once? What must Damian be thinking of me now, as all his co-workers laughed at me?

Manuel was watching my internal struggle play across my face with a sympathetic look. "Hey, it's no big deal," he said, nudging me softly and glancing back over his shoulder at the table of bankers. "They're probably just admiring you." I appreciated his kindness, but it didn't stop me from feeling thoroughly stupid.

"Ryder," came a voice from behind me. I turned to look at Damian, hoping my face had managed to lose its overt rosiness in the past second or two.

"Hey, Damian," I said, not even trying to pretend like I was surprised to see him. "How are you?"

"I'm great!" he replied with a smile. "First day at Feldman, huh? How's it going?"

"Fantastic, so far." I smiled around at my team, and noted the dumbfounded looks on the female faces as they gazed upon his gloriousness. Yes, girls. Trust me, I know.

"Hey, come with me for a sec," he said, grabbing my hand and pulling me to my feet. "I want to introduce you to my friends."

I really did not want to meet his friends. And I wanted to meet them even less when I saw the smirks on their faces as he dragged me toward them.

"Guys, this is Ryder," he introduced, his arm around my waist. I found, despite the looks of bemusement on the faces of the investment bankers surrounding me, that I really liked how it felt there.

"Hi," I greeted with a half-hearted wave.

"Nice to meet you, Ryder," said the man who had first spotted me staring at Damian. I was already predisposed to dislike him, just based on that. He had dark hair, styled in fashionable disarray, brown eyes, and a long, straight nose. I could tell from his demeanor that he was used to being thought handsome, and while some might find him so, my first impression of him was that of a used car salesman. The notion was helped along significantly by the insincerity I could almost see dripping from the corners of the wide, toothy grin he was offering me.

"This is Christopher Morrison," Damian introduced. "But we all just call him Trip. He's one of my fellow VPs at Collins."

I nodded at the smirking man, still not liking the expression on his face. The dude was slimy, I could tell—probably because of how his eyes were traveling steadily up and down my body. Shudder.

"It's good to meet a friend of Damian's from outside work," said another guy to my right. "We don't meet many of those. The guy practically lives at the office." With his olive skin, dark curly hair, and wide brown eyes, this colleague looked much more trustworthy than Trip. I gave him a smile to reward him for it.

"James Handy," Damian introduced me to the curly-haired banker. "He's an associate, reporting to me."

"Oooh," Trip said to James, his voice loud enough to attract notice from other tables in the vicinity. "Put in your place, man! Nothing like being introduced as an inferior."

I had to struggle to keep the distaste off of my face as I glanced back at Trip. Everything about that man repelled me. I turned my attention back to James, and he shrugged carelessly as he held out his hand to me.

"Do you work around here?" he asked. I shook his hand firmly as I nodded.

"For now," I responded. "I'm an audit associate at Durham & Tucker and I'm currently assigned to the Feldman engagement."

"Public accounting," James said, nodding and offering me a sympathetic wince. "You guys have a raw deal. You get all of our hours with about a quarter of our pay."

"Thanks for the reminder," I said, laughing. "You're right, of course, but it's a really good stepping stone to other things."

"Very true," Damian agreed, squeezing me closer to his side and making my heart rate rise. "Ryder just started on Feldman today. They're her first New York client."

"Where are you from originally?" asked the sandy-haired guy to the left of Trip.

"Salt Lake City," I answered immediately. I saw two of the bankers exchange amused glances at my response.

"Salt Lake's a cool place," James commented, and I decided that I liked him best of the table. Except for Damian, of course. "One of my favorite places to ski. Those mountains are incredible."

"Dumbest liquor laws in the country, though," said one of the bankers to James's right. "I end up spending three times as much to get the same buzz."

"I can't believe y'all are admitting you've been to Utah," Trip said, again at a volume calculated to attract attention. "What possible reason would you have to visit a hillbilly place like that?"

This time I couldn't stop myself. I stared at him with a look of incredulity on my face. My inner Utahn was getting seriously annoyed at this condescending heap of investment banker snobbery. It may not be chic or high fashion, but Utah was home . . . what right did he have to knock it? Hadn't he just said "y'all?" Where was he from? I was tempted to ask, but a niggling fear that I was wrong and he was originally from Manhattan stopped me. "Actually Utah is much more sophisticated than you seem to think," I defended instead. "Particularly along the Wasatch Front. Utah's growing economy has been all over in the news for the past few years."

"Yeah, Utah news," Trip snorted, leering at me.

"No, she's right," James pointed out. "I saw a segment just the other day on NBC about how Utah's economy is the strongest in the nation. And I remember reading last year in Forbes about how Salt Lake City is topping national charts for growth. Actually, Feldman itself has been sending tons of jobs out there in the past couple of years."

"What, are you secretly working for the Utah Department of Commerce, Handy?" Trip asked him with a look of disgust on his face.

"Oh, leave him alone, Trip," Damian said, but he sounded amused.

"So, Ryder, is Damian bringing you to the party next week?" asked one of the smirking bankers who had laughed at my humble Utah beginnings. He looked to be a few years older than me, with light blue eyes and a colorless complexion. "I'm Dennis, by the way," he introduced, and his tone sounded as though he thought he was favoring me by doing so. "I report to Damian too." He shot a grin in Trip's direction.

"Nice to meet you," I lied. I was about ready for this meet-and-greet to be over. "And no, Damian is not bringing me to the party next week." I figured I'd just answer the question for Damian so he wouldn't feel pressured into asking me, right there in front of everyone. Besides, if all these charming people were going to be in attendance, I doubted I really wanted to go anyway.

"Damian, dude," said the other banker who'd thought my home state was humorous. His dark hair was styled similarly to Trip's but his face lacked the symmetry and strong jaw. "You should bring her. Show her what partying in New York City looks like. Then maybe she'll change her mind about the apparent sophistication of Utah." Putting the words "sophistication" and "Utah" in the same sentence appeared to be too much for him and he ended up snorting into his napkin.

Wow, I hated these people.

"Shut up, Pierce," said James, a look of contempt on his face. "It's not like your hometown is all that much to brag about. Aren't you from

Oklahoma or something?" He smiled apologetically up at me, and I smiled gratefully back.

"You should come," Damian said to me in response to Pierce's comment. Surprised, I looked up at him. "After all, who else would I bring?"

The absolute dread of spending another minute, let alone a whole evening, with these jerks was tempered moderately by the thought that Damian actually wanted to bring me to a fancy schmancy work function. Of course, it occurred to me that he might just be responding to peer pressure, but I managed to stifle that thought in short order.

"Well, I'd better get back to my table," I said, eager to escape all the eyes currently studying me, some curiously, some impertinently. "It was nice to meet you all."

Damian walked with me back to my table, muttering in my ear. "Sorry to blindside you with a party invite like that. But I'd really love for you to come with me. Should be pretty fun."

I seriously doubted that, but I wasn't about to turn down another opportunity to go out with Damian. "I'm sure it will be. Just text me the details later, okay?"

"Sure thing," he said and smiled warmly at me. He stooped and kissed me on the cheek before turning to head back to his own table. My cheek burned where his lips had brushed it, and my hands clenched the back of my chair involuntarily as I struggled to rebalance myself. My co-workers were all staring at me—the men with amusement, the women with frank curiosity.

"Ryder!" gasped Jie when I finally sat down. "Who was that? How do you know him?"

"His name is Damian Wolfe," I responded, feeling slightly breathless. "And . . . I think I'm dating him."

Seven

That's it. I'm done. I give up."

I smiled to myself as I stirred the macaroni in the pot, trying to make sure it cooked evenly and didn't stick to the bottom. I'd now been living with Lily for nearly three weeks and I was already starting to recognize that tone. It was the sound of "Everything I'm about to say to you should be taken with a grain of salt because chances are, I will change my mind twenty minutes from now. But I require your sympathy, so get over here."

"Sure, Lil," I said, nodding, trying not to let my smile show in my voice. "I agree. You've been trying to get this Broadway career thing off the ground for two full years now, but right now, today, is the appropriate time for throwing in the towel. You've finally reached that point, I think. Time to embrace your future as a perpetual waitress."

I heard something smack into the back of the kitchen cabinet behind me and knew she'd attempted to throw something at me from the living room.

"It feels that way, okay?" she grumped. "This is the four hundred and fifty-seven thousandth audition I've been to, and thus far I've managed a total of two roles, both in off-Broadway theaters that nobody's ever heard of. And one of those shows didn't even make it to opening night, so I don't think it should count."

I made a sympathetic noise as I drained the water from the pot. Through the steam emanating from the sink, I saw Lily sprawled out on the couch, her head hanging off the edge, looking truly pathetic.

"At least you made callbacks on this one," I pointed out. "I thought you said it seemed really promising." I poured the cheese powder from the white packet into the pot and began to stir, my mouth watering as the fake orange color began to coat the pasta. Go ahead, call me weird, but instant mac and cheese was a very significant part of my life in college. I wasn't prepared to give it up yet.

"It did!" Lily cried, sitting up and punching a couch pillow in frustration. "I thought I had it in the bag. The role was perfect for me because it *was* me. It wouldn't even require any real acting on my part. It seemed like the breakthrough I've been waiting for!"

"I'm sorry," I sympathized again. I divided the macaroni between two bowls and carried the other one to her. Being the perfect roommate comfort food that it was, I knew she would appreciate it. After handing her the bowl, I sat down on the other side of the couch, forcing her feet off the edge and nearly sending her and her macaroni crashing to the wood floor. She managed to catch herself just in time, but shot me a dirty look. I ignored her.

"I can't believe that after all that, they didn't even offer you another less prominent role, or at least a spot in the chorus," I said, taking a bite.

"Well . . ." she said, her gaze suddenly shifty as she stirred the mac and cheese with her fork.

"Lily!" I cried, nudging her hard with my big toe. "You turned them down?"

She refused to look at me, and I had a sudden revelation.

"Just how many times have you done this?" I demanded. "How many times have you been offered a minor role but turned it down because it wasn't a lead?"

"It doesn't matter," she muttered, looking mutinous.

"Of course it does!"

"I don't want some two-bit role," she claimed imperiously. "I want to be a star, not a supporting actress."

"Lily, nearly everybody starts as a supporting actress!"

She said nothing, but shoveled some pasta into her mouth, still refusing to meet my eyes.

"Do me a favor," I said through my own mouthful of toxic orange heaven. "The next time you're offered a role, any role, I want you to take it. Even if it's just a chorus role. I'm telling you, a small start is better than no start at all."

Lily glared at me, chewing glumly.

"Lily?" I pressed.

"Fine."

"Good, now on to my problem," I said, folding my legs in front of me and settling back against the armrest.

"You don't know the meaning of the word," she muttered. "You, with your cushy corporate job and slick billionaire boyfriend."

I motioned out the window at the inky black sky. "Yeah, my cushy corporate job in which I worked fourteen hours on my very first day of my very first client." I gave her a pointed look. "And my slick billionaire boyfriend who, first of all, isn't my boyfriend, and second of all, wants to take me to a party with some of the worst people I've ever met. A party where they will get the opportunity to continue to openly mock my lack of sophistication. And they will have an audience. People with whom I would rather never reach "idiot" status. You know, at least until I've actually earned it."

"Uh-huh," said Lily, looking determinedly unimpressed at my tirade. "You said something about a problem?"

I stared at her wide-eyed. "What do I do?"

"Um, don't go?" She looked at me like the answer was obvious.

"But what do I tell Damian?"

"That you're not going?"

"Lily, has anyone ever told you that you are the exact opposite of helpful?"

"You're welcome."

- - - - -

"So how was your first day?" Damian asked me as we sat in yet another swanky restaurant. This time I had decided that I was going to be thoroughly unimpressed, regardless of where he decided to take me. It was step one on my journey of becoming the refined Manhattanite version of myself that I desperately wanted to be . . . if only to save face. I didn't know what step two was yet, but I had to figure it out quickly because the entire transformation process had to be complete before Damian's work soiree the following week.

"It was fine," I answered with a shrug. I had been shrugging a lot that night. It was the only way I knew how to convey a complete lack of awe. My shoulders were beginning to get tired. "Just long. But I can deal with that."

"Are you okay?" Damian asked, studying me with narrowed eyes. "You seem more subdued than usual. Did something happen?"

Dang it. Apparently my efforts were not as subtle as I'd hoped they'd be.

"No, I'm fine," I said, attempting to portray a sense of profound confusion on my face. Let me just say, I did not have Lily's gift for drama.

"Uh-huh . . ." Damian said, looking thoroughly unconvinced. "Seriously, Ryder, what's up?"

I sighed. "Look, I'm just a little nervous about going to this party with you next week." I rubbed my forehead with my fingers, trying to stave off a pressure headache. "Your co-workers didn't make me feel particularly confident about attending."

"Ah, ignore them," Damian said. "Most of them are egotistical prep-school dropouts from wealthy families. They wouldn't know class if it mugged them in broad daylight."

I smiled weakly at him, but it fell off my face almost immediately. "That doesn't really make me feel any better, Damian," I said. "I have so much new stuff in my life right now, I'm not sure I can handle a whole extra layer of social anxiety. Do you have any pointers for me? I'd really like to spare myself any unnecessary ridicule."

"Ryder," Damian said with a kind smile. He reached out and took my hand across the table. "You don't seem to understand what I'm saying to you. Those guys' opinion of you doesn't matter. Anybody whose opinion is worth having will adore you for the amazing person you are. Don't let a bunch of arrogant investment bankers ruin it for you." He squeezed my hand subtly. "Besides, you already have a champion in your camp. I'm fairly certain that James will defend your honor to the death." He smiled at me again, his eyes crinkling at the corners.

"Thanks," I said, squeezing his hand back. "So how are things on your side? Ready to coach me on all the ins and outs of investment banking?"

Damian laughed. "I'm pretty sure you don't really need my coaching. But things are good on my end. I just finished pitching a proposal for a client and I think it went well. Hopefully we'll be signing contracts here, shortly."

"Is that good?" I asked. "Sounds like a big deal."

"Well, proposals like this one *are* a big deal at my level," he replied. "It's kind of how you prove your usefulness to the bank. My main purpose as a VP is to manage existing client relationships, but if you can manage to pitch a new proposal, get it under contract, and handle the transaction on top of that, it's more likely you'll be considered for a director role. Those are hard to get."

"So, based on my understanding, in an investment bank, you go from analyst, to associate, to VP, to director?" I asked.

"And from there to managing director," Damian said, nodding. "If you're very, very lucky. Or very, very cutthroat. Either one." He smiled.

"But what do you actually do?" I asked, scrunching my forehead. "What's the point of an investment bank?"

"Well, our primary function is to help our clients raise funding for their activities," Damian replied. "We also do a lot of work around mergers and acquisitions, or 'M&A.' I'm a VP in the M&A group, so that's what I do. I help clients that are either interested in buying another company or selling their company to another by facilitating the transaction. Really, we operate as a kind of financial advisor for our clients."

I nodded my understanding of this concept. "That sounds pretty straightforward. Is that it?"

He smirked and shook his head. "No, not at all. Those are primary functions, but we have several other business practices." He then embarked on an explanation of each of the services Collins Weiss offered. I nodded like I understood each time he used a new term I'd never heard before in my life. So there was a lot of nodding going on. He didn't stop until he was signing his name with a flourish on the receipt the server had just handed him. "And that's about it," he finished.

"Okay," I said, trying to keep myself from looking as panicky as I felt. I was way out of my comfort zone in this industry. Why couldn't I have been assigned to a fashion merchandising company or something?

"Hey, don't worry about it," Damian said, reaching behind him for his light gray blazer. "You'll pick it up. Plus, you've got a lot of people to help you. Namely, your client, your audit team, and me."

I smiled at him in gratitude. "I appreciate it. I will freely admit that I'm feeling pretty overwhelmed right now."

"Well, let's give you a break, then," he said and gestured to my plate. "You all through?"

I nodded and rose to my feet. Damian took my hand and led me from the restaurant and out onto the street.

"Have you had a chance to explore Central Park yet?" Damian queried.

"Not yet," I responded, still focusing on the warmth of his hand. I hoped he didn't take it away for a very long time.

"Okay, let's head that way," he said. He glanced down my outfit to my feet. I had opted for a more conservative look this time, pairing a cute designer tee with my standard skinny jeans, and throwing on a pair of ballet flats.

"I'm glad you went with the sensible shoes this time around." He winked at me. "Not only are they better suited for getting around the city, but I'm much more secure in our height difference now. What are you, five five?"

"Good eye," I congratulated with a grin, and he laughed.

"Well, my mom is five five, so it was probably easier to assess than it should have been," Damian admitted. He pulled me across the street and we headed into the huge park, lit intermittently with street lamps.

"Tell me about your mom," I said curiously. "You mentioned that she used to be in publishing but she's retired now? What does she do to fill her time?"

"Well, she splits her attention between charity work and attempts to get me advantageously married," Damian replied, looking at me out of the corner of his eye. Gauging my reaction, I assumed. Advantageously married? What was this, England in the 1790s?

"Oh really?" I asked innocently. "Has she sent any good prospects your way?"

"Not lately."

"What a shame," I said, shaking my head in mock sympathy. "But at least you've got the singles ward there to fill the void."

"Indeed," Damian responded, nodding solemnly. "And boy, has it delivered lately." He brought my hand up to his mouth and held it there momentarily, pressing his lips to my fingers.

I felt a soft, warm glow start in the vicinity of my heart and grow steadily brighter. Could this really be happening to me? It was so unusual for me to actually crave the person I was seeing—had I actually found someone with whom I could have a real romantic connection? As we walked under an overhead lamp, I studied Damian's face, admiring the angle of his cheekbones and the strong curve of his jaw. Suddenly, I really needed to know.

"Why are you being so nice to me?" I asked him. My voice was slightly more vulnerable than I wanted it to be, but there was nothing I could do about that now. "You must have *armies* of females after you, but for some reason, you choose to spend your time with a girl from the Utah suburbs who's a full seven years younger than you. Why?"

"Way to throw my age in my face," Damian said, laughing. He looked down at me, and his eyes appeared soft in the yellow light from the streetlamps. "You intrigue me, I guess," he revealed. "Thanks to my mother's matchmaking efforts, I've met all kinds of women, but none as sincere and innocent as you. It's appealing."

I bit my lip as I considered this. I knew I was innocent, but I wasn't sure I liked being pursued because of it. Hence the efforts to become more like my tough-as-nails New York counterparts. He noticed my expression and stopped, pulling me to a halt beside him. He faced me, his expression suddenly enveloped in shadow as he turned away from the lamplight.

"And let's not underestimate the impact of a pretty face," he said, and I could hear the smile on his face, though I couldn't see it. "I'm not sure I've ever seen one I've liked quite as much as this one." He brushed his fingertips across my cheek, and then cradled my face in his perfect hands. He leaned toward me, brushing his lips down my jawbone.

Hmmm . . . that was okay too. I mean, even better would have been an attraction to my fascinating personality and incomparable intellect, but hey, we'd get there eventually. I felt my hands start to shake slightly at his touch. I grasped his forearms, just for something to hold onto, and moved a little closer to him, leaning into his kisses. I felt his breath come a little bit faster at my response. He let his lips glide further down my throat, and suddenly I found that my breathing was accelerating too.

Unexpectedly, an image popped into my head. I imagined the look on my parents' face if they knew I was standing on a deserted, darkened, semi-secluded pathway with a man, letting him enthusiastically kiss my neck. I backed up suddenly, not even really knowing why. My parents couldn't see me, I knew that. It must be an engrained response after so many years of morality lessons at church.

Not wanting Damian to suspect the direction of my thoughts, I beamed brightly up at him.

"Everything all right?" he asked, concerned as he took in my unduly cheerful expression.

"Oh, sure," I lied. "I just thought I saw someone coming toward us down the path." I gestured behind him at the perfectly empty walkway. Then, not wanting him to suspect my fib, I grabbed his hand and started walking again.

I was conflicted. I was more attracted to Damian than I'd ever been to any other guy I'd ever met. Really. Ever. I wanted him in ways I'd never wanted anyone before. Ways that made me blush to think about. But was this crazy, unfamiliar feeling making me reckless? I'd promised my mom I wouldn't forget how I'd been raised, but when it came down to it, I didn't really know what that meant. Sure, I knew all the old church answers when it came to chastity and right and wrong, but the fact was, I'd never really talked details with anybody. Just how far was too far?

- - - - -

"You didn't shut the paper drawer all the way," Hunter contributed helpfully from behind me as the printer started making a bizarre, squealing noise that didn't bode well. I looked down at the paper drawer and noticed that one corner of it was misaligned by a half inch. I slammed it shut and immediately the squealing stopped.

"Thanks," I acknowledged. I hadn't seen Hunter in several days, given that I'd been out at Feldman. My team had sent me back to the office today, however, to pick up some audit files and print off some forms on letterhead for the client to review.

"No problem," he said, leaning against the wall and folding his arms. "Haven't seen you for a while. How is Feldman going?"

"It's going fine," I replied distractedly as I reviewed the pages the printer was spitting out at top speed. "Lots of long hours and mindless tasks, but hey, I'm willing to pay my dues. How have you been?"

"Good," Hunter replied. "Got a new project I'm working on. One of our clients has gotten wind of a potential lawsuit that they may be implicated in, so I'm doing some research on that." He eyed me carefully, as though trying to decide whether or not to say something. "So have you run into your boyfriend at all while you've been over there on Wall Street?"

"He's not my boyfriend," I said, and my voice was strangely monotone. Apparently I said this a lot—it was getting to be a habitual response. "And yes, I have seen him. Why do you ask?" I glanced up at him curiously. He hadn't seemed all that interested in this topic the last time we spoke.

"No reason," Hunter said with a shrug. "I was just wondering. Are things getting fairly serious between the two of you?"

"Not really sure how to answer that," I replied, my eyes once again fixed on the papers whizzing out of the printer and into the tray. "He's taking me to a fancy work party tonight, if that tells you anything."

"With all his Collins Weiss compatriots?" Hunter asked. Okay, yes. This sudden interest in my personal life was definitely strange.

"Yes, I think so," I said with a raised eyebrow, studying him. "Why are you so interested all of a sudden?"

"I've always wondered what those parties were like," Hunter said speculatively, but he had a steely glint in his eye. A glint I didn't trust. "How about letting me come with you?"

"Oh, sure," I said sarcastically. "*That'd* be romantic."

"Not as a date or anything," Hunter said, with a dubious look. "You've already got one of those, remember? Just as a friend who needs something to do tonight." He actually seemed serious about this.

"Um, no," I said with finality. "This situation with Damian is fairly new. The last thing I'm going to do is put it in jeopardy so you can play creepy investigative journalist."

"You're a cruel woman, Red," Hunter said with a disappointed shake of his head. I looked up at him in surprise at the sudden use of the nickname.

"What?" he asked in confusion, noting my expression. I studied him for a second, and then shook my head, realizing that it had been a coincidence.

"Nothing," I said dismissively. "My dad just calls me Red."

"Well, it's a fairly unimaginative nickname, so you can't exactly blame me for stumbling across it," Hunter laughed. He reached out, flicking a lock of my red hair as he squatted to pick up a pile of the audit files I was supposed to be transporting back to the Feldman offices. "Do you need help with this stuff?"

"No, I can manage," I said, pulling the forms off the printer and storing them carefully in my bag. I leaned down to pick up the pile of folders and immediately sent half of them crashing to the floor.

"Obviously," said Hunter, rolling his eyes. He stooped again to pick them up and then headed toward the front desk. "Come on, we'll get you a cab back to Feldman."

- - - - -

I stared at myself in my full-length mirror, feeling distinctly uncomfortable. My work schedule had been a teensy bit (in which case "teensy bit" actually means "a whole freaking lot") more stressful than I had anticipated in the past week, and I hadn't had time to plan for a party outfit. Upon review of my closet, I discovered I did not have a single dress that would be appropriate for a swanky party at a Fifth Avenue penthouse. At which point, Lily came to my rescue.

"Here, wear this," she had said, holding out a hanger.

"Where did you get that?" I asked, staring at the black cocktail dress with obvious designer origins.

"My dad is very important in the business world," she said, her nose in the air. "Which you would remember if you ever actually listened to a word I said. I have a ton of these. But I think this one will show off your figure the best."

And it did. The dress was stunning. But the problem wasn't with the silhouette of the dress; it was with the neckline. Meaning, of course, that it didn't actually have one. And here I stood, in the first strapless dress I had ever worn, knowing that I looked dynamite by New York standards. But also knowing that if my mother could actually have seen me at that moment, she likely wouldn't have been able to find words to communicate her horror.

"You look incredible," Lily said, shocking me with possibly the first sincere compliment she had ever paid me. "Seriously, that dress looks like it was made for you."

"I feel downright naked," I said, crossing my arms over my chest and taking hold of my bare shoulders. "I need a sweater or a wrap or something."

"Are you crazy?" Lily asked, her eyebrows raised. "Why cover up some of your best assets?"

I looked at her disbelievingly, and then back at the mirror. My best assets, huh? "Because, quite frankly, I'd rather Damian not consider my best assets to be physical ones," I said pointedly, looking back at her with a stern expression.

"Oh, we're getting all feminist now, are we?" Lily said, nodding. "I see. Well, let me see if I can find something." She ran back to her room, I assumed to start digging through her closet. I really owed her for all of this. I sat down on the bed, noticing how the dress hiked up my thighs to a point I knew would be considered indecent by many of my acquaintance. I huffed in frustration.

Just then, my phone rang. I was thrilled to see that it was Damian. Just the sight of his name did strange things to my insides these days.

"Hi," I said cheerfully into the phone. "If you're almost here, I'm afraid you'll have to wait a little bit. I'm conforming to the typical female stereoty—"

"Ryder," Damian interrupted, and his voice sounded uncharacteristically urgent. "So sorry to cut you off, but I'm afraid I can't make it to the party tonight."

I was hit by a wave of mixed emotion. Disappointment at not seeing Damian but profound relief that I wouldn't have to attend the dreaded party.

"Are you okay?" I asked, concerned at his tone. "You sound funny."

"I'm at the airport," he explained, and he sounded slightly out of breath, like he might be jogging or something.

"Emergency business trip?" I guessed.

"Not quite," he replied, and I heard him say something about "getting there tonight" to someone in the background, probably an airline ticketing agent. "My dad had a heart attack," he explained, once the person on the other end of the line had stopped talking to him.

"Oh no!" I cried, clutching at the hem of my scandalous dress. "Is he okay?"

"I'm not sure," Damian replied, and he sounded worried. "The hospital called about an hour ago and just said that he was in critical condition. I figured I'd better not wait."

"Of course not," I agreed. "Don't even worry about it. I can't believe you even thought to call me—that was amazing of you. You just focus on your dad and give me a call when you can, okay? I'm so sorry about this."

"Thanks, Ryder," Damian said. "You really are the best. I'm sorry I won't get to see you tonight. I'll call you soon, okay?" He hung up.

I collapsed back on my bed, my feet swinging as they parted company with the floor. I said a silent prayer for Damian and his dad, just imagining how I would feel if I'd heard that my dad had had a heart attack. I shuddered at the very thought.

"How's this?" Lily asked as she burst through the curtain hanging over my doorway. She held up a little black lace bolero jacket. "That dress wasn't made to be worn with a jacket, but I think this one might work okay with it."

"Never mind, Lil," I told her, continuing to lie there and swing my feet back and forth. "Damian just called. He had a family emergency and had to fly to Texas."

"Wait a second, his family is from *Texas*?" Lily said, sounding flabbergasted, letting the arm waving the bolero jacket drop to her side. "I had him pegged as legacy New York royalty for sure."

"He is," I replied with a smile, rolling up on my elbow and supporting my head in my hand. "But his dad is in the oil business and lives in Houston. He just had a heart attack, so Damian's on his way down there to be with him."

"Oh," Lily said disappointedly. "That's too bad. About his dad and about your date. But at least now we have a plan for the next glamorous party he asks you to."

"True," I said, standing up and beginning to shimmy out of the dress. It took quite a bit of active shimmying. The dress may or may not have been a little tight—another aspect that would have appalled my nearer relations.

"So, how about a roommate date instead?" I asked, handing the dress back to her. "I got my first paycheck last week. How about I take you out as a thank-you for helping me get ready for my first official New York social event, even though it fell through?"

"I will never turn down free food," Lily responded. "Just give me a sec to change."

Ten minutes later, Lily and I headed down 50th Street looking for dinner. As we talked and laughed, I couldn't help feeling an overwhelming sense of contentment. This New York life wasn't half bad.

Eight

"Hello?" I asked absentmindedly into my cell phone as I shoved my feet into my black stiletto heels. It was Monday morning and I was already running late. My train to downtown was supposed to be leaving in less than ten minutes, and I still had to walk to the station.

"Ryder?" It was my mom. I stopped short, realizing that I hadn't actually spoken to my mother for nearly three weeks. I'd called to tell her that I'd found an apartment and to provide the address, but that really was it. I'd spoken to my dad a few times since then, like any good daddy's girl would, but I'd never really asked to talk to my mom during those conversations. I'd actually been afraid to, fearing the kinds of questions she was sure to ask me.

"Hi, Mom," I said, attempting to sound cheerful. I glanced at my watch. 8:07 a.m. That meant it was just after 6:00 in Salt Lake. My mother would have just returned home from her brisk morning walk. "How are you?"

"I'm doing well, dear, and how have you been?" There was an undertone in her voice that I didn't miss. She was irritated with me.

"I've been fantastic, thanks," I replied, determinedly keeping the cheerful tone in my own voice. "Sorry I haven't been better about keeping in touch. Work's been kind of crazy."

"Oh, don't worry about it," she said, but the consistent undertone belied her words. "Your father has been keeping me apprised of everything." There it was. The subtle jab. She resented my close relationship with my father—she really always had—but generally she didn't let it show too much. I guess it was different when I wasn't continually under her thumb. Now she needed me to willingly come to her with information on my life instead of just being able to observe and evaluate from across the dinner table.

"Oh good," I said, not rising to the bait. "Well, Mom, now's not really a good time. I'm just heading out for work and I'm going to have to run to make my train. Running in heels while on the phone is never a good idea. You taught me that one." I hoped my attempt at a joke would lighten the mood, but instead it fell flat.

"I also taught you the value of good time management," she pointed out. "If you'd have learned that lesson, you'd never have to worry about being late in the first place." She sighed as though my continued imperfections were the bane of her existence. "Well, I'll talk to you later, honey."

She hung up, but not before I caught the change in her tone. She sounded almost . . . sad. The thought caused a twinge of guilt inside me. I really didn't give her enough credit most of the time. She may be interfering and judgmental sometimes (okay, a lot), but that didn't change the fact that I was her only child. I really did owe her more than I gave her.

Grabbing my oversized laptop bag and some more audit files I'd been tasked with, I headed out the door and toward the elevator. I'd call my mom back tonight, no excuses.

- - - - -

"Ryder, how are those bank reconciliations coming?" Vijaya called to me from across the room. She was talking to Dave and they both looked stressed, so I imagined I must have been holding them up.

"Almost there," I said, trying to keep the strain out of my voice. "There are just a couple reconciling items that I can't seem to get a good explanation on. I'll call up to Katie and see if I can get a better response."

"Think you can have those done by this afternoon?" Dave asked. His voice sounded tense and irritated. Wow, maybe I was worse at this job than I thought.

"Absolutely," I replied, willing the panic to subside. I'd been working on this assignment for a couple of days now, and I hated that it was taking me so long. But I could only take so much responsibility for the pace of the work. After all, I relied wholly on the client for information, and if they wouldn't meet with me, what was I supposed to do about that? I resolved that instead of calling Katie, the manager of the reconciliations team, this time I would camp outside her office until she finally agreed to speak with me. Desperate times call for desperate measures.

I rose to my feet to head to the forty-second floor where the reconciliations team resided, when Bryan, the tall, handsome senior manager, entered the room with purpose. He immediately called for attention, and everyone turned to face him.

"Jim and I have just been speaking to the CFO," Bryan said, sliding a hand into one of his pockets. His intelligent brown eyes scanned the room as he spoke, missing nothing. "It seems that a significant Collins Weiss client has been targeted for acquisition. Collins Weiss has approached Feldman about participating in the transaction. This will be a big deal for Feldman, so we will be staying on top of it throughout the process. We will be getting regular reports from Feldman on the status of the deal as well as the numbers behind it."

There was a buzz around the room and it didn't sound happy.

"I know we already have a lot going on," Bryan said, speaking a bit louder to make his voice heard. He ran a hand through his short dark hair, and his olive-toned face took on a slightly apologetic look. "We'll do our best to keep from overburdening any of the teams with this. We will be pulling a few people off of their current assignments in order to focus on the transaction work." With that, he turned to address one of the managers.

I pondered Bryan's news as I headed for the elevator. I thought it sounded interesting to get an inside look into a big M&A deal, but doubted I would get it. The team was huge, and only a few would get the chance to be solely focused on a transaction like this one—chances weren't good that I would be one of them. But I was curious anyway, especially given that it involved Collins Weiss. I wondered if Damian knew anything about it. I imagined he had to, given that he was a VP on the M&A product team.

As I lounged in a chair outside Katie's office, waiting for her current meeting to end so I could poke my head in, I felt my cell phone vibrate in my pocket. I glanced quickly into the window to the side of her door and noted that she seemed to be as deeply engrossed in her conversation as ever. I pulled out my phone and looked at the screen. It was Damian.

"Hi," I said quietly into the phone. "How are you?"

"Hey Ryder," Damian replied, mimicking my tone of voice. "I'm good, thanks. One question. Why are we whispering?"

"I'm sitting outside a client's office, and I don't want to disturb anyone," I informed him. "People get kind of grumpy around here when they're interrupted."

"Hmmm . . . sounds familiar," he said, and I could hear the smile in his voice. He was in a good mood. That was encouraging.

"How's your dad?" I asked.

"Oh, he's just fine," he replied. "It was touch and go there for a while, but they say he'll recover and with some modifications to his diet, he'll be good as new."

"That's great," I said sincerely. "I've been worried about you guys."

"That's because you're a sweetheart," he said with warmth in his voice. "I've been thinking about you a lot while I've been down here. I miss you."

My heart pitter-pattered away in my chest. "I miss you too," I whispered as an exhausted looking analyst walked by, his arms full of binders. "When will you be home?"

"I'll probably hang out here for another couple of days, but I can't stay long. I have so much to do back at the office."

I didn't think it would be wise to mention the M&A deal over the phone, particularly while I sat within hearing of client ears, so I decided to save that conversation for later. "Well then, I'll see you soon," I said instead. "I mean, provided you want to see me soon." I felt my face redden slightly. There was always the chance that I was blowing everything out of proportion with regard to our relationship.

"Of course I do," Damian said, chuckling. "I'll call you the day I get home and have a chance to assess the work situation, and then we can plan something, okay?"

"Sounds perfect," I said, struggling to keep my sigh of happiness from leaking out. The door of Katie's office opened suddenly to my right and I saw someone leave the room in my periphery. "Hey, I've got to go," I said urgently into my phone. "Talk to you later."

I hung up and stood, straightening my pencil skirt and taking a deep breath before stepping forward to knock on Katie's door. Just then, I saw Paul, a second-year staff on the cash team, walking quickly toward me from down the hall. He was wearing his usual trendy attire, which I liked to refer to as "Hipster Professional." Tight, tapered slacks with a slim-fitting button-up and a skinny tie. He even had the signature hipster faded hairstyle. At least he could pull it off.

When he saw me looking at him, his face gained a great deal of animation (which wasn't unusual—Paul did everything animatedly) and he gestured frantically toward me. I walked forward to meet him, maintaining a steady pace despite his show of impatience. I had learned that he tended to show more urgency than was strictly necessary in just about everything, so chances were, no actual calamity was upon us.

"Oh, good! I found you!" he cried, his short stature coming to a halt in front of me.

"What's the matter?" I asked apprehensively.

"Bryan needs you upstairs," he panted. "He's got a fifteen-minute window and he wants those who have been assigned to work on this new M&A deal to sit down for a briefing."

"Really?" I asked in delight. "I get to work on the M&A transaction?"

"Apparently," Paul said, trying to urge me to a quicker pace as we moved toward the elevators.

"Wait, I promised Vijaya and Dave I would get through this cash reconciliation thing today," I said, gesturing to the papers in my hand. "I need to go back and talk to Katie."

"Here, give that stuff to me," Paul said, taking the files. "I'll take care of it. Just get upstairs ASAP. Bryan's waiting for you."

"Yes, sir," I said, saluting him cheesily. I made it back to the audit room in less than three minutes, despite the slow elevators, and only got a minor glare from Bryan for my tardiness.

"Okay, now that I've got you all here, I just want to run you through the particulars of this deal," Bryan said. He handed each of us a packet, which appeared to contain the administrative information of the transaction. "ManuTech is a tech client of Collins Weiss," Bryan began, crossing his legs as he leaned back in his chair. "They're being bought out by a large Chinese technology company. Collins Weiss, of course, is leading the transaction, but they've asked Feldman to participate. Given the size of the companies involved, this has the potential to be a very lucrative deal for Feldman, thus they informed us of it immediately."

He started walking us through the information in the packet, much of which was financial information on the two tech companies. However, on the last page, I noticed that we had been provided with a list of client contacts at Feldman, as well as a list of contacts from Collins Weiss. Near the top of the list of Collins Weiss contacts appeared the name, "Damian Wolfe, VP, Mergers & Acquisitions Product Team" with his contact information.

Jie was sitting next to me, having also been recruited to the team, and she nudged me. "Hey!" she said in surprise, pointing at Damian's name in my packet. "Isn't that that gorgeous guy who kissed you on the cheek at the restaurant the other day?"

My face colored. I couldn't help feeling that her voice was shockingly loud for someone of her stature.

"Yes," I responded in a whisper. "That's him."

"Hang on," Bryan said, looking over at us. "Did Jie just say that you know someone on the client list?"

"She's dating the Collins Weiss M&A VP!" Jie revealed, sounding delighted. "Damian Wolfe."

"Sort of," I said, my face blushing even darker. "We're not together or anything. We've just been out a few times."

"Are you still seeing him?" Bryan asked straightforwardly. I gawked at him. Was he seriously asking questions about my personal life in front of six random members of the audit team? I usually could be persuaded to make exceptions for ridiculously handsome men, but handsome or not, Bryan was pushing the envelope.

"Um, I think so," I said, raising my eyebrow at him to let him know what I thought of his nosiness. "Why?"

"We'll have to swap you out of the transaction team then," he replied, and my heart sank.

"Why?"

"Independence rules," Bryan explained. "You can't work on a deal that involves someone you have a personal relationship with. We'd get in a lot trouble for that."

Ah, right. Auditor independence. Memories of my audit training as an intern came flooding back. He was right. If Damian had touched the deal, I couldn't have anything to do with it.

"So it's back to cash reconciliations, I guess," I said with a downcast expression.

"Guess so," Bryan answered, and my disappointment must have been pretty evident because he was nice enough to give me a sympathetic look. "Sorry, Ryder, but rules are rules. Hey, on your way over to your seat, can you send over Drita from the debt team?"

"Sure thing," I muttered, standing up and putting the information packet I'd been perusing on my now empty chair for Drita's use.

Darn that Damian. I would make sure to let him know what he'd cost me when I saw him next. He owed me big, and I could think of oh, so many ways that he could pay me back.

- - - - -

"So, I've got a pretty sweet deal for ya." Damian's smooth voice came across the phone line like the best dream I'd ever had.

"Oh really?" I asked. I was lying sprawled across my bed a couple of days later, just having gotten home from Feldman. It was after nine p.m., and I was bushed. But I'd managed to actually push myself ahead of schedule for once on my assigned tasks, so I was feeling pretty good about that.

"Yep," Damian said. "Turns out I'm your favorite person in the world."

"Oh, really?" I asked, wondering if I'd inadvertently told him that once or something. It took me a second to realize that he was teasing. Hey, I was *tired*, okay?

"I got us tickets to see OneRepublic at the Theater at Madison Square Garden next week," he said. "Yes, I know. You can thank me in any way you deem appropriate next time you see me. And really, I mean *any* way you deem appropriate."

I laughed and squealed simultaneously. I'd mentioned that OneRepublic was my favorite band on our last date, and Damian had teased me about it, as he was not a big fan of their style of music. I'd had no idea that they were going to be in New York so soon after my revelation.

"Really? You did that just for me?" I cried. "You don't even like them!"

"But I like you," he replied simply. The man was perfect. I was about to tell him so when I heard a knock on the apartment door.

"You're a sweetie pie," I crooned to him as I hefted myself off my bed and toward the door. Lily wasn't home, so it fell on me to do the menial tasks.

"Next Friday," Damian said. "Don't forget."

"Will I see you before then?" I asked. "Weren't you flying back from Texas tomorrow?" I pulled open the door and suddenly I lost track of my conversation with Damian. Hunter Payne stood in my doorway.

"What the heck are you doing here?" I demanded, my surprise robbing me of politeness momentarily.

"Well, hello to you too," he replied with a raised eyebrow as he sauntered uninvited into the apartment.

"Huh?" Damian asked almost simultaneously on the other end of the line.

"Sorry, Damian," I spoke into the phone. "I just got a surprise visitor. Can I call you back?"

"Oh, don't let me interrupt you, Red," Hunter said, and I could have sworn he increased his volume to make sure Damian could hear him. What a pill.

"Of course," Damian responded. "Have a good time with your . . . friend." I couldn't entirely read his tone of voice, but he didn't sound upset, exactly. More intrigued.

"Talk to you soon," I said, and hung up.

Setting my phone on the table, I turned back to Hunter. "You're a pain," was all I said, and he grinned at me.

"But I'm a *cute* pain, which is by far the best kind."

I snorted unattractively and headed toward the kitchen for a bottle of water. "So, I have a few questions for you," I said, looking back at him over my shoulder as I negotiated around the table and chairs that filled the space. "First question, how on earth did you know where I live?"

"I have friends in HR," he said simply, shrugging.

"That's got to be illegal," I said, pulling a bottle from the fridge. "Want one?" I asked, holding it up to him.

Surprisingly, he declined. I'd rarely seen the guy without a water bottle in his hand. Instead, he began taking himself on a tour of my apartment. "You people have a healthy appetite for furniture," he commented as he took in how little free space there was.

"Yes, well, we prefer sitting to remaining vertical 24/7," I informed him. "Now, second question. How did you get up here? Usually the doorman buzzes us when someone is here to see us. That's kind of the point of a doorman."

"You underestimate my ability to charm people," Hunter said, looking unconvincingly offended. When he saw that I wasn't buying that explanation, he sighed. "I piggybacked off a dude getting on the elevator. The doorman didn't even try to stop me. You should probably report him."

"I might," I threatened, but finally broke into a reluctant smile. "So, last question. What exactly do you want? Did you miss me too much or something? Am I just that lovable?"

"You got me," Hunter said with a smile, shifting the bag on his shoulder. He looked kind of rumpled—like he'd been working for a few days straight without a chance to go home and change. And the fact that he hadn't shaved for probably about that long just aided the impression. "The office is certainly less lively and a whole lot cleaner when you're not around, but I find I like the chaos."

I rolled my eyes as I took a drink from my water bottle, but decided to ignore the blatantly false (ahem) comment. "But, seriously, what are you doing here?"

"Dave Parks was at the office earlier today and happened to mention to me that he'd forgotten to give you the transaction listing you were waiting for. Apparently he got it from the client earlier today. I told him your place was on my way home and I'd drop it by."

I looked at him through narrowed eyes. "I'm on your way home from the office? Where exactly do you live?"

"Murray Hill," he said with a deadpan expression on his face.

I stared at him. "You realize that Murray Hill is in exactly the opposite direction, right? I mean, I'm not even a real New Yorker and I know that."

"Is it?" he asked, feigning a look of bewilderment before grinning slyly at me.

Just then, the door to the apartment opened and Lily walked in with a glum expression on her face. After almost a month of living with her, I was now pretty sure that was just how her face fell naturally. She stopped short when she saw the tall, broad-shouldered, dark-haired man standing in her kitchen. Given her overreaction to me simply telling Damian our address so he could pick me up for our first date, I was sure Hunter was about to be treated to a Lily Specialty. In other words, she was probably about to physically attack him. I got ready to play defense, but she surprised me.

"Well, hello," she said, her face morphing into a *come hither* expression as her voice softened into a seductive purr. She looked him up and down and began to move in his direction. "What's your name, handsome?"

"What the?" I said from behind Hunter, thoroughly taken aback by her reaction. Lily's eyes jumped to me as I came into her line of vision. Her expression of heightened interest disappeared and she sank back into her signature bored countenance.

"Oh, it's you," she said. "I thought we'd just lucked out on the caliber of criminal we'd attracted. But now that I know he's legitimate, it's not quite as exciting."

I shook my head at her in disbelief.

Hunter was laughing. "Hi," he said, holding out his hand to her. "I'm Hunter Payne. I work with Ryder at D&T."

"You know," Lily said as she stepped forward to take his hand, and I noticed that she used the handshake as an excuse to pull him closer to her. "You may not be aware, but Ryder is actually taken. Some investment banker named Damian got there first, unfortunately. But I'm available. Just thought I'd clear that up for you."

"I appreciate that," Hunter said, smiling widely. "And what do you do, Lily?"

"She's a server," I said helpfully, giving her a wicked look behind Hunter's back. "And a bartender. At a pub down in the meatpacking district."

"I'm an actress, actually," Lily said, shooting me a dirty look, but then beaming back up at Hunter. "The bartender thing is just temporary. You know, for fun."

"Sure, for fun. Or survival. Either one," I murmured again from the peanut gallery. "Otherwise she'd starve."

"An actress, huh?" Hunter said quickly, as Lily showed every indication of resorting to profanity in her response to me. "Are you in anything right now?"

I grinned at her openly from behind him, gesturing for her to respond to his question. Baked into my expression was a very clearly communicated *Don't you wish you'd accepted that role now?* dig. She ignored me.

"Not right now, but I have several auditions this week."

"Well, I'll be excited to hear how they go," he replied.

"I'll be sure to let you know," she said.

Hunter turned back to me, his enjoyment evident. "I like her," he said, pointing at Lily.

I rolled my eyes. "Well, now that you've delivered the transaction listing," I said, swiping it up from the table where he'd left it. "I guess we'd better let you get on home." I marched toward the door and opened it for him. He was smart enough to get my point.

"Do you guys have plans for dinner?" Hunter asked, ignoring my blatant attempt to get him out of my apartment.

Lily's eyes lit up. "We most certainly do not," she replied with another suggestive smirk. "Are you in need of some company this evening?"

"Only if you guys are interested," Hunter said, grinning at us. I felt my mouth contort into a grimace, not entirely of my own volition.

"It's almost ten p.m.," I pointed out. "Who eats dinner this late? We'll make ourselves sick."

"Your inner Utahn is showing, Ryder," Lily replied, not bothering to look at me as she continued to check Hunter out.

"Well, why don't you two go ahead?" I suggested. I really wanted to call Damian back. I still wasn't sure when I would get to see him next and I was beginning to feel a tangible need for his presence. I was showing all the symptoms of becoming seriously addicted to that irresistible face.

"Oh, come on, Ryder," Hunter persuaded, moving slowly in my direction. I fought the urge to back up—he looked like he was on the prowl. "You can talk to your boyfriend later. Don't be clingy. Guys hate that. Trust me, I'm a guy. I would know."

It bugged me that he knew I wanted him gone so I could call Damian back. Was I really so transparent in my need? I really didn't want to be the sloppy, obsessive type. I used to roll my eyes at girls like that in college. Now I was becoming one. Ick.

I looked at Lily, hoping she would step in on my behalf. She seemed to be wrestling with two ideals. I knew she'd love nothing better than to have Hunter to herself for the evening, but it was obvious that Hunter wanted me to come along, and she wouldn't want to overplay her hand by urging me to stay home when he so clearly wanted the company of both of us. In the end, her sense of caution won out.

"Seriously, Ryder," she said, tilting her head and letting her ringlets bounce from side to side. "Just come with us. The sparkly investment banker isn't going anywhere, and you know you haven't had a solid meal since Sunday."

That was true. With my insane work schedule, I'd been subsisting off of granola bars and Diet Coke for the past few days. An actual meal would be a tender mercy.

"Okay," I finally agreed. "But it has to be somewhere quick. I have to be at Feldman by seven tomorrow for a meeting."

"Who holds meetings at seven a.m.?" Lily asked, looking scandalized as she walked toward me, snagging Hunter by the arm as she came. "New York workdays don't begin until nine a.m. at the earliest."

"Not in public accounting they don't," Hunter said, patting her on the hand. They waltzed through the doorway together, and I, sighing and shoving my feet into the flats beside the door, followed.

Nine

"So, Lily," Hunter began once we were seated at a table by the window in Pret A Manger, a sandwich place with locations peppered all over Manhattan. I had felt a sense of relief as Hunter had turned into the doorway of the deli. This was so much more my scene than the kind of restaurants Damian frequented. "What's your story?"

"It's really not that interesting," Lily replied as she took a bite of her turkey, provolone, and green apple sandwich. "You should ask Ryder to tell it. She's got an entire fabricated backstory for me because she thinks the real one is dull."

"Oh really?" Hunter asked, turning to look at me as he threw a barbecue chip into his mouth. "So what's the story?"

"I don't remember," I lied, smiling sweetly at him. I unwrapped my own Thanksgiving sandwich (a truly heavenly combination of turkey, stuffing, cranberry, and cheese) and took a bite. A really big one. Mmmm, real food.

"Oh, come on," he prompted, nudging me. "I didn't know you were a storyteller too—that's unusual for an accountant. If anything, you should be proud."

I wrinkled my nose at him, my cheeks round with the food I'd inhaled. Really, I couldn't have spoken if I'd wanted to.

"Fine, I'll tell you," Lily said, giving my stuffed face a disgusted look. "When Ryder first heard that I was an actress, trying to catch a break on Broadway, she decided that I had come from a small town in the Midwest, where I'd dreamed of becoming a world-famous actress since I was a little girl." Her voice rose to a falsely high pitch and contained more animation than she was physically capable of showing with sincerity. I felt like sticking my tongue out at her, chipmunk cheeks and all, but decided that I didn't want to overwhelm Hunter with the childish depths to which I was capable of descending.

"Finally, one day, I managed to scrape together the necessary funds to travel to New York, the only place I knew I could make it big," she continued. She looked at Hunter with an expression that just cried out with theatricality. "Against the wishes of my overly religious parents, I packed my bags and headed for the big city. I was able to find a relatively affordable apartment and a relatively sane roommate to share it with, and I hit the pavement. I spent years auditioning for different roles, never getting a single real part. But I could not—I would not—be discouraged!" Her voice rose in triumph as she lifted a fist into the air with gusto. "On, on I toiled! I took classes in acting, dancing, and singing. I attended conferences and symposiums. I begged directors to give me a chance. I sang and danced my little heart out. But through all the trial and difficulty, through all the tears and despair of my failing dream, I never stopped trying!"

Wow, she was really getting into this. I wondered if she would actually manage to burst into tears at some point. That would be super impressive.

But then she stopped and turned to me. "So, does that about cover it?"

"Just about," I said, daintily placing a potato chip in my mouth. "But you forgot the part about losing the use of your legs when, unused to the unyielding pace of the city, you unwittingly stepped into the path of an oncoming bus." My sarcasm was not appreciated.

Hunter exploded into laughter, his brown eyes shining with mirth. "You guys are great," he said, shaking his head. "The entertainment value is superb." He turned back to Lily. "So what's the real story?"

"Native New Yorker, wealthy parents," Lily said simply with a shrug, taking a sip from her Dr. Pepper. "Needless to say, Ryder was not satisfied."

"It was a boring story," I said simply. "The romantic in me needed more."

"Are you in the habit of creating your own romance?" Hunter asked. His voice was teasing, but the look in his eyes was almost steely.

"I don't even know what that means, my good man," I said loftily, taking another big bite of my sandwich. And yes, I knew exactly what he meant.

"He's asking if you're driving your relationship with Damian forward, or if Damian is," Lily stated helpfully.

I glared at her. We would have words tonight. "Let me put it this way," I said, looking back at Hunter. "I've never once asked *him* out."

"That means nothing," Hunter said, pointing at me. "If you're making your interest too obvious, you're an easy target and he'll keep pursuing you until he gets what he wants from you. Once he's done that, you're toast."

I blinked at him, stunned by the uncharacteristic harshness of his comment. "You do realize that you're talking about your own gender, right?"

"No, I'm talking about Damian," he said emphatically.

I narrowed my eyes, giving him a resentful look. "I thought you said you didn't know him."

"I don't."

"Then how on earth are you qualified to make a judgment like that?" I demanded. "Don't you think you might need to actually meet him first?"

"Maybe," Hunter replied, but he didn't sound like he meant it. "But I know Damian's type. I don't think meeting him will change my mind."

"Well, I'm sorry, but until you do, your opinion means nothing to me," I said incredulously. Suddenly I just wanted to be alone. I needed to think. "Look, guys, I'm really tired. I'll see you later, okay?" I stood up, taking the rest of my sandwich and chips with me, and left the restaurant.

- - - - -

I took the long way back to the apartment, not feeling like going to bed yet, even though I knew I had an early morning. Breathing in the warm Manhattan evening, I took in the energy and the freedom of the city around me, feeling it lift my spirits a little, just by association.

I considered the things that Hunter had said about Damian. I knew I was right, in that he had no place passing judgment on a man he'd never met, but that was just it. I'd gotten to know Hunter quite well in the past few weeks, and a blanket negative statement like that was unlike him. He seemed to be the optimistic sort, and I'd rarely heard him criticize anyone. In fact, he'd even once said to me, "What's the point of thinking the worst of people? I prefer to think the best of them until they prove me wrong—chances are, they never will." But everything he'd just said belied that statement. I chewed on my lip as I considered. What would make him say such things?

As though the uncertainty was driving me to prove Hunter wrong, I pulled out my cell phone and dialed Damian's number.

"Hello?" he said, sounding far away across the line.

"Hey," I said, feeling a warmth well up inside me just at the sound of his voice.

"Ryder," he greeted, sounding delighted. "I was going to call you tomorrow. I didn't think you'd still be up. You've had a lot of late nights this week."

"Yeah," I agreed, feeling the fatigue overwhelm me, almost as though his mentioning it had called it forth. "But we didn't really get the chance to finish our conversation, thanks to Hunter."

"Is Hunter the guy who showed up at your apartment?" Damian asked, his tone politely interested.

"Yes," I replied. "He's just a friend from work."

"A friend who calls you Red," he replied with a chuckle. "Not a very original pet name, although it's certainly accurate. What did he want? You sounded surprised to see him."

"Oh, he was just dropping off some reports for work," I answered nonchalantly.

"After hours? How very employee-of-the-month."

I chuckled and changed the subject. "So, any idea when you are coming home?"

"I'll be home Friday morning," Damian replied. "I have a really important meeting on that new deal I told you about, so I have to be home by then. So how about I pick you up around eight on Friday evening and we'll go do something?"

"Sounds perfect to me," I replied, thrilled that he wanted to see me so soon after getting home. "Hey, speaking of new deals, I'll have you know that you cost me a fascinating assignment by being so brilliant."

"What?" he asked, obviously confused.

"That ManuTech deal you're working on," I said. "I had a chance to work on it from the Feldman side, but as soon as my senior manager heard that I was dating you, I got kicked right back to auditing cash." I gave a dramatic sigh.

Damian chuckled softly. "Well, I can't be sorry about the deal," he said, but his voice sounded apologetic anyway. "It was my proposal, so it's a huge win for my career. And I can't be sorry that we're seeing each other. But I'm sorry you had to miss out on being involved with the transaction because of it. It's their loss, not having you on the team."

"I think so too," I teased. I had just arrived at my building, and nodded at the doorman as he opened the door for me. "Well, I think I'll head to bed now. I'll see you Friday, okay?"

"Have a good night, Ryder," Damian said. "Get some sleep, will you? I worry about you working those long hours."

"Hey, if you can handle it, so can I," I said, laughing. "Bye, Damian."

I hung up, wishing Hunter could have heard that conversation. Damian was an angel. He was *my* angel. And nobody could convince me otherwise.

I went straight to my room and changed into my pajamas—a pair of cotton shorts and a T-shirt. After brushing my teeth, I sat on my bed and pulled out my scriptures to do my nightly reading. Well, nightly was a bit of a misnomer these days, but I was trying. I sat and read in silence until I heard the door to the apartment open. Lily must be home.

"Ryder? You there?" her voice came hesitantly from the other side of the curtain across my bedroom doorway.

"Yes," I called back, still focusing on my reading.

"You decent?"

"If pajamas are considered decent," I replied.

The curtain was brushed aside, and I looked up. Lily stood there, looking at me appraisingly, as though evaluating me. Suddenly, she moved aside to allow Hunter to walk in.

I immediately thought of my makeup-less face and my extremely exposed legs, but quickly pushed away the concerns as I recalled our latest conversation. His insults to Damian.

"Hey," he said, and I was pleased to see the look of remorse on his face, although I didn't acknowledge it. He came to sit on the edge of the bed next to me, resting his calloused hand on my knee. "Look, I'm sorry for what I said about Damian. You're right. I have no right to make judgments like that without knowing him."

I gave him an appraising look. "No, you don't," I finally said. "But thank you for your concern. I know you meant well. And thank you for your apology." I went back to my scripture reading, expecting him to leave, but he didn't. I crossed my legs, forcing him to remove his hand, hoping it would clue him in.

"What are you reading?" he asked.

"The Book of Mormon," I replied simply, not looking up. I was well aware that this response could easily open a can of worms, but I figured that since he'd asked, he could take the consequences.

"Ah," was all he said. He didn't sound surprised at all.

I looked up at him quizzically, despite my best efforts not to.

"Well, I knew you were from Utah," he said as he took in my expression. "Plus I noticed that you drink hot chocolate instead of coffee in the mornings and you never attend any of the office happy hours. So, I figured you must be a Mormon."

"Very astute of you," I said, surprised. "I didn't realize you knew so much about what Mormons believe."

"I've known a few Mormons," he said, shrugging. "In fact, I had a mentor once—a really awesome guy. I looked up to him a great deal, and he was a Mormon. Well, is, I guess . . . he's still alive and everything." He winked. "So I learned a lot about your religion from him. Plus, you know, you guys kind of stand out. It's pretty unusual to find people who so uniformly reject a stiff drink now and then." He smiled teasingly at me.

I felt the corners of my mouth lift slightly. "You know, I never really realized just how different we, Mormons I mean, are until I came out here. But, I guess that's kind of the point. Our church teaches us to live in the world, but not of the world—so it's pretty much inevitable that we're going to stand out."

"Hey, I like it," Hunter said. "Nothing wrong with believing in something bigger than yourself." He got to his feet, smiling down at me. "Well, anyway, I really do apologize for upsetting you. I hope you'll forgive me. And I also hope you'll introduce me to Damian sometime. I'd like to be able to form an opinion of him actually based on his character."

"I'm sure he'd love to meet you too," I replied, thinking that I was probably telling an outright lie. I was fairly certain that Damian would not want to meet the man who called me "Red" at all.

- - - - -

"Here you go," Jie said, setting the Starbucks cup down beside me the next morning. The rich smell of the hot chocolate was pure heaven, especially given that I hadn't had a chance to eat anything yet that day.

We had a cash team morning routine that I was speedily getting used to. Each of the staff took turns picking up coffee (or hot chocolate, as the case may be) for the team. It was an adventure for me to order coffee, not ever having done so before. Thankfully, once I explained to the team at large that I was a coffee virgin and preferred to sip hot chocolate, everyone seemed to accept it as a weird Ryder idiosyncrasy without question. And they all provided me with detailed instructions on how to order their daily lattes, cappuccinos, and macchiatos from the corner Starbucks. Seriously. They even wrote them down for me. Which ended up being a tender mercy, because then I was able to just hand the barista my written order and not have to worry about attempting to spell out the details of a ten-coffee order with the line of forty-seven people behind me.

In fact, one day while I was waiting for the army of green-aproned workers to cough up the coffee, I sat down in one of the cushy Starbucks chairs and copied the order over and over and over again in the little notebook I kept in my bag, so I could just yank out a copy and hand it over to the coffee gods whenever it was my turn to be the delivery girl. Sometimes I simply astounded myself with my own brilliance.

But thankfully, it wasn't my turn to deliver that day.

"Thanks," I said to Jie, raising the paper cup to salute her. "Hey, how's the project going?"

Jie had been working on the M&A transaction for a few days now, and I'd missed talking to her. She'd gone to sit on the other side of the audit room with the other lucky schmucks who'd been selected to handle the transaction work. You know, the ones who didn't happen to be seeing a key player. Sigh.

"Oh, it's coming along," Jie replied brightly. "It's going to be a long, hard slog, though. An M&A transaction is a long process, and they're trying to shove this one through in under a year. We're involved in pretty much every step of the process, so it's going to be rough." Her face took on a teasing grin. "I'm excited to get to know your boyfriend a little bit better, though."

I rolled my eyes. "I feel like I should offer a standard 'he's not my boyfriend' here, but I've done it before and it doesn't seem to have gotten me anywhere."

Jie laughed. "Well, I'm just trying to reign in my insane jealousy. You are a very lucky girl, Ryder Redmond."

I grinned at her as she walked away. I felt like a lucky girl too. And now, with Damian due home from Texas within forty-eight hours, I could feel my heart rate rising with each passing hour. I hadn't seen him in nearly two weeks now, and we were still in the phase where time apart seemed like it weakened the bond between us. My parents used to talk about the "absence makes the heart grow fonder" bit as though it were gospel, but my relationship with Damian sure didn't seem to conform to that ideal. Every day we were separated, I worried a little bit more that he would forget me, or lose interest, or find something better. Let's be honest, it really wouldn't be that hard.

"Hey Ryder, you coming to the happy hour tonight?" Parker asked from the table behind me. It was the partner, Jim Rose's, birthday, and he had invited the entire team down to a bar in midtown for drinks tonight.

"I'm not sure," I replied. I knew it wasn't wise to continue to skip out on office social functions, but they all involved great quantities of alcohol, and I wasn't comfortable with that scene. Granted, I didn't think even my parents would disapprove of me going (provided I restricted myself to non-alcoholic beverages), as functions like this were pretty much expected in the business world. But the fact was, I'd never really been to a bar before. How did one conduct herself, particularly if she wasn't actually drinking?

"You should totally come," Parker urged. "It will be off the hook." It never ceased to amaze me how someone so intelligent could so consistently sound like a California surfer dude—especially given that he was one of the few actual New York natives on the team.

"Where is it, again?" I asked, trying not to wince with apprehension.

"Tavern," he replied. "Even if you're not drinking, and I know you won't, they've still got great food. You should come!" He smiled cheerfully and persuasively at me.

I bit my lip. "Okay," I relented. "Eight thirty, right?"

He nodded and gave me a thumbs-up. "Awesome! You'll have fun. Don't worry."

Regardless of Parker's encouragement, I spent much of the rest of that day dreading the evening. What did one wear to a happy hour? I wanted to ask someone, but I wasn't sure who. As they generally did these days, my thoughts suddenly jumped to Damian. He attended functions like this all the time, didn't he? And he managed, as a member of the LDS Church, to make it all work somehow. Feeling a sense of profound reprieve, I grabbed for my cell phone.

Hey you! I texted quickly. *I have a somewhat inane question.*

He texted me back within minutes.

I love answering inane questions.

I smiled at his response, even as I attempted to phrase my question in a way that wouldn't make me sound like the Molly Mormon I was. *I'm going to my first happy hour at a place called Tavern tonight, and I have no idea what to expect. I don't even know what to wear. You do stuff like this all the time, right? Got any advice for me?*

I saw him begin to reply almost immediately, and I thanked my lucky stars for an experienced boyfr—I mean, uh, man-of-interest.

Oh, that's an easy one, Damian's text informed me. *Most happy hours are right after work, so typically people just head straight for the bar. So whatever you're wearing will be just fine. You'll walk into the bar, show your ID at the desk, and join your party. Easy as that.*

Hmmm, I could handle that. Now all I had to do was actually locate the bar, and I really wasn't even all that worried about that part. I was getting quite good at navigating the city. Suddenly my phone vibrated with another text from Damian.

I have some great drink recommendations for Tavern if you decide to be a little adventurous.

I stared at the text. I felt I knew Damian pretty well by this point, but not well enough to ascertain if he was joking or serious via text message. I decided to treat his question as a joke. He knew I didn't drink. Obviously.

I'm not sure I'm up to getting plastered tonight, I texted with a winky face emoji. *Maybe some other time.*

Damian texted back with his own winky face, and I breathed a sigh of relief, grateful that he had been joking after all. Crisis of man-of-interest's faith averted.

I shoved my phone away and turned back to my laptop to actually get some work done. But my phone began vibrating again almost immediately. I picked it up and saw that my dad was calling. Delighted, I accepted the call and put my phone to my ear.

"Dad!" I cried as I stood and headed for the door to the audit room. Personal calls were supposed to be taken in the hallway so as not to disturb others in the room. "How are you?"

"I'm good, Red, how are you?" my dad's beloved voice echoed over the phone line.

"Really, really good," I answered with a smile. "You don't usually call me during the day like this. Is everything okay?" I thought back to our last conversation. It had been less than a week ago . . . he must have something on his mind to be calling again so soon.

"Oh, sure," my dad said noncommittally. "I was just thinking about you. Wondering how you're doing."

"Well, I'm doing really, really good," I replied again, slightly confused. If he just wanted to know how I was doing, why did he call me at four p.m., when he knew I'd be working like a madwoman? Utah was only two hours behind New York, so he wasn't at lunch or anything . . .

"This is kind of a weird time of day to call me just to inquire about my health, you know," I teased, leaning back against the wall outside the audit room and bracing my foot on the wall behind me.

"Oh, I know," my dad replied. "I was just talking to Kathy—you know Kathy."

"Yes, I know Kathy," I said, still puzzled. Kathy Mayfield was the mother of my best friend, Kara. Both Kathy and my dad worked for Callum Medical, a large medical supply company in Salt Lake.

"Well, Kathy was telling me today that Kara met someone a couple of weeks ago and has been spending every waking hour with him," my dad informed me. I immediately felt a pang of guilt knife through me. It had been far too long since I'd spoken to Kara. Why hadn't she called me to inform me of this exciting new development?

"Oh really?" I asked. "She hasn't told me anything about that, the bum. I'll have to call her tonight to get all the juicy details."

"Good idea," my dad replied and paused. Paused long enough that I wondered if he really had just called to tell me that my best friend was dating someone new. That would be . . . unusual. But then he continued, "So it got me thinking," he said, sounding unsure of himself. "You haven't mentioned anything about your own love life over there in the Big Apple. How are things going on that front?"

He'd called to ask about my dating prospects. I bit my lip as I stared into the empty conference room across the hall. Okay, fine. So I hadn't told my parents anything about Damian. I wasn't even really sure why. He was the kind of romantic attachment that even my picky parents could get behind—a truly good option. But something had been holding me back—probably the fear that they would find the one thing about him that would make him unsuitable husband material for their beloved daughter, and I would be pressured to let the relationship die. And I didn't want to let it die. In fact, *I* would likely die if I had to give Damian up. At least that's what the dramatic teenage romance character in my head was screaming at me.

My dad pretty much never asked questions about my love life, so the fact that he was doing so now had to mean that something had made him feel like he should. Could he sense my hesitancy to discuss this from all the way across the country?

"Um, well, I actually *have* been dating someone," I admitted tentatively. "I didn't tell you guys because, you know, it's just so new. We've only been out a few times, and it's not a big deal or anything."

"Is that so?" My dad said off-handedly, but I could sense his keen interest. That was also unusual. "What's he like?"

"Well, he's a really good guy," I said, and immediately winced. *Way to jump directly into defensive mode, Ryder.* Now he was going to be more suspicious than ever. "His name is Damian Wolfe. He's an investment banker on Wall Street."

"You guys must have lots to talk about then," he replied, apparently trying to be supportive. "With you working at Feldman right now and everything. Where did you meet him?"

"Well I actually saw him for the first time on the street," I answered. "It was the day I moved into the apartment, and he offered to help me with my bags. Lily chased him off, though, so I didn't get the chance to really talk to him. But then I saw him the very next Sunday at church."

"He's LDS?" My dad asked, and he sounded surprised. Why should he be? When had I ever dated a guy who wasn't LDS before? It wasn't like I went around looking for guys who didn't share my beliefs to cuddle up to.

"Of course," I said, not bothering to disguise my indignant tone.

"Sorry, I'm just surprised that you managed to find a boyfriend so quickly and that he also happens to be a member," my dad said.

I raised an eyebrow at the phone, wondering how long it would take him to realize what he'd just said. Not long, apparently.

His voice almost immediately took on a very urgent tone of apology. "Not that you're not beautiful and intelligent and amazing, because you are." Man, he was digging himself a hole that he was going to displace a hip trying to get out of. Another unusual occurrence. "That's great, though, Red. Does he treat you well?"

"He's not my boyfriend, Dad," I said with a sigh. I was really getting tired of saying those words. "We're just dating. You know, casually. But yes. He's an angel, and he treats me like a queen."

"Well, can't ask for more than that," Dad replied, but he still didn't sound quite right. He was worried about something. "Have you met his family?"

"Not yet," I said, checking my watch. I still had a good four hours of work to finish before I headed to that dratted happy hour. I needed to wrap this up. "His dad lives in Texas, so I'm not likely to meet him anytime soon, but his mom lives here in New York. I'm sure I'll meet her sometime. If things continue to go well between me and Damian, of course."

"Well, I'll be interested to hear your thoughts once you've met her," he commented. What an odd thing to say. It must really be freaking him out to have me dating someone he couldn't inspect.

"You know I'm being careful, right?" I prompted, wanting to ease his mind. "Damian is really a fantastic guy, Dad. You have nothing to worry about."

"I'll always worry about you, honey," he responded, and his voice sounded almost tired. "You're my daughter, and therefore my life, and I will never stop worrying. So might as well get used to it."

I chuckled into the phone. "Okay, but try not to worry too much, okay? It's not good for your blood pressure." I checked my watch again. "Hey Dad, I'm sorry to cut this short, but I really need to go. I have so much to do still, and I have a hard cutoff tonight for a company get-together. I'll talk to you later, okay?"

"Okay," he relented. "Love you, Red. Be careful, okay?"

"Sure thing," I replied hastily, shoving away from the wall and heading for the audit room. "Love you too, Dad. Bye!"

Had I not been so busy with my work responsibilities, I'm sure I would have dwelt a bit more on the strangeness of the phone call, but all things being as they were, I admittedly forgot about it. I managed to wrap up my responsibilities for the day around quarter after eight and, along with the rest of the cash team, headed for Tavern and my first experience as a Woman of the World . . . ish.

Ten

The bar was crowded and cold, thanks to the enthusiastically functioning air conditioner, and the two-story open space was unbelievably loud. My team immediately got down to the business of drinking and I got the very great pleasure of watching them all morph into much more exuberant versions of themselves. Dave Parks went from the buttoned-down, somewhat grouchy audit manager of that afternoon to an incredibly talkative, downright bouncy dancing queen. I was tempted to film the transformation on my phone for future use whenever he decided to rake me over the professional coals, but in the end, I decided against blackmail.

While my friends from the cash team did their best to keep me involved and engaged in the revelry despite my lack of what appeared to be pure liquid energy, I soon found the noise, dim lighting, and overall atmosphere slightly oppressive. I told them I needed some air and excused myself from our table on the second floor of the venue to try to find somewhere where I could occupy two square feet with nobody else in it.

I started to make my way through the overwhelming crowd toward the door to the rooftop garden and was oh-so-pleased to make the acquaintance of several very handsy men along the way. I came pretty close to belting one of them, but thankfully he saw something else he liked better almost right away, and I escaped.

Finally reaching a literal breath of fresh air, I moved to the railing at the far corner of the rooftop, which was the only area I could see that looked relatively uninhabited. I leaned casually against the wrought-iron barrier behind me, breathing deeply, and watched the people around me talking, laughing, and dancing. There was a long counter that stretched along the opposite side of the garden, where most of the people enjoying the night air were congregated.

As I carelessly studied those surrounding the high wooden counter, my eyes fell on two men, heads relatively close together as they conversed. I immediately recognized Hunter Payne and the partner, Jim Rose, whose birthday we were supposed to be celebrating. My spirits instantly improved. I had no idea that Hunter had been invited to this shindig. I was tempted to head for him immediately, but then decided that I didn't want to interrupt his conversation, especially since it was being held with my very intimidating boss. I waited and watched as Jim pulled a manila folder out of his shoulder bag and handed it to Hunter, who immediately placed it into his own. Jim said a few more quiet words to Hunter and then walked away.

Aha. My moment of opportunity had come. I pushed away from the railing to move in his direction, right as he looked up and saw me. His face broke into a wide smile and he immediately began heading for me.

"What's up, Red?" Hunter asked, his face bright and cheerful. "I didn't know you were here! Decided you would finally accept a company invitation, huh? This is a big deal!"

I laughed and swatted at his arm. "Well, you were so kind as to point out yesterday that I never attend company happy hours, and as this is the birthday celebration of my boss, I figured I'd better come along. I feel a little out of place, though."

"No one would ever know it," Hunter claimed, shaking his head. "What with you cowering over here in the corner all by yourself." He grinned at me playfully.

"I just needed some air and some space," I defended, laughing. "I'm a Utah girl, after all. And if there's one thing Utah has in abundance, it's space. You don't get much of that here in New York."

"Now that is definitely the truth," Hunter agreed with a nod. He leaned against the railing beside me and let his head fall back to look at the night sky. "So you grew up in Utah, right?"

"Sure did," I replied easily. "Born and raised."

"Are your parents from there as well?" he asked, looking down at me. "Are you one of those Mormons with Utah heritage going back to the 1800s?"

"On my mom's side, I am," I answered. "But my dad is actually originally from the Washington, D.C., area."

"Really?" he prompted. He turned to face me, his hip braced against the waist-high concrete barrier of the roof. "How did he end up in Salt Lake?"

"Well, believe it or not, after getting double degrees in accounting and criminal justice from Georgetown, he went to work for the FBI here in New York," I told him. "He worked in the white-collar division for over ten years. When he was in his mid-thirties, he converted to the LDS Church and decided to move to Salt Lake. I honestly think he got tired of constantly being reminded of how dishonest people can be, and he needed a break from all of that. When he got to Utah, he met my mom, and the rest is history."

"Ooh, the FBI, huh?"

"Yeah, pretty cool, right?" I said, grinning. "But in his heart of hearts, he really is just your average accountant, although totally brilliant, of course. That's a big part of how I ended up here. I followed in his footsteps professionally, and I wanted to get a chance to see what it was about this city that he loved so much."

Odd. Until those words exited my mouth, I'd honestly thought I'd come to New York to escape my mother's shadow. But was that really true? Maybe I actually was just more like my adventurous father than I'd realized. That was definitely a thought process I'd need to explore a bit further.

"Has your dad been back to New York since he moved away all those years ago?" Hunter asked curiously.

"Oh, he used to come back all the time," I replied. "He trained field agents at Quantico for several months of the year and he spent a lot of time up here then. Whenever he could get away from the FBI Academy in Virginia. He did that for nearly all of my growing years."

"Does he still do that?"

"No, he stopped four or five years ago. He said he was getting too old and he needed to make way for the 'new generation.'" I emphasized the words with my fingers. "But I think he misses it. I think he felt like he made a difference in the world when he worked for the FBI. I'm not so sure he feels that way now."

"He sounds like a good man," Hunter commented, with an odd glint in his eye. I wondered what it meant, but didn't bother asking.

"So what about your family?" I asked him. "Where are you from originally, anyway? I don't think you've ever told me."

"Oh, I kind of grew up all over," Hunter said vaguely. "I've spent time everywhere, from Los Angeles to London."

"Oooh, London?" I mooned, letting my envy show all over my face. "I love London. I spent a couple of weeks there with a friend during college, and I've always wanted to go back."

"London is indeed a marvelous place," Hunter said in possibly the most perfect imitation of a British accent I'd ever heard. "I miss it quite dreadfully."

"Wow," I said with wide eyes. "You're good."

"Yeah, well, you pick it up," he said nonchalantly.

"So how long did you live in the UK?" I asked with interest.

"Several years," he replied. "It was a fun place to grow up. Very different from here."

"I'll bet," I acknowledged with a nod. "So was your dad in the military or something? It sounds like you had to move a lot."

"Something like that," Hunter said with a shrug. "He and my mom both died a long time ago though."

"I'm sorry," I said, wincing. This was why asking personal questions was always a bit of a minefield. I decided to change the subject. "So how did you decide you wanted to go into law?"

"Oh, that's an easy one," Hunter answered with a smile. "Money. I actually really like the stuff."

I laughed and nudged him. "That doesn't sound like you at all. I'll bet you actually did it because you had some lofty 'I must save the world from corruption' ideal."

Hunter laughed, but he looked slightly uncomfortable. Bullseye. Man, I was good.

"Hey, it's nothing to be ashamed of," I teased him. "We all need a superhero now and then."

"Yes, well, if I had aspirations to be a superhero, I chose the wrong profession," Hunter said with a laugh. "Not many opportunities for stopping bullets with your chest in corporate law."

"I'm sure we can find something for you," I joked and glanced down at my watch. "Well, I think I've officially met my quota for socializing today. It's nearly ten and I'm exhausted."

"You know, we really should attempt to get you off your Utah interpretation of time and onto New York's," Hunter sighed. "The night is still young."

"Not for me, it isn't," I insisted. "It's my turn to do the coffee run tomorrow, which means I have to be downtown a full half hour early. Ergo, I'm heading to bed." I gave him a stiff military salute and pushed away from the railing. "You should come hang with me and Lil this weekend. She adores you, you know. I have a date with Damian tomorrow night, but we're free Saturday. Feel free to stop by." I winked at him and headed for the door to the bar.

"I may take you up on that," he called after me, and I grinned over my shoulder at him.

"You should," I replied. "If you do, Lily will owe me big, and it's always useful to have the roommate in my debt." I wiggled my eyebrows at him and he laughed. Raising a hand in a wave, he turned his back to me and looked out over the city.

- - - - -

I shoved my foot into my shoe just as the knock sounded on the apartment door. He was here! I thrust the curtain over my bedroom doorway aside and sprinted for the door, determined to beat Lily this time. She didn't even move from her spot on the couch, simply shooting me a look of purest disdain.

"Damian!" I cried as I opened the door. But it was not Damian. It was Hunter.

"Hey," I greeted uncertainly. "Didn't we plan to meet up tomorrow? Did you get your days mixed up again?"

"Not at all," Hunter chuckled, hands in his pockets. "I know you have a date tonight, so I thought I'd stop by and see if Lily wanted any company." He strolled into the apartment, looking completely at ease.

Lily sat bolt upright from her lounging position on the couch. She was dressed in leggings and an old sweatshirt with her ringlets pulled back in a sloppy ponytail.

"Dude, you couldn't have called first?" I said to his back as I closed the door and leaned against it. "A girl always appreciates a few extra minutes to make herself presentable, you know."

Lily snorted as she rose to her feet. "Whatever. I primp for no man."

"I think you look fantastic," Hunter said with a nod and a grin.

Lily blushed. No really, she actually blushed.

"You busy tonight?" Hunter asked her. "Thought we might hang out and watch something." He gestured to the TV.

"I'd love to do something with you tonight," she replied, but she also frowned. "Unfortunately I have to work. My shift at the pub starts in less than an hour." Suddenly her face lit up. "Hey, you can come along and keep me company if you want. It won't be all that exciting, but as a friend, I can offer you a ten percent discount on drinks."

"Sure, I'll come along," Hunter agreed with a smile. "No discount required. I'm actually not much of a drinker, anyway. I'll just chill with you whenever you have a few free minutes. Trust me, it's better than spending the evening by myself at my apartment."

Lily gave him her most angelic smile and headed toward her bedroom to get ready for work, just as a knock sounded on the door behind me.

Oh no. It was Damian. And Hunter was here. Again.

I knew I had told Hunter that I would be happy to introduce him to Damian, but I hadn't actually believed that it would ever come to that. I hadn't had sufficient time to prepare. And now, here I was, having to wing it. Maybe I could just open the door a crack and slip through, using the excuse that Lily was indecent. Yeah, that could work.

I turned to open the door and slide out, but Hunter seemed to anticipate me. He moved up, directly behind me, his head towering over my five-foot-five frame as the door opened. The guy obviously had a death wish or something.

"Hey Ryder," Damian said, before his eyes traveled up to the face that was hanging over mine in the doorway. His brilliant smile faded. "Who's this?" he asked, and I heard his tone slip into cool politeness.

"Hi Damian!" I said, forcing a brightness I didn't feel into my voice as I opened the door to let him inside. "This is my friend, Hunter Payne. The friend from work I told you about, remember?" I looked between the two of them. They appeared to be sizing each other up.

"It's nice to meet you," Hunter said, holding out a hand. "Red talks about you all the time."

Why did he have to insist on using that ridiculous nickname? Was he *trying* to cause trouble? I studied his face and saw the glimmer of mischief under his strictly benign smile. Yes, that's exactly what he was doing.

"Likewise," Damian replied, taking Hunter's hand and shaking it firmly. While his answering smile was completely civil, somehow it didn't look nearly as benign. In fact, he was almost beginning to resemble his name. "Are you here just paying a friendly visit?"

"Oh, he came to see if Lily wanted to go out tonight," I answered quickly before Hunter could do any more damage. "He knew I would be out with you, so he thought he'd come and keep her company. So, shall we go?"

Damian and Hunter were still evaluating each other. Hunter was taller by a few inches and slightly broader through the shoulders, but he had a much less polished demeanor. He looked younger and more spontaneous, with his tousled hair and freckles. Damian resembled a movie star, his thick, wavy dark hair and chiseled jaw truly awe-inspiring. His bright blue eyes were cold as they traveled up Hunter's jeans, T-shirt, and camel-colored leather jacket to rest on his boyish face. He put his hands in his suit pockets, looking slightly satisfied. Apparently he had come to the same conclusion that I had. Physically, there was no comparison between them. Hunter glanced at me, the look on his face slightly amused at Damian's perusal.

"So what's on the docket tonight?" Hunter asked innocently. "An elegant dinner at Le Bernardin? A soiree in a Fifth Avenue penthouse?"

I shook my head and opened my mouth to inform him that we were doing no such thing, just as Damian said, "Something like that."

My head snapped around to stare at him. He was dressed quite formally, in a tailored black suit and blue tie that made his eyes pop to a simply ridiculous degree, but I thought that had been because he'd come straight from work, as usual, and he'd had important meetings today.

"We are?" I asked, trying to keep my voice under control. The very last thing I wanted was to have to split my focus between his glorious presence and not making an idiot out of myself in one of the most exclusive restaurants in the city.

"We're meeting some friends at Jean-Marques," Damian informed me. He looked me up and down, taking in my white skinny jeans and emerald green top, and smiled. "You look incredible, as always, but I did promise you that I would advise you on occasions like these. I'd recommend something a bit more formal."

I did my best to keep the dread off of my face, as I made my way toward my bedroom to change.

"You could always beg off and come with me and Lily tonight," Hunter called after me as I secured the curtain over the doorway of my bedroom to ensure some privacy. I silently cursed his name for so easily reading my expression as I pulled off my clothes and hurled them to the floor.

"No, thank you," I called back. "You guys should probably get going if Lil's going to be on time for her shift." It was a blatant hint and an outright lie as it typically took Lily only ten minutes to get from the apartment to the pub, but I was desperate. Anything to get Hunter away from Damian.

"Hey, I've still got a solid twenty-eight minutes," Lily protested from her room. "Don't rush me; I can tell time."

Dang her and her lack of roommate solidarity. I knew she'd been listening to the entire exchange. Now she was openly declaring her loyalty to the Hunter side of this disastrous equation. I'd show her—she wasn't getting mac and cheese for a month.

I quickly pulled on a fitted black pencil skirt and a flowy black top that I hastily tucked in. I shoved my feet into a pair of four-inch black pumps and studied myself in the mirror. That would have to do in a pinch. Walking the six blocks north to Jean-Marques would be uncomfortable in the skirt and shoes, but I could make it. I grabbed a pair of faux diamond earrings to dress up the ensemble a bit, hoping I wouldn't embarrass Damian too much.

I grabbed my purse and left the bedroom, noting that Hunter and Damian were still eyeing each other distrustfully.

"Stunning," Damian said, his eyes falling on me. "But then, you always are."

"You're going to walk all the way to Jean-Marques in that?" Hunter asked with a scandalized air, his eyes falling on the restrictive, fitted pencil skirt and stilettos. "You'll kill yourself!"

"I've got a car waiting downstairs," Damian informed us both, his eyes looking a bit frosty. "But thank you for your concern." He placed a hand possessively around my waist and led me to the door.

"Bye, Lil!" I called toward Lily's room and heard a muffled response. I gave Hunter a half-pleading, half-infuriated look, and left the apartment with Damian.

Eleven

Once we were free of the competitive atmosphere in the apartment, my head snapped back to the excitement I'd been feeling the past couple of days at seeing Damian again.

"Oh, I'm so glad you're here!" I cried, throwing my arms around him as we waited for the elevator. He laughed and squeezed me tightly.

"I missed you like crazy," he said with a warm smile. His fingers trailed up my arms to my shoulders and then up my throat to cradle my face in his hands. Then, there in the hallway while we waited for the elevator, he kissed me softly. It was brief and sweet and I felt my heart stutter happily as the elevator dinged. We boarded and Damian pushed the button for the lobby, just as a massive freckled hand stopped the doors from closing.

Lily, dressed in her black T-shirt and jeans, with her black apron clutched in a wad in her hand, boarded the elevator with a wicked smile at me. Hunter was right behind her. His eyes were fixed on me, and his gaze was thunderous. In that moment, I knew he'd seen the kiss. I looked back at him steadily and unapologetically, chin raised. As protective of me as he seemed to be, he didn't have the right to dictate who I kissed. And it was time he realized that.

We stared each other down the entire way to the lobby, Damian eyeing us both with interest. By the time we made it out to the waiting car, he had an amused smile playing around the corners of his lips. Lily and Hunter took off down the sidewalk toward the subway entrance without a backward glance.

Once seated in the backseat of the sleek black car, Damian turned to me with a smile. "So what's the deal with you and Hunter? At first I got the sense that he might be interested in you romantically, but now, having met him, I think he's more of a domineering older brother."

I sighed. "Yes, he seems to have christened himself my protector for some reason. Don't take it personally. I have a feeling he'd be this way about anyone I dated. It's not just you."

"Oh, I think it probably has something to do with me personally," Damian replied as he reached over to take my hand. "Nobody really trusts Wall Street these days, thanks to the credit crisis and certain Hollywood portrayals thereof, so I'm not surprised he's not thrilled that you're dating an investment banker."

"Well, it's none of his business," I said loftily, looking out the window at the passing city. "He doesn't get to dictate my social life like that."

"I agree," Damian said with a nod, and his eyes crinkled at the corners as he smiled. "But don't give him too hard of a time. If you've got another person in your corner concerned about your well-being and your safety, I'm not going to complain about it."

I gazed at him with what was probably a pretty soppy look on my face. Yep, I was falling hard for this one.

- - - - -

We made it to the restaurant in less than ten minutes, and I felt my nerves clench a bit as we headed up the familiar stairs and into the building. Carmen stood behind the hostess desk again. And just like the last time we'd been here, her eyes lit up when she saw Damian. And also just like the last time, they dimmed a bit when they saw my hand clasped in his.

"Hello!" she said in a determinedly cheerful voice, her earrings swaying as she glanced down at her table chart. She looked incredible in a sleeveless black dress with gold accents that complimented her beautiful olive complexion. Her black pixie cut was gelled into spikes, and her eyes were lined with black, which made her light green eyes almost glow. She wore the same gold locket around her neck I'd noticed the last time I'd seen her. "Jean-Marques tonight, Damian?" she asked with a smirk.

"Yeah, thanks," Damian replied with a smile. "We're meeting Trip, Pierce, and James. Have you seen them, by chance?"

"Yes, they're already seated," she informed him. She was staunchly refusing to acknowledge me. "I'll take you back right now."

Trip and Pierce? I cried out mentally. Really? I had to spend the entire evening with his arrogant, slimy investment banker pals? Suddenly I wished very much that I had gone with Hunter and Lily tonight and skipped the drama that was sure to ensue. I hoped I could manage to get through the evening without placing my Utah-born-and-bred fist directly in Trip's sneering face.

"Damian!" Trip's voice echoed throughout the otherwise quiet restaurant when he saw us approaching the table. "Dude, where've you been? We've been here like a half hour!"

"More like ten minutes," James countered in a softer tone. He smiled at me. "How are you, Ryder?"

"I'm great. Thanks, James," I replied, smiling sincerely at him. I quickly claimed the chair next to his so I wouldn't have to sit next to Trip's date, which would have undoubtedly condemned me to an evening of attempting to converse with Trip. Let's face it; that was a punishment no one should have to bear.

Damian sat next to me and smiled around the table at large. Pierce sat across from me, his date to his left. She was a very small, thin girl with shoulder-length dark brown hair and deeply tanned skin. She smiled at me in a friendly way, and I smiled back.

"I'm Tricia," she said, reaching across James and his date to shake my hand. She wore a strapless, navy blue dress and simple but elegant jewelry.

"Ryder," I said to Tricia, shaking her hand. I noticed that while she was thin, she was well-muscled and looked fairly sturdy. I therefore formed the assumption that she likely worked in the fitness industry.

"I'm Maelin," said the girl to James's right. She was beautiful, with smooth, black skin and shining black hair pulled into a slick ponytail. "It's nice to meet you."

"And you," I replied with a smile. They all seemed to be several years older than me, and I tried not to feel intimidated at being included in their sophisticated little gathering.

"This is Trip's wife, Leigh," Damian gestured to a woman with platinum-blonde hair seated next to him. I tried to hide my surprise at the revelation that Trip was married. For some reason, his level of skeeziness indicated in my head that he would be single. Especially given the marked up-and-down once-over he'd given me when we first met. The idea that he was married and had still openly checked me out made me like him even less.

I glanced around at the other women at the table, noticing that Maelin had a sparkling diamond on her left hand, but Tricia did not. I wondered if James was married as well.

I allowed Damian to order for me again, not wanting to demonstrate my ignorance of fine cuisine in front of an audience. Throughout the meal, I kept most of my conversation directed at James, Tricia, and Maelin, which worked out well, as it seemed that Damian preferred to talk with Trip, Leigh, and Pierce.

I found out that Tricia was indeed a personal trainer and I congratulated myself on my instinct. I also discovered that Maelin and James were engaged, and that Maelin was a successful actress. I attempted to stifle my inclination to get all starstruck at the news.

Between entrées and dessert, I excused myself for a quick trip to the ladies' room. I walked out to the lobby between Jean-Marques and The Bistro at Jean-Marques, and found Carmen at the hostess stand as usual.

"Hi!" I chirped cheerfully as I approached her. She looked up and gave me what can only be described as a deadeye.

"Can I help you?" she said coldly.

I tried not to take it personally, as I knew perfectly well why she was not disposed to like me. "I'm just looking for the restroom," I said, keeping the smile pasted on my face, despite her look of contempt. "Can you point me in the right direction?"

She pointed behind her at a hallway to her left and wordlessly looked back down at the screen on the hostess stand. I looked at her for a second and then shrugged.

"Thanks," I said, determined to be the adult in this conversation, and walked toward the hallway.

"He'll never stay with you, you know," I heard from behind me. I turned to look at Carmen, who was back to glaring at me with her magnificent green eyes.

"Pardon?" I asked.

"He has women all over this city fawning over him, and as soon as he finds something he likes better, he's gone," she informed me with a slightly triumphant smile. "So if you're thinking that you're going to be able to keep him, you won't."

"Well, thanks for the warning," I said, taken aback. Hadn't Damian said that he and Carmen had been friends since childhood? Why would she talk about him like this? I tried not to let this question trouble me as I turned my back to her and headed down the hallway.

- - - - -

As Damian and I left the restaurant later that evening, both Tricia and Maelin pulled me aside. They informed me that they got together for brunch with a group of other ladies once a month, most of them attached to other investment bankers.

"Girls like us have to stick together," Maelin said, winking. "Usually we just whine about the hours our men keep, but it's fun to have some girl time."

"We'd love for you to join us," Tricia said with a smile.

I had to work hard to keep from showing how flattered I was at being included, but at the same time, the thought made my middle twist unpleasantly. As I was so often complaining to Lily, this was not my world. The thought of "brunching" with an entire crowd of New York's elite without Damian there to serve as a buffer sounded downright terrifying.

"Um, that sounds fun," I replied, infusing my voice with enthusiasm I didn't feel. "When is the next one?" Maybe I would have a legitimate excuse to turn them down.

"A week from tomorrow," Maelin replied. "We're meeting at Dulce in the West Village at ten a.m. We have a standing reservation there."

Dang it. I was wide open. I glanced back at Damian who was waiting a few paces away, his expression guarded. "Oh, um . . . well, I . . . I guess I'll be there," I capitulated, buckling under the pressure of their expectant faces. "Thanks for the invite."

The girls smiled and waved at me as I walked with Damian down the stairs toward the car.

"So, invited to *the* brunch, huh?" Damian asked with a raised eyebrow as he seated himself next to me in the car. "They're choosy about who they invite to that get-together. You must have impressed them." He smiled at me, but I couldn't help noticing that it didn't quite meet his eyes. Did he not like the idea of me mixing with the wives and girlfriends of his friends? While there was something almost mortifying in that thought, I smelled a way out of the stressful outing, and that was far more important.

"Oh, should I not go?" I asked, hopefully. "Trust me. I'm totally okay with backing out."

If Damian had misgivings, he covered them expertly and chuckled. "No, not at all! It speaks well of you that Tricia and Maelin want you to come. You should definitely go." He smiled as though he were making my wildest dreams come true.

Well, if I hadn't been thoroughly stuck before, I certainly was now. Biting my lip in consternation, I turned to look out the window.

- - - - -

"How was Jean-Marques?" Lily asked from my bedroom doorway, not bothering to notice the fact that my light was off and I was under the covers. All very good signs that I was asleep. Lucky for her, I was not. I'd been having a hard time drifting off, due to the thoughts and worries about my relationship with Damian streaming in living color through my head.

I sat up and reached over to turn on the lamp next to my bed.

"It was fine," I replied with a shrug. "Unfortunately we met up with some of Damian's less likeable colleagues, but their dates were awesome. I've been invited to brunch with all the girls next week."

"Ooh, brunch," Lily said in a lilting aristocratic tone. "How very upscale."

"Damian actually didn't seem terribly happy about it," I said with a meaningful look. "I'm not really sure why. Although he couldn't be less excited about it than I am. I really am not made for this kind of thing." I let all my breath out in a whoosh, collapsing back into my pillow.

"So are you going?" Lily asked curiously. She kicked off her shoes and seated herself on the end of my bed, reaching back to pull her hair free of its ponytail.

"I think so," I replied, shoving an arm under my head to tilt it upward. "I told them I would, anyway. Hope I don't end up embarrassing myself. Why do I always feel like I'm out of my league with these people?"

"They're a different species," Lily replied simply, picking at a fingernail.

"Different species, huh?" I asked, grinning at her. "Don't you come from the same kind of background? New York royalty?" I nudged her teasingly with my foot.

"I'm a defector," she claimed loftily. "I've officially hit 'starving artist' status, according to Hunter." She was quiet for a second, smiling softly to herself. I watched her, a grin spreading over my face.

"Sooo . . ." I began. "What do you think of Hunter? 'Cause from where I'm sitting, it looks like you may have developed a bit of a crush."

"Oh, you know . . ." Lily said vaguely. I waited in silence, an expectant look on my face, until she finally met my gaze. "Oh, fine," she admitted. "I like him, okay? Kind of. You know, a bit. He's just . . . respectful and funny and, you know, he's not that hard on the eyes either. Which is rare. Honestly, I feel like I haven't met a guy like that in years . . . or maybe ever. Oh, stop it."

I was beaming at her and apparently she couldn't take it. But I was thrilled. "He's a great guy, Lil. I'm happy for you."

"Well, to be honest, you have no reason to be. We're seriously just buds at this point. So, don't get all gooey about it yet, okay? And please don't say anything to him."

"Oh, come on," I said indignantly. "Would I? But you better keep me in the loop on this. I'm pretty sure that's implied in the roommate contract somewhere. Unwritten clause."

"Sure, whatever," Lily said carelessly, but I saw the glimmer in those brown eyes. She was excited about this one. She jumped to her feet and headed for the doorway. "Oh, by the way," she said suddenly, turning on her heel. "Hunter will be here at two p.m. tomorrow. We decided that it's time you experience New York's shopping scene. We're taking you to Fifth Avenue."

"You *both* decided?" I said with considerable skepticism. "Hunter agreed to go shopping with us tomorrow?" He didn't seem to me to be the type to adore shopping, particularly with two women in tow.

"I guess I mean 'we' in the royal sense," Lily capitulated. "But what Hunter doesn't know won't hurt him. We just won't tell him what we're doing until we get off the train." She gave me a brilliant smile and left the room.

- - - - -

"You guys realize that I'm going to be required to turn in my man card for this, don't you?" Hunter complained as he followed us into Saks Fifth Avenue the following afternoon. "No self-respecting guy spends his Saturday afternoon shopping. At least not guys like me, who prefer football to . . . Fendi." He read the designer name off a sign as he passed by. "That said, what exactly is Fendi?"

Lily looked back at him with disdain. "The only reason we dragged you along is because we require a male eye to tell us what to buy and what to bag. The female psyche is completely different than the male psyche, and I prefer to dress for the appreciation of the opposite sex."

"And I had you pegged as a feminist," Hunter replied, shaking his head in mock disappointment. "What would Mary Wollstonecraft say?"

"Who?" Lily asked in confusion.

"She was one of the first . . . never mind," Hunter replied with a sigh.

He stood uncomfortably outside the dressing room, waiting for each of us to come out and model our wares for his approval. At first he would only offer half-hearted nods or shakes of the head, but after several remonstrances from Lily for his "bad attitude," he started to put more effort into it. Finally, outside a dressing room in Bloomingdale's, I got this golden nugget out of him.

"The color is fantastic on you," he said as he studied me in the emerald green sleeveless dress. I had picked it up because the style reminded me of what Carmen had been wearing the night before at Jean-Marques. She'd looked incredible in it, but now, looking at myself in comparison, I was realizing that I lacked her tall, willowy frame and spectacular curves. Apparently Hunter agreed. "But it hugs your figure in all the wrong places," he informed me. He walked around me, a fist to his mouth, looking for all the world like he belonged on a fashion reality show. "I'd say go for something that will emphasize the trimness of your waist and maximize your bust line and your hips."

I'm not kidding. He actually said that.

"Quite frankly, I'm not sure whether to be offended or flattered at your attention to detail," I said, staring at him.

He looked up at my face innocently. "Well, you're the one forcing me into the role of fashion consultant. You get what you ask for."

Lily stood in the doorway of the dressing room in her next getup, waiting for her turn to be evaluated. Poor girl.

"Fair point," I muttered, as I hopped off the dais in front of the mirror and headed for my dressing room.

Lily sashayed up to the dais in her next outfit, which was a tight-fitting cocktail dress that revealed much more than it concealed. I gave her a raised eyebrow as she passed me, but my reaction was nothing to Hunter's. His face burned red and he couldn't seem to make himself look at her.

"Um, I'm not sure I'm qualified to judge on this one," he said, looking steadily at the floor. "I can't tell if that's a dress or a bathing suit, to be honest."

I laughed from the doorway of the dressing room, watching them. "I think he wants you to put on something a little more conservative, Lil," I called to her with a grin.

"Don't get me wrong," Hunter said quickly, obviously not wanting to offend her. "You definitely have the body for it." His face burned even brighter. "I mean, I'm not saying you can't pull it off or anything. I just feel almost like I'm taking advantage of you, just by looking at you. And, you know, my mum taught me better than that."

"Your mum?" I teased him, laughing. "What, does your inner Brit shine through when you're flustered or something?"

He looked at me with an expression that was momentarily horrified and it made me laugh harder.

"Fine," Lily huffed as she jumped off the dais and moved in the direction of her dressing room. "I can barely move in it, anyway."

Hunter was much less inclined to give his opinions after that. I think he was probably afraid to. We ended up grabbing dinner from a hot dog vendor (both Hunter and Lily were frankly disturbed by the idea when I suggested it, but it was a New York experience I hadn't had yet) and then headed back to the apartment with our purchases.

"So what are you guys up to tomorrow?" Hunter asked nonchalantly as he lounged on the couch, his feet resting on the coffee table.

"I'm working. Ryder has her usual religious rituals," Lily answered, her head buried in one of the kitchen cupboards. She hadn't been able to stomach more than a bite or two of her hot dog, so she was scouting out the rest of her dinner.

"Religious rituals?" Hunter looked at me with a raised eyebrow.

I rolled my eyes in Lily's direction. "She just means I have church tomorrow," I answered. "I go every Sunday morning at nine a.m."

"And she's gone for *hours*," Lily emphasized to Hunter, removing her head from the cupboard to give him a significant look. "Ryder's serious about her religion."

I shrugged carelessly and continued flipping through the magazine the girl at Saks had thrown into my bag with my purchase.

"Plus, there's the possibility that Damian will be there, so she wouldn't dream of missing out," Lily commented, again with head pressed between two cereal boxes as she reached to the back of the cupboard for whatever it was that she wanted.

"Really?" Hunter asked, looking back at me. "Damian is a member of your church?"

I nodded, keeping the nonchalant look pasted on my face.

"That surprises me," he said, studying my face closely.

I looked up at him. "Why do you say that?"

"Well, let's just say that Damian Wolfe is very different than most Mormons I've met, you included."

I stared at him dubiously. "You barely know him, Hunter. You've had, what, one conversation with him?"

"I'm a very good judge of character," Hunter stated plainly.

"I've already tried that one," Lily informed him from the kitchen, a spoonful of peanut butter in her mouth. "It doesn't work."

"What is it with you two?" I demanded of them. "Damian has been nothing but polite and respectful to both of you, and all you can do is talk crap about him behind his back."

I expected them both to look ashamed, but not even close. They even had the audacity to give each other an exasperated look. You know, like I was the one who was being totally unreasonable. Throwing my hands up in frustration, I rose to my feet and headed for my bedroom.

"Hey, where you going?" Hunter called after me.

"To my bedroom. The air's feeling a bit judgy in here," I said snottily, leaving them both smirking behind me.

- - - - -

"You excited for the concert this Friday?" Damian asked me at church the next day. He'd come to sit with me in sacrament meeting, and I noticed an increased level of conversation around us as soon as he'd done so. Most Sundays he sat by himself in the back, when he was able to come. He'd told me that with his work and travel schedules, he missed church more often than he'd care to admit.

"I can't even begin to tell you," I whispered back excitedly. "I've never seen OneRepublic in concert, but I know all their songs by heart. This is like a dream come true."

"Good," Damian said, and he reached over to take my hand. I noticed the girl sitting across the aisle peeking over at us behind her hair.

The whispering through the ward increased when Damian walked to Sunday School with me, his hand still cradling mine. Men and women alike were gawking at us now, and I wondered why we were such an item of interest. I mean, sure, Damian was dreamy, and he appeared to have chosen me as his current romantic interest (yes, there was still some element of the surreal to that), but he had to have dated girls in the ward before now, right? Was I just *that much* less attractive than his usual love interests? Honestly, it wouldn't have surprised me.

"Why are people staring at us so much?" I hissed at him as we sat in the Sunday School classroom. I attempted to stare down a girl with curly brown hair who was gaping unabashedly at us.

"Are they?" Damian replied carelessly, staring at his phone. "I hadn't noticed."

"Probably because you're used to people staring at you," I muttered.

Damian glanced at me and laughed, his eyes lighting up momentarily. He slid his arm around me and pressed his lips to the side of my forehead. "I'm sure they're just curious. Singles ward rumor mills are constantly active and focused on couples in the ward. Try not to let it bother you."

"Couples?" I asked. Yes, I was indeed attempting to start a *define the relationship* chat right in the middle of Sunday School. And no, I wasn't sorry. "So . . . are we a couple, Damian? I haven't really been able to arrive at a firm answer on that point yet." I eyed him surreptitiously out of the corner of my eye, gauging his reaction.

He turned to face me again, his expression unreadable. "You really want to talk about this right now?" he asked. It was a sincere question, thankfully, not an incredulous one.

"A simple yes or no will suffice," I replied with a smile. "Just so I know where we stand on the issue."

His look softened as he studied my face for a moment, turned up toward his. "Yes," he said, kissing my forehead again.

Twelve

I walked on cloud nine for the rest of the week. I was so happy about the new development in my relationship with Damian that I wanted to tell absolutely everyone about it. I wanted to shout to the heavens (or at least to the sixty-eighth floor) about my new official significant other and how amazing and sweet and beautiful and perfect he was. I managed to hold myself back, however, not wanting to alienate my small group of New York comrades. Not the least of which were Lily and Hunter, who were still not completely on the Damian fan wagon. Or anywhere near it, really. Still, despite this, I functioned in a state of ever-present smiles.

In fact, I even managed to keep that goofy smile on my face when Amelia Applewhite (the mousy-haired, saber-toothed wad of bad manners I'd met on my first day with the firm) walked into the Feldman audit room on Wednesday morning and looked around like she owned the place but really wished she didn't. She saw me almost immediately and just couldn't seem to stop herself from rolling those wire-rimmed eyes. You know, as though the fact that I was sitting in the same room amounted to a really trying day for her.

"Hi, Amelia!" I cried in unwarranted delight, waving furiously at her. Hey, if she was going to be unnecessarily unpleasant, I'd be the opposite . . . to an annoying degree.

She just studied me with a look of disgust on her face. I had to bite my lip to keep from laughing out loud.

I watched as Dave walked up to her with a rare look of welcome on his face. He exchanged a few quiet words with her and then turned to the room at large and clapped his hands.

"Okay, guys!" he called out. "This is Amelia Applewhite. We've pulled her onto Feldman since we've had an increase in work with the M&A transaction and we've had to reassign people. We're assigning her to the cash team to take Jie's place."

Usually I'm a pretty "go-with-the-flow" type personality. But I'll admit that it took a great deal of effort to stifle my groan at the thought that Amelia and I would be working together on a daily basis. We didn't exactly mesh well.

Amelia didn't seem to be all that thrilled, either, as Dave led her over to where my team was sitting. He introduced her quickly, and she managed to glower steadily at all of us. I glanced around to my team members, noting that they all seemed about as happy to have her as she was to be joining us.

"Cash?" Amelia said, turning to glare at Dave. "Really? You realize that I just spent the past month doing detailed work on collateralized debt obligations over at Monarch Bank, right? I think I can handle something a little bit more complicated than *cash.* I thought I would be working on the M&A deal."

I whistled quietly through my teeth at her moxie and Manuel chuckled beside me.

Dave did not appear to be impressed either. "While I can appreciate your superior experience," he said, "Feldman is about ten times the size and complexity of Monarch, so you'll find that auditing cash here is a much more complicated enterprise than you'd think. Sit down." His voice held the finality I'd come to associate with him. Amelia glared at him even more fiercely but sat. Directly into the seat next to mine.

Why? I cried internally to the heavens. Why did she have to choose the seat next to me?

"I guess I'm not surprised to see that *you* are on the cash team," she sneered quietly at me. "I wouldn't imagine that you could handle anything much more complex than that."

Wow. How could someone be so needlessly unpleasant?

"You're delightful," I said to her in an overly cheerful tone, hoping that my sarcasm was shining through adequately.

She ignored me and pulled her laptop out of her bag. We didn't say a word to each other for the rest of the day, but I watched as she steadily offended, disrespected, and insulted every member of the team in turn. I had to keep myself from shaking my head in disbelief. Did she honestly believe that this was the best course of action? I knew she was ambitious, but did she really not realize that alienating everyone around her was not going to help her in the long run?

As I walked toward the elevator that evening with Parker and Jie, Parker turned to me with a significant look on his face.

"That Amelia is something else, isn't she?"

"She sure is," I replied with a smile. "But something else of what, I couldn't say."

"Is she terrible?" Jie asked eagerly. "I thought I heard her call Tarin, that senior on the investments team, an idiot, but I figured I must have misheard her. It seemed unlikely that someone would be that rude."

"I can hardly believe it," Parker said, shaking his head with an expression of amazement. "I wonder if she realizes how off-putting she is. I hope she doesn't last long. I'm not sure I can put up with many more days of that. Did you hear her tell me that someone my age will never be taken seriously in this profession? What's that all about? With that kind of attitude, she'll be out of this firm within a year."

"Oh, I'm sure she's just feeling a little inadequate," I said. For some reason, a strange sense of first-year solidarity was welling up inside me. After all, we all handled stress differently. Maybe being unpleasant was just Amelia's coping mechanism. Not that that was acceptable, but at least it might explain her repellent attitude. "She's still trying to get the hang of things. She probably doesn't like feeling so off-kilter. I know I don't. We shouldn't be so hard on her."

Parker opened his mouth to say something else, the look on his face indicating that it would probably be in disagreement with my view. But then, Amelia came up behind him, just having left the audit room. I shook my head almost imperceptibly at him, and he shut it again, glancing over his shoulder in just about the most obvious way possible.

Amelia glanced at us, and I knew immediately that she'd heard our conversation. But she didn't look mad, or irritated, or even superior. In fact, the look on her face was different than anything I'd seen on it yet that day. She looked troubled. She glanced at me one more time before getting on the elevator and standing silently in a corner, looking at the opposite wall. We all boarded silently after her.

- - - - -

Amelia maintained her usual sour demeanor throughout the rest of the week, but I noticed that it was much less aggressive than it had been on her first day. Regardless, I found that listening to her constant negativity just exhausted me, so I usually ignored her.

"Any fun plans this weekend, Ryder?" Dimitriy asked as he handed me a stack of work papers he'd just finished reviewing.

"Yes!" I crowed. "I'm going to see OneRepublic tonight!"

"Ooh, I love them," Jie said. She was on a rare break and was lounging in the chair next to me, on the opposite side of Amelia. "I wanted to go to that, but I couldn't afford the tickets. Is Damian taking you?"

"Yes," I responded, trying not to sound too smug. "He bought tickets for me a couple of weeks ago when I told him I liked them."

Jie sighed. "You are so lucky. That guy is gorgeous. And he's obviously successful. The name 'Damian Wolfe' is splattered all over those transaction work papers. He's super important to that acquisition. You've found yourself a total winner, Ryder."

"Ooh, speaking of which," I said, glancing at my watch. "I have to get out of here. I still have to go home and change." I rose to my feet quickly and started packing my bag. Yanking it up onto my shoulder, I headed for the door, calling back to my team, "See you all Monday! Have a good weekend!"

The entire cash team, save Amelia, called their good-byes. As I turned back toward the door, I could have sworn that I saw Amelia watching me with half resentful, half curious eyes.

- - - - -

"Yay or nay for a rock concert?" I asked Damian, turning in a circle in front of him. I wore tight black skinny jeans with black leather booties and a green tank top that made my eyes almost radiate with color. I had a leather jacket slung over my shoulder, just in case the venue was overly air-conditioned.

I knew I looked good, but I also knew that I had never worn anything like that outfit in public before. *It's just a tank top*, I told myself, stifling the guilt nibbling at me. Sure, it was a little tight, and maybe a little bit low cut, but I was bringing a jacket. If I felt like I was drawing too much unwanted attention, I'd just put the jacket on and cover it all up. No big deal.

"You are probably much more qualified to answer that question than I am," Damian said with a chuckle. "But for what it's worth, I can't take my eyes off of you."

And that was exactly why I'd decided to wear the slightly more revealing outfit. I really, really liked it when Damian looked at me like that. It was satisfying knowing I could have that effect on him.

I grinned and grabbed my little black purse, ready to head out the door, but Damian sidled up to me, halting my progress. He reached out to take my hand, weaving his fingers through mine. He slid his other hand around my waist and pulled me tightly against him. His mouth claimed mine almost urgently, and suddenly I forgot all about my favorite band and the concert we were supposed to be attending.

My head was swimming with Damian's kiss, and slowly, he began to move those kisses down my jawline toward my neck. I clutched at him, my fingers scraping across the back of his jacket, pulling him closer. I felt his breath begin to accelerate against my skin.

This was bad. I really needed to stop this. But I didn't *want* to stop it. This hunger for him was so different than anything I'd ever felt before. Damian's fingers, pressed against my waist, began to move southward.

Just then, the door to the apartment opened and Lily whirled in. It was exactly the wake-up call I needed. My eyes snapped open, and I stepped backward. I ran my fingers over my face and hair, and then down my shirt, making sure everything was in place.

"Hi, Lil," I greeted in an overly casual voice.

She didn't respond, but stood there, looking at me. Her expression was wary, almost worried. Then she turned to survey Damian and her eyes hardened. "What are you two up to?" she asked with steel in her voice.

"Oh nothing," I replied in the same awful off-the-cuff tone. "We're just heading out to the concert. You working tonight?"

She nodded silently, studying me.

"Well, have fun," I said, moving past her toward the door, Damian behind me. Lily grabbed my arm, holding me in place as Damian left the apartment.

"Ryder," she said urgently, glancing at Damian's back and lowering her voice. "Be careful, okay? Don't do anything that will cause you to hate yourself in the morning."

I felt myself blush. "Lily!" I exclaimed. "You know me better than that!"

"I do," she said emphatically, eyeing Damian with distrust. "But I'm also pretty sure I know *him*."

I rolled my eyes and walked out the door. Yes, maybe Damian and I had gone a little bit too far once or twice, but Damian was just as much a member of the Church as I was. He had the same standards and the same ideals, right? He wouldn't let it get out of hand any more than I would.

Once in the car heading for the concert, Damian began kissing me again, although in a much more controlled fashion, and I enjoyed getting to know his lips a bit better. By the time we arrived, I was thoroughly giddy.

The concert was fantastic, made even better by the fact that Damian never really let go of me. Either he held my hand or stood behind me, his arms around my waist. I saw woman after woman gaze at him in admiration, and I couldn't help but feel how lucky I must be to be the one he'd chosen.

On the car ride back to my apartment, Damian played with my hand, tracing his fingers over my palm.

"I have to ask you something," he said, his attention focused on our entwined hands. He brought my palm up to his lips, brushing them softly over my skin.

"Yes?" I asked, goosebumps raising on my arms.

"My mother would like to meet you."

Something told me he'd been buttering me up with his tingle-inducing lips before dropping this on me. Everything inside me came to a screeching halt. "Your mother?" I asked.

"Yes," he answered with a smile that told me I'd been right about his motives. "She attempted to set me up with another one of her society protégés the other day and I told her that I was unavailable for match-making. Once I told her about you, she informed me that she would like to meet you. She wants you to brunch with her sometime soon."

Another brunch. Apparently this was what the wealthy set did in New York.

"Just me and her?" I asked nervously. The idea of brunching with a society matron of the Upper East Side sounded incredibly daunting to me.

"I'll be there," Damian assured me. He was studying my face closely. "You look worried."

"I am, a little," I admitted. "Something tells me that I won't have much in common with your mother. I'm fairly certain she won't approve of me."

"I wish I could say that you were wrong," Damian said with an apologetic expression. "But I won't lie to you. My mother is a difficult woman to please, and I doubt that a sweet, beautiful little accountant from Utah is what she had in mind for me. But just know that no matter what opinion she forms of you, it won't impact mine."

This did not help me. "Okay," I said in resignation. "When?"

"I'll give her your phone number when I see her tomorrow and she'll give you a call," Damian replied. He laughed at my expression of discomfort and pulled me again into his arms. Within ten seconds, I'd forgotten my own name.

- - - - -

I walked into the Dulce restaurant the next day with a slight fluttering in my middle. I had been dreading this "brunch with the girls" for over a week now, but at least I'd had time to prepare myself mentally.

Looking around as I entered what looked like a whitewashed pueblo, I noted that the atmosphere had an understated southwestern influence. Clean adobe walls and a simple, elegant color scheme. I saw Tricia almost immediately, sitting over in a corner of the restaurant with a group of very chic-looking young women. I was suddenly very glad I'd decided to go with the blue striped skirt, sleeveless flowy white shirt, tan booties, and sunglasses. Unbelievably, I looked like I fit right in with the crowd. Relieved I had taken the time to google "brunch outfits" before getting dressed that morning, I headed toward the group in the corner.

"Hi Ryder!" Tricia said as I walked up to them. "Ladies, this is Ryder Redmond. Maelin and I met her the other night when a group of us went out to dinner, and we adored her. We decided to invite her to our little gatherings going forward. She's Damian's girlfriend, so we figured that was recommendation enough." She winked at me.

Just hearing the words sent a rush of warmth through me. Yes, I was Damian's girlfriend. How on earth had that happened? The entire table seemed to be wondering the same thing, because I saw them all perk up at her words. I immediately felt the mental sting of six pairs of eyes studying me from head-to-toe.

"Really?" A lovely blonde woman with piercing blue eyes asked. She subtly bit a manicured fingernail as she watched me sit down next to Tricia. "I'm impressed. I've never heard Damian refer to any woman as his girlfriend before. He's not a big fan of commitment and generally prefers to play the field."

"It's relatively new," I replied with a smile, trying not to betray any kind of negative reaction to her words. Still, the blonde looked like she expected the answer.

"Let me make introductions," Tricia said. She gestured to each young woman as she recited her name. The girls smiled in turn as she pointed to them. The blonde-haired, blue-eyed Jennifer continued to eye me speculatively.

"And I'm Maelin," came the voice from behind me. The sleek-haired Broadway star seated herself between ruby-lipped Lucy and blonde-haired Tait and grinned at me. "Good to see you again, Ryder."

"Hi!" I greeted, grateful she was here. I could use as many allies as I could get.

"So, what do you do, Ryder?" asked the voluptuous, brown-haired Clara. "You'll find we're a pretty humdrum set around here." She smiled at me in a friendly way, and I noticed with gratitude that her brown eyes were kind and sincere. "Three publicists, two fashion designers, and one model. Along with the personal trainer and the actress you already know."

I resisted with great difficulty the look of incredulity that wanted to assault my face. Did she say humdrum? With fashion designers, models, and actresses among them?

"I'm an accountant," I replied simply, determined not to apologize for being the odd one out in this fashionable set. Honestly, the word "accountant" sounded almost comical in this company. "Hardly as glamorous as a fashion designer, but there you have it. So who does what?" I looked around at the table curiously, wondering if I could pinpoint which graceful figure engaged in which profession.

I easily identified the fashion model. Tait Carlson was tall and willowy, with cheekbones that looked like they might successfully cut through filet mignon. She had an unusual face . . . a memorable face. It practically screamed fashion model. Sure enough, she identified herself as the runway queen.

"Publicist," said the brunette Lucy, raising a hand with glossy blue fingernails, not bothering to look up from the brunch menu.

"Same," said the raven-haired Evynne, taking a drink from her ice water with pouty lips.

"Ashley and I are the fashion designers," said Jennifer, flipping her shiny blonde locks over her bare, tanned shoulder. She wore a simple, strapless, floral print dress, and I admired how the clean lines of it complimented her slim figure and delicate bone structure. I wished I had natural fashion sense like that. Jennifer gestured to Ashley, who sat beside her, as she spoke.

Ashley had light brown hair and skin almost the same shade of brown. It gave her a slightly monochromatic look, but she had vivid green eyes that kept it from being overwhelming.

"And I'm your third publicist," Clara replied with a grin. She put an elbow on the table and rested her chin in her hand as she studied me. "So who do you work for?"

"I work as a financial statement auditor at Durham & Tucker," I answered, reaching for my water glass. "Right now I'm spending all of my time over at Feldman Partners downtown."

"Oh, so you're close to Damian every day," Lucy said with a wink. "That must be nice."

I laughed. "Well, it would be, if I felt like it did us any good to be geographically near each other. Unfortunately we still really only see each other on weekends when we have time. Our hours are fairly similar, so weekdays are impossible."

"I just can't get over the fact that Damian has settled down," said Tait, shaking her head at me. "You must have him thoroughly whooped."

Whooped. I really fancied that idea. Jennifer didn't appear to, however. She gave Tait a split-second glance of nastiness before covering it up quickly with a sweet smile. I wondered if I had a case of sour grapes on my hands. I found myself suddenly very interested in Damian's reputation with these women.

"So, have you girls met many of Damian's love interests in the past?" I asked, keeping my voice light and airy, as though I were merely curious.

"Well, you're currently sitting with four of them," Ashley said with a smirk. "Lucy, Tait, Jennifer, and Tricia have all dated him."

"Really?" I said, eyebrows raised, looking at Tricia. "You didn't mention that."

"Oh, it was ages ago," Tricia said, waving a hand through the air. "At least a year. Damian was the one that introduced me to Pierce. Pierce is much more my speed."

"What does that me—," I started to ask, but the server stopped by just then to inquire about our orders. I held on patiently while the group ordered, determined to pick right back up where I'd left off as soon as the server walked away.

"So, how did you and Damian meet?" Lucy asked me when the server headed back toward the kitchen.

"We met at church," I answered quickly, wanting to press Tricia for an answer to my earlier question.

"Church?" Jennifer said with raised eyebrows. "Since when is Damian religious?"

"He's a Mormon," Tricia said, taking a drink of her orange juice. "I always knew that, but he never really talks about it."

"So you're a Mormon too?" Tait inquired. She was studying me as though expecting to see something bizarre about me that would identify me as such.

"I am," I said, taking a bit of the pecan banana bread the server had put on my plate.

"Oh, well that explains why he's settled down this time," Clara said with a nod. "You share his religion."

I shrugged offhandedly, but in my head I could see many more differences between me and the glamorous group comprising Lucy, Tait, Jennifer, and Tricia than just my religion. While I wasn't unattractive, I hardly possessed their level of class, style, and polish. Maybe Damian liked how much more ordinary I was. That thought wasn't exactly comforting, but if that was what appealed to Damian about me, then who was I to complain?

"So what did you mean when you said Pierce was more your speed?" I asked, turning to Tricia.

Tricia seemed to be avoiding my eyes. Or maybe I was just paranoid and she really was struggling that much with spearing a piece of pineapple on her fork.

"Oh, Damian's just pretty intense when it comes to his work," she commented, brushing a strand of her brown hair behind her ear. "Pierce is determined to be successful, but he doesn't immerse himself in his ambition quite the way Damian does."

I considered this, wondering if it was something I should be concerned with.

"There's nothing wrong with ambition," Jennifer defended, tossing her magnificent head haughtily. "Damian works a lot, yes, but he grew up in a very successful family. His parents are loaded. I think he just wants to prove himself."

"He's already one of the fastest rising at Collins Weiss," Tait pointed out. "At least that's what Dennis says."

Tait must be Dennis's current love interest. I nearly shook my head in amazement. Was there some kind of rotation program or something?

Damian appeared to have dated all of his friends' girls before they did. Wasn't it awkward when the whole group got together?

Finally, the conversation moved away from me and Damian and I had a chance to contemplate under the guise of listening to everyone complain about their latest bikini wax, manicure, or hair treatment.

Was it okay with me that Damian had been around the block with all of these girls? I searched my feelings, digging around to see if I could find any kind of resentment hiding away somewhere. I was surprised to find that there wasn't any. So Damian had an active social life. Did I honestly expect that he wouldn't have dated anyone before me? Absolutely not. Yes, the fact that many of those girls were still around him on a regular basis was an interesting dynamic to deal with, but it sounded like he hadn't really ever been serious with any of them. At least not serious enough to "settle down," as Tait had put it. That thought was especially gratifying.

Thirteen

"So," Hunter said as he lounged on the couch later that day, tossing a throw pillow up into the air. He was starting to look far too comfortable in my apartment. "Lily tells me she walked in on you and Damian going at it last night."

I choked on the spoonful of ice cream I'd just shoveled into my mouth. "What?" I cried, coughing. "That is completely overstating what actually happened."

"Uh-huh," Hunter said, wholly unconvinced. He continued throwing the pillow into the air and catching it, single-handedly. He kept his back to me, and I suspected that he was purposely avoiding my eyes.

"We were just kissing," I defended, feeling my cheeks go pink. "No law against that, is there?"

"Depends entirely on whose law book we're referring to," Hunter said, still not looking at me. "You're a Mormon. Your law is much higher than many others. You should probably remember that."

"Are you seriously sitting there, preaching my own religion at me?" I demanded, tempted to throw my spoon at the back of his presumptuous head.

"Consider it a reminder," Hunter replied calmly. "Sometimes we need those."

"Yes, well, I think I can remember the rules all on my own, thanks."

"Sounds to me like you're already starting to break them," Hunter continued in that same maddeningly tranquil tone. "And you and Damian have been dating, what, a month? Moving right along, I see."

I drew in a breath through my nose, trying to calm my boiling blood. "Mind your own business, Hunter," I seethed. I might have thrown a mild profanity in there as well. Possibly.

Hunter finally looked back at me, the couch pillow stilling in his hands. "Just be careful, Ryder, okay? Please." He looked so concerned that it was difficult to maintain my rage.

"Why does everyone keep saying that?" I questioned desperately. "Damian has been nothing but incredible to me. He's one of the kindest, sweetest, most respectful—"

"Yeah, I've heard all that," Hunter said, and his voice hardened. "But it doesn't change the feeling I've got. There's just something about all this that doesn't sit well with me."

"Unfortunately, I don't give a flying hoot what you think about him," I replied loftily. "The only thing that matters is what I think about him. And as of right now, he's the most interesting man I've ever met, present company included."

"Ouch," Hunter said, wincing at me.

"You asked for it," I said, rising to me feet and moving toward the kitchen. "I wouldn't have even thought to mention it if you hadn't pressed me into it."

Hunter snorted.

- - - - -

"Sister Redmond!"

I stopped in my progress down the blue-carpeted church hallway and turned to face Bishop Elias, a friendly smile on my face.

"Hi, Bishop!" I chirped. "How are you this morning?"

"I'm doing well, thank you," the distinguished man replied. "I'm glad to see you looking so cheerful. I'd like to have a little chat with you, and the positive response rate for meeting with the bishop tends to be much higher in happy people, I've found." He winked at me.

"Oh really?" I said, attempting to keep the smile on my face. "What would you like to meet about?"

"Why don't we step into my office?" the bishop requested, gesturing back down the hall. I nodded uncertainly. In my experience, meeting with the singles ward bishop led either to uncomfortable conversations about dating or an invitation to accept a calling in the ward. Neither sounded like fun to me.

The bishop waved me into a seat inside his office, shutting the door. He sat down on the other side of his desk, folded his hands on top of it, and beamed at me.

"Sister Redmond," he said warmly. "We're so happy to have you in our ward. You've been here, what, about a month and a half now?"

"Just about," I replied hesitantly. I knew that a month and a half was considered plenty of time to get used to a ward before getting a calling. I could practically feel the words forming themselves in his head.

"We'd love to get you more involved in the ward."

I bet you would, I responded mentally. "Okay," I said, trying to force some enthusiasm into my voice. "What did you have in mind?"

"How would you feel about serving as a ward missionary?"

I studied him carefully, mulling his words over in my head. I'd never served as a ward missionary. I'd never served as any kind of missionary.

"What does that entail, exactly?" I asked.

"Well," the bishop began, his voice kind. "Your main responsibility would be to find and prepare people for the full-time missionaries assigned to our stake to teach. We'd also love for you to help with fellowshipping and teaching current investigators. So what do you think?"

"I'm not sure I'm cut out for missionary work," I said with a wince. "I've never done it before."

"Where the Lord calls you, He paves the way," the bishop said. Rather unhelpfully, I thought.

"Well . . . okay," I reluctantly agreed. "But you'll have to be patient with me."

"You'll be great," Bishop Elias encouraged. "I'll have Patrick, our ward mission leader, give you a call to fill you in."

"Thanks, Bishop," I said, trying to keep the lack of enthusiasm out of my voice and off of my face. I rose to my feet to leave.

"Just one more thing," the bishop said, reaching out a hand to stop my departure. He gestured to the chair again.

"What's up?" I asked curiously.

"I understand that you have recently begun dating Damian Wolfe," he began.

Oh man, I thought. *Dating and a calling, all in one meeting. What a rip.*

"Yes, we've been dating just over a month now," I replied straightforwardly.

"And how are things going?"

I knew he was just being a good, concerned bishop, but I was getting a little tired of dissecting my relationship with Damian for people.

"Just fine, Bishop," I replied, and I was mortified to hear the subtle undertone of irritation in my voice. I attempted to mold my face into a more pleasant expression to counteract it.

"Good to hear, good to hear," Bishop Elias replied, but his face looked concerned. "We don't see Damian around these parts much."

"No, he tends to work a lot of Sundays," I countered. "He's especially busy right now with an M&A transaction that's on an accelerated timeline."

"I see," the bishop responded, but he didn't appear any less troubled. "How well do you know Damian, Ryder?"

"I feel like I know him quite well," I said, eyeing him uncertainly. Just where exactly was this going?

"He's a very charismatic young man, to be sure."

"Yes, he is," I agreed. "Among other things." This felt an awful lot like talking to Hunter and Lily. I almost wished he'd just get around to the accusation so I could refute it and get out of there.

"Does he treat you well?" Bishop Elias inquired with sincerity. "He's lucky to have you. I hope he realizes it."

"He treats me very well," I insisted, feeling like I was defending myself, but not sure why. "Better than anyone I've ever been with."

"I'm glad to hear it," he said, studying my face closely. "Well, your relationship is obviously none of my business, but I just wanted to make sure you knew that you have people who love you and are concerned about you. If you ever need to talk through anything, please don't hesitate to let me know."

I nodded my hasty thanks at him and rose to my feet again. But he wasn't finished.

"You have been blessed to have the gospel all your life, Sister Redmond," Bishop Elias said. "You know the path. Do your best to stay on it. That's my advice."

"Have you been talking to my mother?" I asked, narrowing my eyes. The bishop looked surprised at the question.

"No," he said honestly. "Why? Do I sound like her?" I could see a hint of amusement playing around his lips.

"Just a little," I admitted with a self-conscious smile.

"She's a wise woman," the bishop said, also smiling. He rose to his feet and extended his hand to me. I shook it warmly, deciding to focus on his concern for me other than what seemed like constant attacks on my relationship with Damian.

"She really is," I responded. "See you later, Bishop."

- - - - -

"What exactly is a ward missionary?" Lily asked with her mouth full of cereal. We sat at the kitchen table, legs propped up on the unoccupied chairs, except that Lily's wasn't actually unoccupied. Instead she rested her legs on Hunter's lap as he silently read the *New York Times*.

"It's a missionary assigned to the ward," I said, choosing to leave the description at that. I was busy watching Hunter as he read the paper, thoroughly ignoring us.

"So are you going to move in, or what?" I asked, reaching out to dig my finger into his arm. "I feel like every time I turn around, you're here."

"What's wrong with that?" Lily asked, milk running down her chin. She wiped it away and then reached out to cup Hunter's face in her hand and squeeze his chin. "He's adorable. Why not keep him around?"

Hunter's eyes didn't vary from their perusing of the paper. He must have been reading a riveting story.

"Nobody should ever be that engrossed in the business section of any newspaper," I commented, shaking my head.

Lily rolled her eyes and nodded her agreement at me as she poured herself another bowl of Cocoa Puffs. I took a bite of my grilled cheese and girded my loins to broach a new subject with her.

"So, Lil," I started. "How was your audition yesterday?"

Hunter and I had waited around for her return the day before, wanting to hear the outcome. She'd finally stormed in at roughly four p.m. and grunted a peeved greeting before marching directly into her bedroom, slamming the door behind her. After that, I'd been afraid to ask.

She looked up at me with an annoyed expression on her face, but she answered anyway. "Sucky," she replied. "I messed up everything and I walked away completely humiliated."

"Well there's always the next one," I comforted her.

"That's the thing!" she raged, her look truly frightening now as she glared at me. "I promised you I would accept the next part offered to me, so I did. Now I'm stuck on this show in a minor part and surrounded by people who saw me at my worst. Thanks a lot!"

"Wait a second," I said, holding up a hand. "You had a horrible audition and you *still* managed to score a part?"

"Yes, a tiny, miniscule, hardly-any-lines part, where I'll never be noticed."

"You have *lines*?" I cried. "It's not even a chorus part? Lily! That's amazing!"

Lily looked at me incredulously. "You are so weird," was all she said, before Hunter managed to put down his newspaper and look around at us.

"Did someone say something to me?" he asked. "I thought I heard someone say my name." He wiped a hand across his chin and it came away wet. "Why do I have milk on my face?"

"No idea," Lily said brazenly. "What were you so mesmerized with in there, anyway?" She nudged the edge of the newspaper with her foot.

"Oh, just an article about insider trading," Hunter replied. "A whole group of bankers over at Pingree & Clare, you know, that investment bank over on Hanover, were charged with several counts of it yesterday. I find that kind of thing fascinating."

"You should have gone into prosecution instead of corporate law," I said. "Then you could be on the front lines."

"Meh," Hunter replied. "Corporate law is more lucrative. You know how I feel about money." He winked at me and I laughed.

"You coming to the pub tonight?" Lily asked him, using her foot to turn his head in her direction.

"You're working tonight?" I asked, just as my phone started to ring. I picked it up as Lily made some comment about how increased hours were necessary if she was expected to ruin her future prospects with such piddly acting roles as the one she'd just accepted. I chuckled as I put the phone to my ear.

"Hello?"

"Is this Ryder Redmond?" It was a very cultured, refined voice on the other end.

"This is Ryder," I acknowledged, heading into my bedroom where I wasn't distracted by Hunter and Lily's conversation.

"This is Victoria Wolfe," said the woman. "Damian's mother."

"Oh!" I cried in surprise. "That's right, Damian said you would be calling. It's great to hear from you."

"Yes," said Victoria, which made me smile involuntarily. So far she was conforming perfectly to my expectations, formed on Damian's description of his mother. "I'd like to invite you to brunch with me sometime soon. Damian has spoken so highly of you and I'd simply love to meet you." She said all the right things, but her voice sounded less than sincere. This should be fun.

"I'd love to meet you as well," I said. "What date works best for you? As long as it's on a weekend, I'm quite free. I work full-time on weekdays."

"I'm afraid my social calendar is far too busy on the weekends," Victoria said, and given her tone, it sounded like it was said with relish. "My next available date is two weeks from Thursday at ten a.m. I'll plan on seeing you and Damian then."

What now? Was she serious? No "will that work for you?" or "can you make that?" Just an expectation that I would obey her ridiculous directive?

"Um, I'm sure I can make that work," I said, obeying her ridiculous directive. *You can't make that work! You can't make that work! You have a job, lady! You can't make that work!* My brain was screaming at me.

"Wonderful," said Victoria. "Well, dear, I'll see you both then. Bye-bye now." She hung up. I stared at my phone in disgust.

"You have a very odd habit of displaying bizarre amounts of emotion to that phone," said Hunter from the doorway of my bedroom. "Didn't I catch you once almost snogging that thing?"

"Snogging? Your Englishman is showing," I replied, not bothering to look at him. I threw my phone down on my bed and collapsed backward next to it, making my mattress springs creak. I stared listlessly up at the ceiling.

"What's your problem?" Hunter asked, coming to sit next to me.

"Damian's mother just commanded me to brunch two weeks from Thursday," I complained, throwing an arm dramatically over my face to block out the sunlight coming through my window. I could feel a migraine coming on.

"Thursday?" Hunter verified. "Um, don't you have a full-time job or something that requires you to be there on Thursdays?"

"Yes," I replied, my voice muffled by my arm. "She doesn't seem to care about such tawdry details as my job security."

"What are you going to do?"

"Throw myself on Dave's mercy, I guess. Or maybe I'll just negotiate an earlier lunch that day." Then, spurred into motion by that idea, I sat up. "Hey! I'm brilliant. That will totally work."

Hunter shrugged. "I don't see why not. Dave's a reasonable guy. I'm sure he'll be fine with that." He studied me a second before continuing. "So what's Damian's mom like? Sounds like she's a piece of work."

"I'm not under any illusions that we'll be best buds," I replied glumly.

"Does that bother you?" Hunter asked with a significant look. "After all, if things work out with you and Damian, she'll be your mother-in-law."

"Thanks for pointing that out."

"Well, you have a tendency to ignore reality when it doesn't suit you, so I'm acting to offset that unfortunate part of your personality."

"Bless you," I said. And then I smacked him hard across the face with my pillow.

Fourteen

"Hey, Mom," I greeted into the phone as I walked quickly down the street toward Feldman. It was early September and the mornings were starting to get chilly. "How are you?"

"I'm good, honey, and you?" She replied. Her voice was strikingly upbeat. Alarmingly so.

"I'm great," I said, hesitantly. "What's up with you? Did Dad clean the kitchen without being asked again? You sound positively giddy."

"Oh, it's just a nice day," she said. "How is work?"

"It's fantastic," I replied, this time with enthusiasm. "I love my team so much and finally, after two months, I feel like I'm starting to get the hang of things."

"That's wonderful," Mom said, really sounding like she meant it. We were almost a full minute into this conversation, and I hadn't detected a judgmental comment or disapproving tone yet . . . what was going on?

"How did the End-of-Summer Bash go last week?" I asked, referring to the neighborhood's annual late summer party. My mom was always a driving force behind it, and I was convinced that *she* was convinced that it wouldn't happen without her help. "I know you were working hard on that. Did you win the award for best peach pie for the eighth year in a row?"

"Actually, I didn't enter this year," she said. I nearly tripped over the doorframe into the Feldman building at her words. My mom's peach pie was legendary, and I'd never known her to not enter it.

"You what?" I asked, shocked. I waved absentmindedly at the security guard, Carlos, who I'd come to know over the past several weeks, and I ignored his teasing comment about my lack of grace. I focused all of my attention on the voice on the other end of the phone. "Why not? You always enter. And you always win."

"I decided to simplify my life this year," Mom said. And she sounded thrilled about it. "I'm cutting out some things that I feel aren't necessarily adding to my happiness. And I'm trying to spend more time on those things that do. And number one on that list is you."

"Huh?" I said, rather indelicately.

"Ryder, who do you consider to be your best friend?" Mom asked.

"Um, Kara," I said, confused. "Or Lily. Or maybe Dad. Maybe all three. Can you have three best friends?"

"Exactly."

"And I repeat: huh?" I said. My mom appeared to be having some kind of episode. Who was this woman?

"What happened to us?" she asked. "When you were little, we were buddies. We did everything together. But I feel like the moment you hit thirteen, we became enemies."

Her voice sounded tight with emotion and for a moment I feared she would cry. I am not good with crying. I hardly ever cry myself, and I'm terrible at comforting others who cry. I cringed as she continued, but her voice sounded quite steady, thankfully.

"I understood that raising teenage daughters was difficult. Heaven knows I heard it enough from others. And I was willing to be your enemy temporarily if it meant that I raised you to become a well-adjusted, contributing member of society," Mom continued. "But I thought that phase was supposed to pass eventually. I thought that once you hit eighteen or twenty that you'd forgive all the teenage discipline I heaped upon you, and we'd become friends again. But here you are, twenty-three years old, and you still can't stand me."

"Mom!" I exclaimed, completely flustered at what she was saying. "That's not true! We're not enemies!" I looked around the elevator bank, hoping nobody was listening in on my conversation. I wasn't sure how to explain to my mom what we were, exactly, but I never would have used the term *enemies*.

"Ryder, I want to fix this," she said firmly. "I'm tired of being unsure of my footing in my relationship with my own daughter."

"Okay," I said as I boarded the elevator to the fifty-second floor. What exactly did she intend to do about our relationship? She sounded positively fierce, and it was making me nervous.

"I want to make it clear that I'm not blaming you for where we are," she continued. "I am just as much to blame as you, if not more. But I've had enough. We're turning the corner, you and me."

"How so?" I asked, thankful nobody had boarded the elevator with me. This was not a conversation I wanted to have with an audience. It felt shockingly like a DTR, albeit a different kind than I was used to.

"Are you coming home for Thanksgiving?" Mom asked.

"I wasn't planning on it," I said, unsure where this was going. "I can't really afford a plane ticket right now. And I actually have to work the day after, so I wouldn't be able to manage a trip that substantial."

"Okay, then I'm coming to you," she said. "You don't have to put me up. I'll find a hotel or something, but I'm coming out there to see you."

My first reaction was dread. I know that sounds despicable, but it really was a knee-jerk response. My mom and I had had a rocky relationship for as long as I could remember. I'd always said that one of the primary reasons I'd moved to New York was to escape her judgment and seemingly unreachable standards. And now she was declaring her intention to invade this nice, independent little life I'd made for myself. What if she didn't approve? What if she didn't like Lily, or Hunter, or worse, Damian? Would my knowledge of her disapproval ruin everything for me? I knew I'd been silent on the line for too long, but I didn't know what to say.

"Please, Ryder," Mom pleaded, and her voice was achingly defenseless. A pang of guilt shot through me.

"Of course you can come," I said quickly. "I'd love to see you, Mom."

- - - - -

"Well, this is great!" Damian said.

We were in the car, on the way to his mother's apartment for brunch. I'd been successful in convincing Dave to let me move up my lunch break a couple of hours, and he hadn't even seemed too irritated about it.

"What is?" I asked as I checked my makeup in my cosmetic mirror.

"You meeting my mom, me meeting yours," he replied. I'd just told him about my mom coming for Thanksgiving. "I like the idea of us meeting each other's families. Bodes well for our future."

I gave him a smile, but refocused on the state of my eyeliner. I felt a driving need to look perfect, and I felt fairly certain that I was failing miserably. The car pulled up to a beautiful building on the Upper East Side that seemed to be almost all sweeping windows.

"Karan," Damian greeted as we walked through the doors and past the desk in the lobby. The doorman nodded at him in response.

"I'll buzz your mother that you're on your way up, Mr. Wolfe," the man called after us as we headed toward the elevators. Damian pressed the penthouse button, and we went sweeping skyward.

I studied my reflection in the elevator door with a critical eye. Since I'd had to work that day, I'd worn the most appropriate outfit I could find for both the office and for brunch, settling on a tan pencil skirt and dark brown pumps with a short-sleeved button-up shirt and a wide, dark brown belt. I had a light, cream sweater in my hand, but I hadn't decided on whether to put it on or not.

"You look incredible," Damian said, watching me as I examined my outfit. He pulled me against him and leaned over to nibble on the edge of my jaw, just beneath my ear. Goosebumps rose on my arms.

We exited the elevator and Damian led me toward a door with a plate next to it that proclaimed "Penthouse D." I took a deep breath as Damian knocked. The door opened almost immediately. The woman who opened it nodded demurely at Damian and informed us that his mother was in the breakfast room.

The apartment was lovely. The walls were a stark white, but decorated with bold artwork. The furniture was all in neutral colors, and I realized immediately that the artwork was meant to be the focal point of every room. Each exterior wall was made up purely of windows, and the apartment glowed with natural light. And it was monstrous.

"How many rooms does this place have?" I inquired quietly as we walked through a large living room and into a spacious kitchen.

"Only four bedrooms," Damian answered. "It's the smallest of the penthouses in this building, but my mom decided she didn't need as much room as when I was younger, and she moved from Penthouse B to this one. Penthouse B is almost double the size."

I stared at him. Why would a family of three require so much space? I decided not to ask, as just then, we entered the breakfast room.

It was the same glowing white as the rest of the apartment, with cream carpets and beige furniture. The far wall was entirely glass, and French doors were open to a balcony with a small, round table, set for three, situated in the doorway. A lovely, statuesque woman with brown eyes and dark hair swept into a low bun stood to greet us as we approached. She took my hand and pressed it gently. Her skin felt like velvet.

"Ryder, it's so nice to meet you," she said, her dark eyes glittering. I did not believe her for one, solitary moment.

"And you as well," I returned, hoping I was more believable. "You have an absolutely beautiful home."

"Thank you, dear," she said, gesturing me to the seat on her left. Damian sat on her right around the small, circular table. "I hope I didn't inconvenience you too much. I know you work during the day. You're an accountant, correct?" I detected the small curl of her lip as she said it. Hardly the accomplished socialite she wished for her son.

"Yes," I replied, trying not to smile. I found that, now in her presence and having gotten an immediate sense of just how determined she was to disapprove of me, I no longer cared about impressing her. It was abundantly clear within ten seconds of meeting the woman that she would never be impressed by me. So now I felt free to be amused by her sense of superiority. My entire body relaxed. "I work as an auditor for Durham & Tucker."

"An auditor," she repeated, staring at me. "How nice. Damian described you as a professional, but for some reason I immediately jumped to the conclusion that you were an attorney or something similar. Silly me."

"Well, you weren't too far off," I replied, my smile climbing higher on my lips. "I have an advanced degree and a professional license, so I am definitely considered a professional in most circles, much like an attorney."

"Well, of course you are, dear," Victoria said, reaching out to pat my hand. I nearly choked on the level of condescension in her tone. "Why don't you tell me about your family?"

Ah, the subject of my unqualified career was too painful for her delicate ears. Little did she know, my origins would likely be much worse. "Well, I grew up in the Salt Lake area," I began, but she interrupted me almost immediately, apparently already displeased.

"Utah?" she asked, eyebrow quirked.

"That's right," I replied. Ooh, the entertainment value was spectacular.

She turned to Damian and gave him a falsely surprised look. "Damian," she said with smile. "I didn't realize that, all this time, you were craving someone whose background was so overtly pastoral. How progressive of you."

Damian just laughed and reached out to squeeze his mother's hand. "I'm more open-minded than you think, Mom," he said with a wink.

Despite what Damian had told me on our first date about his mother being indifferent to him as a child, they had obviously healed the breach since. They were close, by the looks of things. I wasn't sure exactly how I felt about that. On one hand, it was great that a mother and son could have a good relationship, particularly after what Damian had described as a fairly unhappy childhood. But on the other hand, when that mother was, well, less than welcoming, the circumstance became a bit more complicated. I didn't know how I would deal with the situation in the long-term, but I found I wasn't up to solving that particular problem at the moment.

"Pardon me, my dear," Victoria said, turning back to me. "You were saying?"

"I grew up in Utah," I started again. "My dad is a CPA like me, with a background in white-collar law enforcement, and my mom is a housewife." Victoria was so kind as to offer another smirk at this. I wondered if she'd press charges if I poured my grapefruit juice over her head. "She's also the best cook in the world and spends a lot of time doing service in our community. I believe that, in that way at least, she's much like yourself?"

Yes, I admit it. It was a desperate attempt to change the subject. But can you blame me? I only have so much self-control, and the look of superiority on Victoria's face as she listened to me talk about the people I loved most in the world didn't bode well for the welfare of her cream-colored carpet.

"Oh, yes," Victoria said with a sanctimonious nod. "I do a lot of work in the community."

Blessedly, this subject carried us through the next twenty minutes, and I was required to say very little. She addressed most of her words to her son, who seemed to know most of the people and places she spoke of. As they conversed, I had the opportunity to study them both in detail. They looked very much alike, and it was obvious that Damian had inherited his looks from his mother. With the exception of his eyes. He must have gotten those from his dad.

"I'm so sorry, Ryder," Victoria said, turning back to me with a faux expression of contrition. "We're neglecting you. How do you like your omelet?" She gestured to my plate, which still held the majority of a plain egg white omelet, some stewed spinach, and a piece of dry wheat toast. I'd only nibbled around the edges of the toast and taken a few bites of the omelet. Glancing at Damian's plate, I noticed that he'd gotten a real omelet, complete with tomatoes, onions, peppers, cheese, and what looked like ham. Apparently his mother didn't think *he* needed to watch his girlish figure.

"It's just fine, thank you," I said, not feeling the need to pay a false compliment. The food was bland and boring, and pretending otherwise wouldn't change her opinion of me.

"You've hardly touched it," Victoria pointed out. She raked her black eyes over my figure as I sat, legs primly crossed, arms folded. "I assure you, it's very low-calorie, so you needn't worry about that. I assume that's something you take into consideration, given your, ah, size."

Wow. She was playing nasty. Tempted to kick her in the shins but knowing Damian would probably break up with me if I did, I gave her a saccharine smile instead.

"Actually, no," I replied. "I never count calories. And eating is one of my very favorite pastimes. For that reason, I usually go for something more like a danish." I grinned at her, fully enjoying the look of disgust on her face. It was a downright lie—I actually wasn't much of a breakfast food person at all—but the falsehood was worth it for her reaction. I could practically read her mind. Her son just couldn't end up with a girl who one day might end up (gasp!) *fat*.

Damian laughed again. It seemed to me he had been doing a lot of that in the past thirty minutes. "Don't have a coronary, Mom," he said. "Ryder is a very reasonable eater." He winked at me behind his mother's back.

"Well, we'd better be going," I said, getting to my feet. I knew we'd barely been there a half hour, but I really did need to get back to work, and it wasn't as though I was enjoying myself being continually insulted by the Queen of the Manhattan Socialites. Besides, I was starving. I'd definitely be stopping for a sandwich along the way.

Damian stood as well, taking my cue. "Yeah, I guess we should take off. Both of us have to get back downtown." He leaned down to kiss his mother on the cheek. "Thanks for the invite, Mom. I'll stop by this weekend, okay?"

"Please do," she said, getting to her feet. "It was so nice to meet you, dear," she said to me, not bothering to smile. I knew that she knew that I knew that she didn't really mean what she said.

"Have a nice day," I said to her with a courteous smile. Again, why lie? She'd hate me anyway. I turned and left the room, Damian behind me.

"Well," he said as we left the penthouse. "That was interesting."

"Was it?" I inquired disinterestedly.

"You could have been more polite," he pointed out. I gave him an incredulous look and he responded quickly, "And I guess she could have as well."

"Probably," I agreed. "But it doesn't matter. We both knew she was never going to like me."

Damian didn't bother to disagree with me.

- - - - -

"I'm still wigging that she said that to you," Hunter said as we walked toward Wall Street. I'd stopped off at the D&T office to drop off some work papers at the retention center on the thirty-sixth floor, and had run into Hunter in the lobby. He was also heading to Wall Street for a meeting with another client. We'd decided to keep each other company on the journey, and because I have no sense of self-preservation, I'd started telling him about my brunch with Damian's mother the day before.

"Yes, well, it wasn't exactly a surprise," I said. "We both knew she wasn't going to like me. She has very firm ideals about the kind of woman she wants Damian to end up with. And trust me, I'm not it."

"How did Damian take it?" Hunter inquired. "Did it upset him that his mom wasn't very nice to you?"

"Not really," I replied. "Like I said, neither of us were expecting anything better."

"He didn't even defend you when she called you fat?" Hunter said, staring at me in disbelief. "You're not fat!"

"I know I'm not," I said with a smile. "But he didn't need to defend me. I know he doesn't think I'm fat either, and how would getting into a fight with his mom over something so petty have helped either one of us?"

"I don't think I've ever met a girl anything like you before," Hunter said, shaking his head as he threw a dollar into the can of a transient holding a cardboard sign. "Most women would have a first-class freak-out if their boyfriend's mother spent a half hour insulting them to their face and he didn't bother to jump in and defend them."

"It was more funny than anything," I said, pulling my laptop bag more securely onto my shoulder. I winced slightly as the balls of my feet radiated an ache more intense than usual. I usually took the subway from the office to Feldman, and therefore I hadn't dressed for a walk as long as this one. But Hunter had suggested we walk the full distance instead of taking the train. I should have argued with him.

"Well, more power to you," Hunter stated in the same dubious tone. "So I haven't talked to you for almost a week now. How are things going with ol' Damian?"

"Good," I said, cringing again at the pain in my feet.

"What's up with you?" Hunter asked, finally noticing the look of discomfort on my face.

"Nothing, my feet just feel like I'm walking on razor blades, that's all," I said through gritted teeth. "I've already walked roughly ten blocks in these shoes and I hadn't planned on trekking quite so far today."

"Oh, sorry about that," Hunter said, glancing down at my feet. "I didn't bother to take your shoes into account. Here, let me help." He stepped in front of me, his back to me, and squatted down about a foot.

"Um, what are you doing?" I asked, puzzled.

"Get on my back," he prompted. "I'll carry you the rest of the way."

"You want me to piggyback down the streets of New York?" My tone clearly demonstrated my disbelief. "What if I see someone I know?"

"So what? Tell them your feet hurt."

I considered for a moment, then shrugged. I braced my hands on Hunter's broad shoulders and pushed myself up on his back, clasping my stilettos around his waist. I shoved my shoulder bag behind me so it rested across my back. Hunter threaded his arms under my legs to keep them snugly secure against his torso, and started off down the street.

Yes, people stared. But mostly they just smiled at us. I'm sure we made quite a sight—the man dressed professionally in slacks, a collared shirt, tie, and a sweater, and the woman in a sleek gray business suit . . . but we did it anyway.

Hunter carried me thus all the way to the doors of Feldman, where we ran smack into Jim Rose as he was entering the building.

"Hunter," he greeted with a raised eyebrow. "What exactly is this?"

"Hi, Jim," Hunter said casually, gently setting me down on the pavement. "Ryder hurt her foot a ways back, so I operated as her transportation to get to Feldman. You doing okay?" he asked solicitously as he turned to me.

"Oh, sure," I said quickly, hoping my face wasn't reddening. "Much better, Hunter. Thanks."

"Well, see you later," Hunter said, and headed on down the street.

"Remind me of your name again," Jim said as we headed through the revolving door into the Feldman building.

"Ryder Redmond," I answered with a confident smile. Yes, the partner of my audit team had just caught the legal counsel of our firm giving me a piggyback ride down Broad Street. What else was there to do but act like it was totally normal?

"You're a first-year staff, correct?" Jim verified as we headed for the elevator bank. "Cash team?"

"Yes," I confirmed in surprise. "I'm impressed you knew that, with a team the size of this one."

"I've heard good things about you," Jim said, holding the elevator door for me to board.

"Oh really?" I said with raised eyebrows. "That's nice to hear."

"Both Dave and Bryan have been very impressed with you," Jim said. "I believe you were originally part of the transaction team, correct?"

"Yes," I confirmed again. "But I had to rotate off."

"Why is that?"

"Well, I'm currently dating the Collins Weiss VP who is managing the M&A transaction," I explained. "It was an independence issue."

"Damian Wolfe?" Jim asked, turning to face me. He sounded dismayed. "You're in a relationship with Damian Wolfe?"

"Ye-es," I answered hesitantly, surprised by his tone. "Is that okay?"

"Of course," Jim replied, turning back to face the elevator doors as they opened. "I just would have expected Bryan to mention that to me."

"He probably didn't consider it to be worth mentioning," I said honestly. "After all, my place has been taken by someone just as competent. Probably more so." We walked toward the audit room in relative silence, and I felt extremely awkward.

"Well, it was nice to talk with you, Ryder," Jim said, heading toward his desk in the corner of the room.

"Same," I said to his back as he walked away. Smiling to myself and shaking my head, I turned toward the cash team corner of the room.

Fifteen

I was roused one Saturday in early November by the persistently ringing cell phone on my tiny nightstand.

"Hello?" I croaked into it, noting as I did that my alarm clock was flashing 7:46 a.m. at me. Who in heaven's name was calling me at 7:46 a.m. on a Saturday morning?! Whoever they were, they were crow fodder.

"Hi, Ryder?" came an unfamiliar male voice on the line. "This is Patrick Sweeten. I'm the ward mission leader. I understand you're my newest ward missionary!"

First of all, he sounded way too cheerful for the crack of weekend dawn. Second of all, he hadn't even apologized for waking me at the crack of weekend dawn.

"Hi Patrick," I said in a deadly tone. "Hey, quick question for you, do you happen to know what time it is? Just curious."

"Ah," Dead Patrick didn't sound the least bit contrite. "Not a morning person, are you, Ryder?"

"Not on Saturday mornings, Patrick," I replied with a yawn. "But you've got me up anyway, so why don't you just say what you need to say, and I'll do my best to remember it, despite my livid and exhausted frame of mind."

"Sounds good," Patrick replied, laughing. "I just wanted to let you know that we're having a ward missionary council meeting tomorrow after church. Also, I just wanted to challenge you to keep an eye out for good investigator prospects for the missionaries. They're all around us, if we will just sincerely look for them."

I was dozing off again. When the line fell silent, I jerked awake. "Sure thing, Patrick. See you tomorrow." Without waiting for a response, I hung up.

But, hours later when I finally arose for the day, I actually managed to remember his directive. And if I were being completely honest, I had two prime candidates for missionary work in my two closest New York friends. The question was, did I have the courage to do anything about it?

- - - - -

"Got any fun plans for Thanksgiving, Ryder?" Jie asked from my left, the Tuesday before the turkey-centric holiday. As usual, she had decided to spend her rare breaks from the transaction team sitting next to me, and was currently, from the looks of it, doing a little bit of online Christmas shopping. "Going back to Utah for the weekend?"

"Can't," I said distractedly as I examined a bank statement on my laptop screen. "I have to work Friday."

"What?" Jie said, turning to look at me. "Why?"

"Well, first of all, I have lots to do," I said pointedly, glancing at her. "Second, I haven't accrued enough vacation to take the whole weekend off and still be able to go home for Christmas. I'd rather go back to Salt Lake for Christmas than for Thanksgiving."

"Makes sense, I guess," she capitulated. "So what are you doing for Thanksgiving, then? Are you going to spend it all alone? How pathetic." She gave me a facetious grin.

"No, my mom is coming from Utah. I'm picking her up from the airport in exactly forty-five minutes. Which is why I have to get this done," I hinted, staring back at my screen. She completely ignored the hint.

"Ooh!" she cried and reached out to grab my arm, making me jump. "This is the first time she's going to meet Damian, isn't it?"

"Yes," I acknowledged, giving her a strange look. "Why?"

"He's meeting your family!" Jie crowed. "This is a huge step!" She looked absolutely overjoyed at the idea. Was this my relationship or hers, exactly?

"How are things going with the two of you, anyway?" Jie prodded. "I haven't talked to you about it forever. Last I heard, you locked horns with his mom."

"It's going great," I said sincerely. "We haven't seen each other as much lately because he's getting so busy with this M&A deal. I actually haven't seen him for nearly two weeks. But he texts me almost every day."

"Two weeks?" Jie cried. "That's an eternity! Are you sure everything is okay with you guys?"

"Pretty sure," I said, struggling not to laugh at her distress on my behalf. I reached for my cell phone and pulled up my messages. "Take a look at his last text to me." I held it out to her.

You are the most beautiful woman in the world, Jie read off of the screen. *Can't wait to see you this weekend.*

I heard a derisive snort from Amelia behind me, but I focused instead on Jie, as she squealed in borrowed joy and raised her little fists to her face in delight.

"Oh, that's so sweet!" she sighed. "You guys are adorable."

I laughed and stowed my phone back in my bag. "Well, I just hope my mom agrees with you. I'd hate for her to dislike him as much as his mom dislikes me."

"Trust me. One look, and your mom will be swooning," Jie assured me.

"I'm not sure I want my mother swooning at the sight of my boyfriend, but thanks for the comforting sentiment anyway."

"Well, you better remember everything and tell me on Monday," Jie threatened. "I can't seem to get a single date these days, so I have to live vicariously through you and your charmed existence."

"I'll take notes," I promised. I glanced at the clock again and groaned. "Okay, you have officially destroyed my productivity. And I have to go. I'll have to finish this tomorrow." I shut my laptop with a snap and shoved it into my bag. Reaching for my coat, I headed for the door.

"I'm out until Monday," Jie called after me. "So I'll collect your notes then. If they're lacking in sufficient detail, you're toast!"

I waved a hand vaguely over my shoulder as I left the room.

- - - - -

"Mom!" I called, as soon as she appeared on the escalator. "Mom!" I waved my arms like a crazy person above my head. She finally caught sight of me, and her face relaxed into a relieved smile.

She looked frazzled, and I wondered if something had happened to her on the flight over. Had she been pinned into a corner of her seat by someone with little regard for personal space? I could imagine something like that thoroughly freaking my mother out.

"Oh, I'm so glad you're here!" she said as she threw her arms around me. "I wouldn't have the first idea of what to do if you weren't."

I looked at her in surprise, unable to imagine my self-assured, always-in-control matriarch ever being unsure of what to do.

"You'd just grab a taxi," I said with a shrug. "Easy peasy."

My mom looked scandalized. "I don't even know where I would find a taxi," she claimed.

"Have you never traveled by yourself before?" I asked. "I guess I've never really bothered to ask you, but I figured you came out here to see Dad all the time when he did his Quantico trainings. You know, before you had me."

"Nope," she said, shaking her head. "Never once. I've only ever traveled with your dad. And I feel pretty helpless without him. That's one of the reasons I'm so impressed by you and your level of independence. I don't think I could ever do what you've done."

I stared at her. We were less than two minutes into our reunion, and she'd already paid me a sincere compliment. She must be really serious about this mend-the-relationship thing.

"Thanks," I murmured, reaching past her to grab the handle of her suitcase. "Well, let's head out. I requested an Uber, and he should be here any minute."

"You requested a what?" my mom asked in confusion.

As we headed out toward the curb, I explained the mechanics of the car service taking the world by storm. We were settled in the car and heading toward Manhattan within five minutes.

"So, what's the plan for Thanksgiving?" Mom asked. "Is it just you and me?"

"No," I replied, pulling out my phone to see if I had an angry text from Dave for leaving work an hour early. "Lily's family decided to head to Barbados for Thanksgiving . . . for some reason. She has rehearsals, so she's staying in New York instead of joining them. So she'll be there. We invited Hunter, so you'll get to meet him too. We were thinking we'd just hit a restaurant somewhere in midtown."

"A restaurant?" Mom looked scandalized. "For Thanksgiving?"

"Yeah, why not?" I said casually. "None of us love to cook, and I guarantee that a restaurant would be preferable to anything we could manage to whip up."

My mom studied me steadily for a moment before shaking her head. "No," she said with finality. "No way. There's no way I come all the way out to New York to see my daughter for the first time in months and we have Thanksgiving, the consummate family holiday, at a restaurant. I will cook."

"No!" I protested hotly. "You didn't come all the way out here just to cook us all a big Thanksgiving dinner, either!"

"We'll cook it together," Mom said slyly. "I'm sure all of you independent young hoodlums could use a good cooking lesson."

I looked at her through narrowed eyes. "Our apartment kitchen is roughly the size of your linen closet. It will be very crowded."

"The more the merrier," she said with a wink.

- - - - -

"This is so nice of you," Hunter said gratefully to my mom as he walked through our apartment door on Thanksgiving. "I can't tell you how long it's been since I've had a real Thanksgiving dinner. Seems like a lifetime."

"My pleasure," Mom said, beaming up at him. She took the store-bought pumpkin pie he handed to her and tried not to cringe at it. Yes, my mom makes all of her own pies.

"I felt like I should bring something," Hunter whispered to me as he passed. "It felt too moochy to just show up empty-handed."

"Since when do you care about being moochy?" I whispered back. Like the mature attorney he was, Hunter pulled a face at me.

"Hey, you," Lily greeted, running up to throw her arms around him. He gave her a squeeze and kissed her cursorily on the cheek.

My mom watched them bantering back and forth as they headed toward the kitchen and whispered to me, "Are they together?"

"I don't think so," I replied. "At least neither one of them has said so to me. But I know Lily really likes him."

"What about you?" Mom asked with a knowing look.

"What about me?" I asked, truly baffled.

"Do you like him?"

"Of course I like him," I said. "But not like that. I'm with Damian. You know that."

"Oh, yes, I know that," Mom said softly, but she didn't sound convinced. "When will I get to meet this Damian, anyway?"

"He's having Thanksgiving with his mom," I answered, moving toward the kitchen. "But he said he'd drop by tonight to meet you."

"Can't wait," she replied with a bright smile.

It was her bright, fake smile. Trust me, I knew it well. What was up with that? She hadn't even met Damian yet. How could she possibly already not like him? I decided to ignore her reaction until later. I was sure that as soon as he charmed her, like he did everyone else (except Hunter and Lily, of course), that she would change her mind.

"So, what's first?" Lily asked, grabbing an apron out of the mountain of grocery bags piled on the table.

Mom, Lily, and I had spent the evening before shopping like crazy, even going so far as to purchase color-coordinated aprons. Mine was red, of course. Lily's was purple, as she said she preferred the assumption of royalty that came along with it. Hunter's was green, because Lily thought it would go well with his hair, and my mom's was white. Since she was the real chef amongst us all.

"First, I'm going to set you slicing potatoes," Mom said, pulling a cutting board from the grocery bags. Lily went to the kitchen for a knife, and Mom cleared a space at the table for Lily to operate on the root vegetables. "Now, I want you to slice like this," Mom said, illustrating to Lily in the air. "I've already washed the potatoes, so you can start now. Put all the slices in here." She handed Lily a bowl, then turned to me.

"You can watch the turkey," she informed me. "It's the easiest of the jobs, and that's why it's yours—I know your history in the kitchen."

I opened my mouth to retort, but she ignored me.

"You," she said, pointing at Hunter, "can be in charge of the stuffing. We'll start you off by breaking the bread into chunks. I'll show you what I mean." I watched them together as my mom demonstrated the size of the pieces of bread she wanted for her stuffing. Hunter bent his head close to hers, his eyes focused on what she was telling him, nodding his understanding. It was frankly adorable to see him like that. No wonder Lily was crazy about him.

The afternoon went on in this manner, with Mom issuing orders and Lily and Hunter jumping to obey. It was warm and pleasant in the apartment, and we all talked and laughed while we worked. By four p.m., the dinner was looking professional and smelled incredible.

"Not bad," Mom said, surveying our progress. "Ryder, why don't you set the table? The turkey should be done any minute."

While I set about laying places on the table, Lily ran to change her shirt (she'd splattered large amounts of gravy while stirring too enthusiastically) and Hunter and my mom sat in the living room chatting. I couldn't hear what they were saying, but they seemed to be deep in conversation. As I watched, Mom reached out and laid an earnest hand on Hunter's arm, a grateful look on her face. I wondered if she was thanking him for watching out for me and Lily. I got the sense that New York overwhelmed my mother a bit, and the thought of me living here by myself was probably downright frightening to her.

"Let's eat!" Lily cried as she emerged from her bedroom in a clean shirt. "I'm starving!"

"You bet!" Mom said, quickly standing. She braced a familiar hand on Hunter's shoulder as she stood, and I found my heart warming at the idea that she could take to my friends so quickly. Maybe this whole suggestion of being best friends with my mom wasn't such a bad idea after all.

- - - - -

Long after the turkey was devoured, the three of us sat around the table, talking and laughing. Lily told my mom all about her life growing up in Brooklyn, in far more detail than even I had ever received. My mom told her own stories of growing up in a small town in Utah, and Lily and Hunter marveled at the oddities of small-town life, never having experienced them.

Hunter didn't share any of his own past, which didn't surprise me. He rarely talked about himself, and I figured it was something he was uncomfortable with. I admired my mom for not prying into his background. Hunter had just hinted at the possibility of breaking out the pies (which had been my mom's primary activity that day), when there came a knock at the door.

"Oh!" I cried, jumping to my feet. "That must be Damian. Geez, is it six already?" I glanced at my watch as I skipped toward the door.

"Hey, beautiful," Damian greeted as I opened the door, beaming. "Happy Thanksgiving."

"Happy Thanksgiving!" I cried, pulling him into the apartment and throwing my arms around him. "Oh, I haven't seen you in ages!"

"It has been a while, hasn't it?" Damian said, laughing as his arms encircled me tightly. "I've missed you." He pulled back to plant a kiss on my lips.

Suddenly the silence of the room around us seemed to envelope me. I pulled away quickly and turned to face the table of observers. Hunter and Lily were giving me looks that clearly said, *Really? You couldn't have waited to invite him over until after we found an excuse to leave?* My mom looked like she was trying to paste a welcoming smile on her face. It was partially successful.

"You must be Damian," she said, rising to her feet and walking toward him with a hand outstretched. "I'm Emma Redmond."

"It's wonderful to meet you, Emma," Damian said, taking her hand and leaning in to kiss her cheek in signature New York fashion. She looked startled by the overt show of affection. "You're the first member of Ryder's family I've been able to meet, so this is a really big deal for me," Damian said with a killer smile. "I simply adore your daughter."

"I can see that," Mom said, her friendly smile hitching a little. "Why don't you come and sit down, Damian? We were just about to have some pie."

She gestured toward the table, to the seat between me and Lily. Lily's eyes clearly said, *Come near me and I'll gladly pull your lip over your head*, but Damian ignored it.

"So, how has your Thanksgiving been, Damian?" Mom asked from the kitchen as she gathered the pies and whipped cream, juggling them like a master.

"Here, let me help you with that, Emma," Hunter said, rising to his feet quickly to relieve her. She gave him a smile, much more sincere than the ones she'd been offering my boyfriend. *Hmmmm.*

"It's been very nice, thank you," Damian replied, his eyes also flicking between my mother and Hunter. He hadn't missed the difference in sincerity either, it would seem. "My mother is a society woman, so Thanksgiving is a bit more formal than I prefer, but at least the food's good." He winked and my mom laughed lightly. Lily rolled her eyes and Hunter gave a courtesy smile at the joke.

"Ryder tells me that you're an investment banker," Mom said. Moving right along down the line of conversation topics, apparently. "That must be a stressful career."

"For the most part," Damian agreed with a nod. "I have the odd window of freedom, but unfortunately that has not been the case lately. I've been working on a big M&A deal, and it's kept me from being able to see Ryder much these past few weeks. I hate it when that happens."

He smiled at me, his eyes crinkling at the corners. I grinned back at him and reached out to take his hand, ignoring the show Lily was making behind Damian's back of pretending to vomit into her water glass.

"Well, I'm sure Ryder understands, being a busy professional herself," Mom said, her voice sounding quite proud as she cut into Hunter's store-bought pumpkin pie. "Ryder's very ambitious, so I'd hope that she would encourage you in your own career as well."

I stared at her, trying valiantly to not look as stunned as I felt. I had never heard my mom speak in such glowing terms about my professional ambitions. In fact, I'd always assumed that she held nothing but disdain for them. After all, it was those very ambitions that she saw as being in the way of my marrying and settling down to create a houseful of grandbabies.

"Yes, Ryder's fantastic," Damian agreed emphatically. "She's always very understanding when my schedule keeps us apart."

"So Damian," Hunter said, nearly interrupting him. "What big M&A deal are you working on currently?"

"Well, unfortunately, Hunter," Damian replied, his eyes taking on a bit of a frosty look. "I can't really discuss that here. Confidential, you understand."

"Oh, confidential, of course," Hunter said, nodding sanctimoniously. "We wouldn't want you breaking any kind of law, now would we?"

Damian just watched him. "No," he finally said smoothly. "We certainly wouldn't."

I looked between them hopelessly, despairing of ever getting them to play nice. My mom appeared slightly amused as she, too, glanced between the two of them. Finally deciding to stop the stare-down, she turned to Damian.

"Pie, dear?" she asked.

Damian didn't stay long after that. He made a half-hearted attempt at swallowing his piece of pumpkin pie, and said all the right things, asking questions about my childhood and about my family, but I could tell he really just wanted to leave. And I didn't blame him. It couldn't be particularly enjoyable, attempting to make conversation when half the room disliked and mistrusted him.

I walked him out to the street after he shook my mother's hand again, smiled at Lily (who didn't bother to smile back), and nodded stiffly at Hunter.

"Sorry about all that," I apologized as we walked toward the elevator. "I don't know what Hunter's problem is. He acts like an overprotective guard dog every time you're around. I'm sure he'll get used to you."

"I doubt it," Damian said, but he smiled. "It doesn't matter, though. It was all worth it, just to have a few minutes alone with you." He pulled me solidly into his side and pressed his lips into my hair as we waited for the elevator to arrive. "Hey, I've got a proposition for you," Damian said once we were aboard, whizzing toward the lobby.

"What's that?" I asked curiously.

"What kind of vacation time do you get for Christmas?"

"I'm planning on taking pretty much everything I've got," I replied. "It'll amount to about a week and a half. I have to be back in the office between Christmas and New Year's. Why?"

"I'm heading down to Houston to spend some more time with my dad around the holidays," Damian said, watching me. "He's still recovering, you know, and a lot of the folks working on the M&A deal are taking time off then. That's about the only time this business stops to take a breath." He grabbed my hand and pulled me off the elevator and toward the lobby. "Anyway, I'm planning to take off to see him around the sixteenth of December, and I wondered if you'd like to come with me."

I stopped, pulling him to a halt beside me. "What?" I asked, dumbfounded. "You want me to come to Houston with you for Christmas?"

"Well, I wouldn't want to pull you away from Christmas with your family," he said, tucking a hand into his pocket. "So I was thinking, maybe we could spend a few days with my dad and then head to Salt Lake to spend the rest of the time with your family. What do you think?"

I tried to put into words what was running through my head. The inside of my skull was reverberating with *Yes! Yes! Yes! Yes!* but I also had the facial expressions of my mother and father flashing in my mind, and they didn't look all that thrilled at the idea of me cutting out part of my trip home to visit my boyfriend's father. But I'd still have plenty of time with them, and traveling with Damian sounded like heaven.

"I think that's a fantastic idea," I said, smiling warmly at him. "I'd love to meet your dad."

"Then consider it settled," Damian replied, reaching out to pull me close to him as he moved toward the door to the street. "I'll book our flights first thing when I get home tonight."

- - - - -

"Knock, knock."

My mother's voice came from the doorway to my room later that evening. She was in her flannel pajamas and holding two mugs of what smelled like hot chocolate. Even though she had offered, I had shouted down her intentions to stay in a hotel, instead telling her that our couch was plenty large enough for a good night's sleep, and she could take my bed while I slept in the living room. She had finally agreed to stay in the apartment, but only if she slept on the couch. I had begrudgingly accepted.

"Hey," I greeted, looking up from the novel I was reading. "What's up?"

"Just thought it would be nice to get in a private word or two with my daughter," Mom said, handing me the warm mug and seating herself on the corner of my bed. "Especially on a day as momentous as this—the meeting of her first real boyfriend." She smiled playfully at me, and again, I was struck by how different she seemed than the woman I used to know. "I know he wasn't treated as well as you would have liked by your friends today. Was he all right?" She sounded sincerely concerned.

"Oh, he was fine," I said with a shrug. "He doesn't get ruffled easily." I took a sip of the yummy drink she had provided and, taking a deep breath, looked up at her. "So what did you think of him?"

She looked as though she had been expecting the question. "He's probably one of the handsomest young men I've seen in quite a while," she said with a smile and a wink. "I imagine you could look at that face for long periods of time without complaint."

"Yeah . . ." I said, feeling my face redden.

"I hope there's more to it than just that, however," she said pointedly. "You haven't told me much about him, but I hope he's more than just some pretty features. I hope that he's a good man. And that he shares your values."

"He does," I assured her, setting my mug down on my nightstand. "I did meet him at church, after all."

"You did," Mom conceded, but her expression looked strangely hesitant. "But that doesn't necessarily guarantee anything, does it?"

I threw up my hands so suddenly that my mom jumped, almost spilling her hot chocolate all over my comforter.

"I don't get it," I said in frustration. "What are all of you seeing that I don't see?"

"Pardon?" Mom asked, eyebrows scrunched.

"You all seem so unimpressed by him. Hunter and Lily outright hate him. And I just don't understand why," I complained. "He hasn't done anything to deserve it. He's been consistently polite to them, regardless of how they treated him in return, and he's so good to me. Yet they still have nothing but contempt for him. Why? What am I not seeing?"

Mom smiled softly to herself as she studied the mug in her hand. "They're just worried about you," she said finally. "They're good friends,

Ryder. You're blessed to have found such good people so quickly after moving here. I think the Lord was watching out for you."

"I'm sure He was, but that doesn't answer my question," I pointed out.

"Doesn't it?" she said with a significant look. She smiled to herself again as she got to her feet. "Look, Ryder, you're a smart girl. Nobody is going to tell you who you should date and who you shouldn't. But don't discount the opinions of the people who care about you. Sometimes they have a clearer perspective than you might think."

She pushed aside the curtain in the doorway, pausing to look back at me. "I love you, honey. I'm so proud of you. I hope you know that." With a smile that looked slightly wobbly around the corners, she bade me goodnight and disappeared.

Sixteen

The weeks between Thanksgiving and my Christmas vacation were brutal at work. I was determined not to leave a single thing undone, given the somewhat snide comments I'd been getting from Amelia over the past month that "long vacations were generally not the fastest way to the top."

Now, I was far from taking career advice from Amelia, but I couldn't help but notice that, despite her nasty attitude, she appeared to be doing quite well at Feldman. I'd overheard Bryan, the handsome senior manager, telling Jim Rose that she was performing above her peers (ouch) and that she was asking for more responsibility. I was determined not to let that go unanswered, so my formerly eighty-hour weeks had taken on an additional ten hours, mostly just so nobody could complain that I wasn't doing my job.

But now, with the miserable period of non-stop auditing behind me, I could focus ahead on my week and a half of pure freedom with Damian. My parents had taken the news of my shortened visit with good grace, so I wasn't even feeling guilty about it. Damian and I arrived in Houston on Friday evening and took a car from the airport to his dad's house in the River Oaks area.

As we walked up the path toward the front door of the house, it opened and out stepped a thoroughly average-looking man with a pleasant face and striking blue eyes.

"Ryder," he greeted, as though he'd known me all my life. "It's so great to finally meet you. I'm David."

"It's wonderful to meet you," I replied, stepping into his warm embrace. I was struck by how oddly comfortable I felt with him, almost immediately. "Thanks so much for having me."

"Of course," David said with the warmest smile I'd ever seen. "I'm just thrilled to be meeting a young lady of Damian's. He typically doesn't bring them around. Must be ashamed of me." He winked at his son, who laughed and stepped forward to hug his father.

"Hey, Dad," he greeted, pounding him on the back. "You look great! Feeling better, I hope."

"Much better. Thanks, son," David said, leaning down to pick up my suitcase. "Well, come in, come in! I was just about to put some burgers on the grill."

David's house was incredible. It wasn't massive—in fact, it was probably quite a bit smaller than his penthouse apartment in New York had been. But it was professionally decorated in a contemporary masculine fashion, with a black and tan color scheme everywhere, and vibrant artwork on the walls. In that way, it reminded me of Victoria's New York apartment, and I wondered if her decorating style had influenced David.

After instructing us to leave our bags in the front entryway, David led us out onto the back patio in front of a deep-blue-tiled pool. It was unseasonably warm, nearly seventy degrees, as we sat at the glass patio table and chatted while David grilled burgers and veggie skewers. The conversation was casual and easy, and David's sense of humor was charming. Even Damian seemed more easygoing than usual.

After dinner, when it started to get a little chilly, we moved into the house and David offered to show me where I'd be sleeping. I started to get a little nervous about the possible sleeping arrangements as we dragged our suitcases to the second floor, but I needn't have worried.

"Damian, you know where to go," David said carelessly, gesturing down the hall. "Ryder, you come with me." He took me down the hall in the opposite direction, finally opening the door to a beautiful room decorated in dark red, tan, black, and white. There was a set of French doors directly by the bed that led to a balcony out the back of the house.

"This is beautiful," I assured him. "Thank you so much."

I wouldn't have dreamt of voicing how grateful I was that he didn't assume that Damian and I wanted to share a room. I assumed that he knew that Damian was a Mormon and didn't hold with such things, but I wasn't sure if Damian really talked about his religious beliefs with his family. He barely discussed them with me, and I actually shared them.

"Of course," David said with a smile. "Just let me know if you need anything, okay? There are clean towels in the bathroom." He nodded toward the doorway on the opposite side of the bed from the set of French doors. Then, setting my suitcase inside the room, he respectfully backed out, shutting the door behind him.

Damian stopped by my bedroom shortly before I turned out the light, staying just to wish me a goodnight and kiss me briefly. I fell asleep feeling more content than I had in a very long time.

- - - - - -

The more I got to know David Wolfe, the more I liked him. He was gracious and sincere, complimentary and conscientious. In the four days we spent with him, he took us all over Houston, wanting to keep us busy and engaged at all times. But my favorite times were those evenings when, exhausted from our busy days, we just sat in his living room and talked.

David told me hilarious stories about Damian as a child—things that I was sure Damian never would have shared himself. I was impressed by how David spoke about Victoria—which was always with the utmost respect. He never used profanity, or even, it seemed, spoke negatively at all. I was enamored, and I told Damian so.

"Yeah, like I said," Damian laughed. "He's a thoroughly decent guy."

Our last night in Houston, Damian gave me a mysterious look before dinner and told me he had "errands to run" (which I took to mean last-minute Christmas shopping), leaving me alone with David. Our conversation was cheerful and humorous, as usual, but David seemed to become almost introspective as we sat down to a simple meal of oven pizza and salad.

"So how long have you and Damian been seeing each other now?" David asked, taking a bite of his pizza.

"About five months," I replied, likewise taking a bite of my slice. "It's been an adventure for sure."

"Has he told you much about his past?" David asked.

"His past?" I said, raising an eyebrow. "He's told me about growing up in New York and about you and his mom, if that's what you mean."

"His religion?" David prompted. His gaze seemed a little too focused on his plate as he meticulously pulled cheese strings off of his slice of pizza.

"He's a Mormon, like me," I said simply.

"And me," David said with a smile, glancing up at me. "Well, sort of."

"You're a member of the Church?" I asked, trying to keep the astonishment out of my voice. Damian and I had attended sacrament meeting in a ward in Houston the day before, but David hadn't accompanied us, which had cemented my assumption that Damian was the only Mormon in his family.

"A very negligent one," David replied with a somewhat pained smile. "I joined the Church when Damian was a child, only about five or six. I took him to church with me every Sunday, hoping that it would provide him with the opportunity to meet people outside of Victoria's circle. It worked, and Damian wanted to be baptized when he turned eight, like all of his friends in the ward. We continued to go to church together until Victoria and I divorced when Damian was fifteen. After that, I tried to stay around as much as possible for him, but I think he always felt like I abandoned him." David looked back down at his plate, and it appeared to me that he was blinking more rapidly than usual. "He seemed to want to separate himself from everything that had anything to do with me. He stopped going to church and he wouldn't even see me for several years. It was at that point that I figured I'd give him his space and I left New York for Houston."

I looked at him in surprise. "Didn't you think he might feel even more abandoned by that?"

David gave me the same mirthless smile. "You're much more astute at your age than I was at forty-five," he said. "It definitely didn't help matters. But Damian eventually came around. One day, about eight years after I moved here, he suddenly called me. We started talking on the phone every couple of weeks, just casually, and eventually he even made time to come down to see me. He told me he was going back to church, and it had made him want to get back in touch with me. But by then, I'd let my own religious fervor lapse." He winked at me.

"When was this?" I asked curiously.

"Oh, about two years ago," David replied. "He tries to get down here at least a couple of times a year, and sometimes I'll go up to see him." He took a deep breath and shook his head. "I love my boy, Ryder." He blinked furiously again, still shaking his head. "He's very much like his mother."

"Do you still love her too?" I asked, not thinking.

David gave me an appraising look, and I felt my cheeks burn.

"I'm sorry," I said, mortified. "What a thoughtless question to ask."

David chuckled and reached out to place a hand on mine. "There is a part of me that will always love Victoria. At least the way she was when we first met. She's very different now, and sometimes I see shades of her in Damian that really concern me." He looked steadily into my eyes, and I felt like his soul was attempting to speak directly to mine. "In fact, sometimes I think it might be a lost cause."

I looked at him, not sure what to say. Damian seemed as far from a lost cause as anyone I'd ever seen. He was confident and self-assured, put-together and firm in his ideals. "You seem worried about something," I finally said to David. "How can I help you?"

David smiled at me, the corners of his blue eyes crinkling just like Damian's. "Oh, you sweetheart," he said, pulling my hand to his lips and kissing it. "You do me good, just being here. Seeing your goodness. Just don't let that fade, okay? Damian could use someone like you in his life."

I nodded readily. I was more than happy to stay in Damian's life for as long as possible. Picking up my forgotten pizza, I took a bite.

Sensing my desire to move on to less weighty topics, David began chatting about old Christmas traditions that they'd had in their family when Damian was small, telling more humorous stories about his childhood. We were just loading the last dish into the dishwasher when we heard the front door close.

"In here!" David called without preamble. A few seconds later, Damian came sauntering into the room, hands in his pockets.

"How was your errand?" I asked, giving him a teasing grin.

"Completed satisfactorily," Damian replied with a smile of his own. He walked up to me and kissed me quickly on the cheek. As he moved away, I noticed that the smell of his cologne, which was divine by the way, was powerful enough to make my eyes water . . . had he just sprayed himself again? And if so, why? I wondered idly where he'd been.

David was watching Damian carefully, his expression somewhat saddened. I immediately felt guilty for encouraging him to talk about the past. A past where he had had a marriage and a family. I was sure it was a sobering thing for him to think about.

"Did you two have a good time?" Damian asked, sitting heavily at the table and pulling a pitcher of water toward him.

"We had a wonderful chat," David answered, smiling at me. "You've got a good one here, Damian. I hope you realize that."

"I sure do," Damian said, giving me a wide, toothy smile. I laughed.

"Well, I still need to pack," I said, heading for the stairs. "I'll let you two freely discuss all my virtues out of my hearing while I do so." I grinned playfully at them and headed for the stairs.

- - - - -

We arrived in Salt Lake City the evening of December 21. Coming down the escalator into the baggage claim area of the Salt Lake airport, I had to hold myself back from potentially maiming the people around me in order to get to my dad, whom I could see waiting below.

"Excuse me, excuse me," I gasped to people around me as I skirted them. Running into my dad's open arms felt like home. Damian, dragging my carry-on along with his own, followed me.

"Hey, Red," Dad said, squeezing me tight enough to let me know that he'd missed me just as much as I'd missed him. "So good to have you home for a bit."

"I can't tell you how good it is to be here," I said into his shirt. "I actually teared up a little when we started descending into the valley and I saw the mountains. I didn't realize how much I'd missed them."

Once I'd finally pulled back from my dad, my mom stepped in for her hug. "Glad you made it okay," she said, kissing my cheek and then reaching up to hug Damian as well. I loved her for the willing show of affection to him. He seemed gratified as well as he hugged her back.

"It's great to see you again, Emma," he said.

"You must be Damian," Dad said, stepping forward and holding out a hand to him. FBI alumnus that he was, I knew he was sizing Damian up. Given his law enforcement poker face, I couldn't tell if he was impressed or dismayed by what he saw.

My dad was slightly taller, only by an inch or two, but the men were built along the same lines. Slender through the waist and powerful through the shoulders. My dad had always kept up on his physical fitness, even while working as a CPA. I think he considered it a matter of FBI pride. But I noticed, as I took the opportunity to look, that he had softened a bit around the middle.

"What's up with this, Dad?" I asked, reaching out to pinch his slightly softened abdomen. "Getting a little cushy, aren't we?" I winked at him.

He laughed. "Hey, it's your fault," he said, putting his hands up defensively. "I've been missing my running buddy these past several months."

"Ah, I haven't really kept up on it either," I admitted. "But I do so much walking around the city that it thankfully hasn't made much of a difference."

"You look fantastic, Red," my dad agreed, leaning down to kiss the top of my head. "Now, let's grab your bags and get on home." He reached out to take my carry-on from Damian, somewhat territorially I thought, and headed toward the baggage claim.

The drive home was slightly awkward. Damian attempted to get some conversations started by asking my mom how the last month had been and my dad about his work. My mom was pleasant enough, answering his questions amiably, but apparently not much had happened in the past month—which was a testament to her crusade to simplify her life, because usually December much more closely resembled hell than heaven in the Redmond household.

My dad insisted on giving simple, single-sentence answers to Damian's questions, despite Damian's attempts to get him to elaborate. I was embarrassed. The discrepancy between how David Wolfe had received me and how my dad was receiving Damian couldn't possibly have been more distinct. Eventually, Damian gave up. I gave him an apologetic look, but he just smiled at me and reached out to take my hand.

"Any plans to see Kara while you're home?" Mom asked me as we turned onto our street.

"Probably," I answered, looking out the window as we passed her house. "We haven't talked about it, but it would be a crime not to get together with her."

"Have you spoken to her often?" Mom asked, not looking at me. She seemed to already know the answer to her question.

"Not as often as I should have," I admitted. "I just got busy when I moved, and I . . . well, I totally dropped the ball. I probably owe her a big apology."

"Probably," Mom agreed. I wondered if Kara had said something to her.

Dragging our suitcases into the house, I headed toward the basement where the guest rooms were located.

"Where are you going?" Mom asked in confusion, watching me.

"The guest rooms," I said with a puzzled look. "Why?"

"Why wouldn't you stay in your own room?"

"I thought you turned it into a craft space," I replied, matter-of-factly. I thought I saw Mom wince a little.

"No, it's still there," she said, taking one of my suitcases and heading toward the second floor. "George, will you take Damian down to one of the guest rooms?" she called over her shoulder.

"With pleasure," Dad said, and I knew he was relieved that Damian and I would be sleeping with two floors between us. Fathers.

"So what changed your mind?" I asked my mom as we climbed the stairs. "You seemed pretty gung ho about the craft space conversion idea when I was packing to leave."

"Well, it's amazing the things a person will say and do when they're angry and hurt and don't know how to deal with it," my mom said as she opened the door to my bedroom, revealing it to be exactly as I'd left it.

"What do you mean?" I asked, hefting my suitcase onto the bed and unzipping it to unpack my clothes.

"Well," Mom said. She sounded slightly uncomfortable. "Let's just say that I took your moving to New York a little personally and leave it at that."

"Ahh," I said, nodding in comprehension. I started transferring clothing from my suitcase to the bureau across the room, not looking at my mom. "Well, just for the record, I didn't leave because of you."

"What?" Mom said, and I noticed that she sounded genuinely surprised. I didn't blame her. I'd certainly been unguarded enough in my comments six months before to make her feel that way.

"Look," I said with a sigh, sinking onto the edge of my bed. "I don't blame you for thinking that. I certainly did my best to make you feel like I was running away from you. And I even thought I was for a while. And I'm truly sorry about that. But it wasn't you. It never was." I looked up at her and was surprised to see her eyes shining with tears. The idea that I'd left Utah because of her must really have been bothering her. "I needed the independence. I needed to feel in control of my life, and I'd told myself that it was you holding me back," I continued, looking down at my clasped hands. "But it wasn't until I was talking to Hunter a few months ago that I realized, my moving to New York had nothing to do with you. It just took me a while to see it."

Mom sat next to me on the bed, wrapping her arms around me and leaning her head to rest against mine. "I love you, sweet girl," was all she said. And my eyes started to feel a bit shiny too.

- - - - -

I woke the next morning to the sound of a slamming door. I sat bolt upright, turning to stare at my closed bedroom door and the five-foot-seven blonde figure leaning against it.

"Well, if it isn't my absentee best friend," Kara said, eyes blazing. "Did I wake you? I'm so sorry." Her tone virtually guaranteed that sorry was the very last thing in the world she was feeling.

"Hey Kara," I croaked in my early morning voice. "What a surprise."

"I don't blame you for being surprised," she replied, flipping her long blonde hair over her shoulder as she took a step closer to me. She looked like she was ready to pounce, and I fought the urge to burrow under my covers for protection. "After all, you haven't spoken to me in months, so I assume you thought I was dead. Right? Otherwise why would you never have called me?"

I cringed at the expression of hurt on her pretty face. "I'm sorry," I said. "Really, I am. I've been neglecting a lot of people. When I got to New York, it seemed like I had stepped out of my old life and into a new one, and I kind of just let the old life slip away. You deserved better than that. I'm really sorry, Kara."

She studied me for a minute before shrugging and coming to sit on the bed next to me. "Well, it's not entirely your fault," she admitted. "I could have called you too. Turns out phones work both ways."

"They do," I agreed with a nod. "Truce?"

"Truce," she agreed. "Which means I can now tell you all the stuff I couldn't tell you when we were fighting." She crossed her legs and turned to face me, her expression eager.

"I met someone," she said with relish. I could tell by the way her eyes were shining that she really liked this one.

"Oh really?" I said, bringing my knees up under my chin. "Do tell."

"His name is Jordan," Kara began. "He's tall and blond and wonderful and I couldn't imagine my life without him."

"Wow, that's quite a description."

"It doesn't do him justice," Kara said, shaking her head, wide-eyed. "I can't wait for you to meet him. Actually, I have already arranged for you to do so."

"You have?"

"Yes," Kara said imperiously. "I ran into your supermodel boyfriend in the kitchen, and he told me that you two would be happy to come to lunch with Jordan and me today. So you'd better get your butt in gear, because it's after ten."

"You met Damian already?" I asked in surprise.

Kara nodded, and I could tell she was making a serious effort to keep a straight face. Gradually though, a smile started to blossom until she was beaming at me. "Besides Jordan's, that might be the most gorgeous face I have ever *seen*."

"Isn't it?" I swooned. "I never get tired of looking at him. And he's so sweet to me."

"Well, I definitely see why you brought him home to meet your parents." Kara stood, heading for the door. "I'm having Jordan meet us here, so I'm going back out there to get to know your love interest a bit better while you shower and *brush your teeth*." She said the last words emphatically to let me know she'd noticed my morning breath.

Man, I'd really missed her.

- - - - -

Having Kara around was a saving grace for me. She treated Damian with all the warmth and kindness that none of my other friends had been able to manage. She seemed to approve of him by default, just because he was my choice, and I loved her for it.

In return, I treated Jordan with the same level of warmth and approval, although it didn't take much effort. He was perfect for Kara, and watching them together was like living in a particularly cheesy romantic comedy.

We spent much of our time in the days before Christmas hanging out with them, and I couldn't help but feel warm pleasure at the thought of my best friend in the world and the man I adored getting along together.

Christmas Day was a low-key affair for us. Damian and I exchanged gifts privately that morning, and I was, as usual, outdone. I had purchased him a new silk tie in the color blue that exactly matched his eyes. It was a completely lame gift, as I well knew, but Damian acted as though it were the most thoughtful gift in the world. He kissed me soundly and told me he would wear it faithfully.

He gave me a beautiful diamond earring and bracelet set. The thought of how expensive the jewelry must have been made my face glow with embarrassment at my own piddly gift.

I wore the earrings and bracelet to our Redmond family Christmas dinner. My dad's eyes had bugged nearly out of his head when he saw the glistening diamonds on my wrist as I descended the stairs into the living room, coat in hand.

"Where did you get that?" he demanded, pointing at the bracelet.

"Damian gave it to me, along with these," I informed him, pointing to my ears. "Aren't they incredible?"

"What exactly is going on with you and that boy?" Dad challenged in a voice that was far too loud, given that Damian was only one floor below us. "Why is he giving you gifts that cost thousands of dollars, and why are you two vacationing together over the holidays? Is this more serious than you've let on?"

"Dad," I warned, my voice a soft hiss. "This is not the time to discuss this."

Damian was coming up the stairs, and given the controlled expression on his face, I knew he'd heard my father's questions.

"Well, are we ready to go?" My mom asked cheerfully, jumping up from where she'd been sitting on the couch, watching my exchange with my father.

Damian nodded, and I followed suit.

My father's control lasted impressively through the family gathering (where Damian was constantly hounded by my fawning aunts and female cousins), through the drive home, and even well into the next day. But eventually, as I knew it would, his concern resurfaced.

As we sat around the dinner table the day after Christmas, Dad finally turned to the two of us and asked straightforwardly, "Damian, I need you to indulge a concerned father for a minute."

Damian looked up at my dad, his face wary. "Okay," was all he said.

"I need to know why you're pursuing my daughter," Dad declared.

My mouth fell open. "Dad!" I protested.

My dad held up a hand to me. "Let him speak," he insisted. I turned to give Damian an apologetic look, but he wasn't looking at me.

"Well, sir, it seems to me you give Ryder far too little credit," he said, his voice smooth and controlled. "Why wouldn't I pursue her? She's beautiful and intelligent. Our personalities complement each other."

"I give my daughter all the credit she deserves," Dad said. His face was stony and unforgiving—a face I almost didn't recognize. "It's *you* I don't trust. What makes you think you're good enough for her?"

I gasped, a hand to my mouth. But Damian didn't seem surprised.

"Ryder thinks I'm good enough, and that's all that matters to me," he said, his voice still maintaining its measured silkiness.

"But Ryder doesn't have the life experience that you and I have, does she?" My dad said pointedly.

"You have so little faith in your own daughter's discernment?" Damian asked, and I saw his lip curl slightly. Uh-oh.

"This has nothing to do with my daughter's discernment!" Dad roared, making both me and my mom jump. "This has to do with you thinking you can pull the wool over everyone's eyes. This is you, coming to my daughter, a wolf in sheep's clothing, convincing her that you're the man of her dreams. But I know you. I've known men like you."

Damian stood, his blue eyes aflame. "Excuse me," he said, and stalked out of the dining room. I heard the front door slam seconds later.

Dad turned, his face softening, to look at me. I stared at him in shock and anger, disbelief radiating from me.

"Red—" he began, but I interrupted him.

"Don't."

Without another word, I went after Damian.

Seventeen

Damian was gone. Despite how quickly I had shoved my feet into boots and my arms into a reasonably warm coat, by the time I exited the house, Damian had disappeared. I figured he probably wasn't starving for my company right then anyway, so I didn't bother attempting to follow.

I went back in the house and up to my room, not bothering to look at my parents as I passed the doorway to the dining room. Even though I could feel them both looking at me. I sat on my bed, my forehead resting on the knees folded up to my chest, and wondered if my relationship with Damian was over. How could I expect him to be okay with staying with me, when all of my friends and family, with the exception of Kara and my mother, seemed doomed to hate him for reasons that made no sense to me?

Knowing Damian didn't want to talk to me, but needing to do something anyway, I pulled out my cell phone and sent him a short text.

I'm sorry. Please come back.

- - - - -

The next day, our last day in Salt Lake, Kara came over to say goodbye before we left for the airport.

"Are you okay?" she asked as soon as she saw me. I must have looked worse than I realized.

"Not really," I replied. Damian was barely speaking to me, although he had assured me when I saw him that morning that he wasn't angry. At least not with me. I knew he was still sorting out what had happened the night before and likely deciding if a relationship with me was still worth it.

"What happened?" Kara asked.

"Damian and my dad had a huge blowout," I said, biting my lip. "My dad accused him of being a 'wolf in sheep's clothing,' whatever that means. Then Damian stalked out and disappeared. I don't know if he just went for a walk, or if he got a ride somewhere, but he didn't come back until this morning."

Kara watched my face carefully for a minute, considering my words. "So what now?" she finally asked.

I continued to chew on my lip. "I guess I'm waiting for Damian to tell me that."

Kara give me a tight squeeze and told me she loved me before leaving. She stopped in the doorway and gave me one last look of uncertainty—almost as though she had something to say—but finally, she just shook her head and left.

My mom had been given the dubious honor of driving Damian and me to the airport, as my dad had gone into the office early that morning. Before he had left, however, he had stopped by my room, where I was methodically repacking my suitcase. He stood in the doorway, hands in his pockets, looking apprehensive and a little sheepish.

"I'm sorry, Red," he apologized. "What I did last night—it wasn't fair to you."

"To me?" I said, eyebrows raised. "It wasn't fair to *him*, Dad. You had no reason and no right to speak to him like that. What is going on with you?" Without meaning to, my voice had gotten louder and more high-pitched with each word, clearly indicating my frustration with my favorite guy in the whole world. This did not happen very often.

"I just . . . worry about you," Dad replied, wincing slightly at my tone. "It's what dads do, Ryder."

I was getting really tired of that excuse. That's what Hunter kept saying too. Why was everyone so worried? It made no sense! What reasons did they have? Was I not an adult, capable of making my own informed decisions?

I shook my head and turned my back to my father, continuing to pack my suitcase. I heard him sigh and walk back down the hall toward the stairs. I didn't go after him.

The drive to the airport was only a little bit awkward, thankfully. Mom kept up a steady stream of chatter, and Damian responded pleasantly. Still, I was almost relieved to say good-bye at the terminal.

"Love you, hon," Mom said as she hugged me tightly. "And so does your dad."

"I know," I said begrudgingly. "I love you both too. Tell him that for me, will you?"

Mom watched me silently for a moment before pulling me to her again, her hand stroking the back of my head. "You'll understand someday," she said softly in my ear. Letting me go, she smiled almost sadly at me.

"I'm not sure I will," I replied. "But it doesn't matter now."

Damian hugged my mother quickly and thanked her for her hospitality before dragging his bags toward the terminal. I hugged my mom once more and followed, wondering what the next several hours alone with Damian would bring.

- - - - -

Not much, it turned out.

"So, are you ever going to speak to me again?" I finally asked Damian once we were seated on the plane. He hadn't said more than a few words to me for the hour and a half since we'd said good-bye to my mom.

"I'm just processing," Damian responded, barely looking at me.

"Are you upset with me?" I asked, and I hated how timid I sounded.

"I'm not mad at you and I don't blame you for anything," he assured me with a more substantial look this time. "But I do need to consider the things your father said. Can you understand that?"

I nodded, but felt the fear welling up inside me. Was this the beginning of the end? If so, it wasn't like I could blame him for dumping me.

We barely spoke during the five-hour flight back to New York, and it wasn't until we were sitting in a car headed to my apartment that Damian finally turned to me.

"No," he said firmly. His blue eyes were steely and determined.

"No, what?" I asked, confused. Confused, but relieved that he was once again communicating.

"No, I'm not ready to give up on this yet," he said. He put an arm around me and pulled me close to his chest. "I can appreciate the fact that your father doesn't like or trust me, but I want to be with you, and I think you feel the same way."

"I do," I assured him fervently. I leaned into him, pressing my lips to his cheek, relief filling me to the brim.

"Then that's all that matters," Damian said with a smile. He covered my lips with his, and my mind went blissfully blank.

- - - - -

"So how was the trip?" Hunter asked the following day.

It was still the week between Christmas and New Years, and therefore the Feldman offices were a ghost town. I'd opted to work from the D&T offices until after the New Year, and apparently so had my team. I'd come in that morning to find them scattered all over, typing away in their cubicles. I'd also found Hunter stationed in his office, poring over paperwork.

"Pretty good," I said, refusing to mention the horrific last couple of days. The last thing I needed was Hunter finding out about that. "I really enjoyed meeting Damian's dad. He's an incredible guy."

"Glad to hear that," Hunter said. He wasn't really listening. He was skimming over a piece of paper, his eyebrows scrunched as he studied it.

I watched him, remembering suddenly the challenge I'd been given in my last meeting with the ward missionary council a few Sundays before. If I were being honest, it was the same directive I'd been given since the beginning. I usually managed to ignore it. But this time, staring at the face of one of my potential missionary prospects, I felt a subtle nudge from my conscience.

"Hey, so, just curious, how much do you know about my church, exactly?" I asked, oh-so-subtly.

Hunter must have been listening at least a little bit, because he looked up, formerly scrunched eyebrows now raised. "Pardon?" he asked politely, if somewhat dubiously.

"Well, I've noticed that you seem to know quite a bit about the LDS Church, and I wondered if you'd ever done any serious investigation into it," I said. I was totally winging this.

Hunter appeared to be seriously considering my words. "Well," he said, biting his lip at the corner. "I haven't done much *serious* investigation, as you call it, but I probably know more than the average Joe on the street." He went back to perusing his sheet of paper.

"Would you have any interest in knowing more?" I asked, screwing up all my bravery to form the question.

"Sorry?" Hunter asked, looking up at me again. He didn't look incredulous this time, just curious.

"Well, I wondered if you might want to come to church with me this coming Sunday," I invited, trying to keep my breathing from betraying my nervousness. Man, this was hard.

Hunter watched me for a minute, silently considering. Then he shrugged. "Sure, why not?"

I blinked. "Really?" I asked.

"Don't look so surprised," Hunter said, setting his paper down on a very large pile. "I told you I had a mentor once who was a Mormon. And I know you. So, yeah, I'll admit I'm intrigued. I think it would be interesting to know more about what you guys believe."

"Well, I'm glad," I said with a smile. "Meet me at my apartment at eight thirty a.m. on Sunday and we can go over together."

"Sounds like a date," Hunter said, winking cheekily at me.

I laughed and stood, giving him a wave before heading toward my cubicle and the mountains of catch-up I had to do.

- - - - -

I'd been working steadily for a couple of hours when I heard someone clear their throat behind me. Bryan stood there, leaning against the cubicle wall.

"Hey," I said, uncertainly. Senior managers didn't come visit me very often.

"Hey Ryder, how was your holiday?" He asked pleasantly.

"Great, thanks," I replied. I moved on from the niceties quickly, knowing he didn't actually care about my holiday all that much. "What can I do for you?"

"I actually have a project for you," Bryan said. "Jim Rose recommended you for it, and I think he's right. I think you'd do a great job."

"Okay. Thanks . . . I think," I said with a hesitant smile. "What's going on?"

"We found an error in Feldman's last quarterly filing," Bryan answered, gesturing toward my laptop screen. "I sent you an email about it a couple minutes ago. They're going to need to refile, and obviously, we'll need to sign off on their numbers before they do. I'd like you to be our feet on the ground. You know, organize the project and take care of all the heavy lifting."

"Really?" I said, half in excitement, half in fear. "That's kind of a big job. I've only been here six months."

"And you've performed very well in that time," Bryan answered with a kind smile. "I have complete faith in you, and so, it would seem, does Jim." Bryan bent down, resting his hand on my desk as he leaned nearer to me. "I know you were disappointed to not get a chance to work on the M&A deal, and this is a great way to distinguish yourself, Ryder," he said somewhat conspiratorially. "You do this job well, I think you'll be pleased at what may come of it."

"I'll do my best," I answered. There was no question of accepting. Not when the partner himself had suggested I take the assignment on.

"Glad to hear it," Bryan said, straightening. "I'll send you the documentation and set up some time for early tomorrow to walk you through it." With that, he walked away briskly. I watched him go, until I registered that a pair of eyes were resting on me from the cubicle across the row. It was Amelia, and she was glaring.

"What?" I said, raising my hands in self-defense. "What have I done now?"

"Nothing," she said scathingly. "That's the whole point. You've done *nothing*." She turned back to her laptop, but I could practically see the steam pouring from her ears.

I sighed. I'd never understand that girl.

- - - - -

Hunter's knock came a few minutes before eight thirty a.m. on Sunday, which meant I was unprepared for him. Lily, therefore, answered the door. Still in her pajamas, I might add, as she usually was at pre-ten-a.m. on a Sunday.

"Hunter!" I heard her exclaim in ecstasy. "What are you doing here?"

"Ryder didn't tell you?" Hunter replied. "I'm going to church with her this morning."

"You are?" Lily said, aghast. "No, she didn't tell me. Excuse me for a second, won't you?"

I knew what was coming. Sure enough, the curtain over my bedroom doorway was tossed violently aside as Lily stormed into my bedroom.

"You invited Hunter to go to church with you?" she hissed at me. She looked very unhappy about this.

"Yeah, so?" I asked innocently, staring at myself in my cosmetic mirror. She was playing right into my hands . . . just as I knew she would.

"Why would you do such a thing? Are you trying to date him behind my back?"

"Lil, since when does church constitute a date? May I remind you that I am currently seeing a gorgeous hunk of masculinity named Damian? I ain't no two-timer." I finished swiping on my lipstick and used my ring finger to tidy the corner of my mouth before looking up at her.

"Does *he* know that?" she demanded. "How do you expect me to get anywhere with him if you're spiriting him away to convert him to your religion?"

I shot her a withering glance at this frankly comical mental leap and rose to my feet. "You realize there's a very simple solution to this problem, right?" I said, slipping my feet into my gray stilettos.

"Oh really, what's that?"

"You could come with us."

Lily stared at me, her look of incredulity sharpening into something almost calculating. "How much time do I have to get ready?"

"I'd say about five minutes."

"Done."

Ten minutes later, the three of us were headed down the sidewalk toward the subway station. And I was a ward missionary extraordinaire.

- - - - -

Damian was less than pleased when I walked into sacrament meeting flanked by his two biggest anti-fans. I could almost hear him groan from across the chapel. But he pasted a polite smile on his face and greeted them both pleasantly. Hunter greeted him back just as pleasantly, although his smile seemed a little forced. Lily completely ignored him.

"What are they doing here?" Damian whispered to me as the opening song began. "I didn't think they were churchy types."

"They're not . . . yet," I replied, winking at him. "Let's just say I'm totally rocking my calling right now."

"I didn't realize you were so gung ho about missionary work," he commented, reaching forward to pull out a hymnbook. He didn't look particularly happy about my success.

"I haven't been, until now," I admitted. "But who knew I'd be so good at it?"

I winked at him again, but he didn't reply.

Church passed quickly, with my communications including either Damian or Lily and Hunter but never all at the same time. I felt like I was operating in two separate dimensions. It was slightly exhausting, to be honest. Finally, once Damian had begrudgingly agreed to drag Hunter with him to priesthood meeting, I pulled Lily with me into Relief Society.

"So, what do you think so far?" I asked her.

"Meh," she said, looking around at the room full of young women, studying the faces surrounding us. "You know, I give you far too little credit."

I eyed her in confusion. "What do you mean?"

"With all this competition, Damian still singled you out? I salute you, sister."

I gave her an exasperated look and turned to the front of the room as the meeting began.

After church, we met Hunter as he was strolling comfortably down the hallway, studying the artwork hanging on the walls. He was alone.

"Where's Damian?" I asked, glancing around him.

"Oh, he delivered me to the meeting as you instructed, and then he promptly departed," Hunter informed me. "Seems my company was just too much for him to bear for an entire hour."

"Oh," I said in disappointment, but brightened almost immediately. "Well, what did you think?"

"Very interesting," Hunter said, nodding. "A lot of what I heard today was familiar. I think my mentor worked a lot of what he believed into our everyday conversation without me knowing."

"That was wily of him," I chuckled. "Think you'll ever come back? Or have we scared you away for good?"

"You know, I think I just might make a return visit," Hunter said, and he gave me a knowing smile before heading toward the door into the winter sunshine.

Eighteen

"I'll pick you up at eight," Damian informed me. It was ten thirty p.m. on Saturday, the week before Valentine's Day, and I had just gotten home from the office. Damian had called me while I was on the subway, wanting to discuss our plans for the romantic holiday. Our first Valentine's Day.

Both of us had been incredibly busy over the past month, he with his M&A deal, and I with my new project at work. I was just about finished, however, and I was very pleased with how it had gone. I thought my superiors were actually quite impressed with me, which felt nice. But I hadn't had much free time to spend with Damian, nor him with me, and I'd really missed him.

"Works for me," I replied with a yawn. "I'm glad you're staying up on things like Valentine's Day, because I'm so exhausted I didn't even remember it was February."

Damian laughed. "Well, what can I say? I'm a glutton for punishment. Most men would just let the holiday slide right on by, relieved that their significant other had forgotten it."

"But not you," I cooed at him, collapsing backward on my bed. It was a struggle to not fall asleep immediately.

"Not me," he replied. "Anyway, I haven't actually figured out what we're going to do yet, but hopefully I'll come up with something spectacular. Stay tuned."

"Will do," I said, and I could feel myself fading. Apparently I sounded like it too, because he chuckled in my ear.

"I'll let you get some sleep. Have a good night, beautiful."

"Mmmm," I replied with a smile and managed to hang on long enough to disconnect the call before losing consciousness.

- - - - -

The next day at church was spent ignoring Hunter's snide comments about my Valentine's Day date with Damian (who was working again and therefore wasn't at church at all).

"Oh, I can already hear it in my head," Hunter said, wrinkling his nose. "All the sighing and mooning about the restaurant he takes you to and how he held your hand and nuzzled your ear all night. Details of the roses and the chocolates and the cheesy music. Revolting." He faked a shudder as he grabbed my arm and yanked me into the Sunday School classroom, which I'd been too distracted to notice we were passing.

"Oh please," I replied with a snort. "Why on earth would I tell you anything about it? You've never been particularly supportive of my relationship with Damian. Trust me, you and Lily are the last people I'll be gushing to."

"Speaking of Lily, is she ever going to come with us again?" Hunter asked we sat side by side in the steadily filling classroom. "She seemed so enthusiastic that first Sunday that I thought she might actually be interested in religion. It was kind of shocking, actually."

"I think she was more interested in the company than in the actual destination," I said with a grin. One corner of his mouth quirked up in a signature half-smile, but I noticed that it didn't quite reach his eyes. "Speaking of which," I said, elbowing him. "Are you *ever* going to officially ask her on a date? She's crazy about you, you know, even if she doesn't say it."

"I know," Hunter admitted. He glanced down at his hands in his lap. "I'm not sure. I've thought about it."

"What's to think about?" I asked, nudging him again. "Lily's a catch!"

"I know she is," Hunter said, still not looking at me. "But I'm not sure we're all that well-matched, to be honest. She's so independent. She doesn't . . . I don't know, *need* anyone. I think I'd like to be needed."

"Who's to say that she wouldn't grow to need you?"

Hunter lifted a shoulder halfheartedly, and he looked relieved when the teacher started talking at the front of the room, effectively putting an end to our conversation. I watched his face for a moment more, and then turned to focus my attention on the instructor. But I couldn't help feeling a sense of impending doom. What would happen to our happy little threesome if Hunter decided that he didn't want to be with Lily? How would she take that? I shuddered at the thought.

- - - - -

"Okay, change of plans," Damian said over the phone on Valentine's Day. I was sitting at my laptop at four p.m., wishing it were four hours later. "Don't be mad at me, okay?"

Just for the record, things I wanted to hear pretty much never started out that way.

"Okay . . ." I replied, drawing out the word.

"So you know we're wrapping up this deal," Damian began, and he sounded excited. "We just submitted the proposal to the regulators for approval today, which means, provided they don't have any issue with it, we're almost done."

"That's great!" I said, trying to sound enthusiastic, but really just wanting him to get to the point.

"Well, we're having a little party at Uptown6 tonight to celebrate," he said, and I could hear in his tone how much he really wanted to go. "I know it's awful timing, but I figure you and I can have a romantic dinner any time, and this party is to celebrate a really big milestone in my career. Would you mind terribly if we hit up the party instead of doing dinner tonight?"

I felt my heart sink just a little bit. The last thing I wanted was to spend the evening with his investment banker pals, but he was right. This transaction was a big deal for him, and that was something I really did understand. If I were a good little girlfriend, I would support him in that.

"Of course we should go," I replied. "It's a big day for you. We can celebrate Valentine's Day another time. What time should I meet you at Uptown6?"

"Around eight," Damian said, and the happiness in his voice made me immediately glad I had agreed to the change of plans. "You're the best, babe. See you in a bit."

I hung up and tried to drum up some enthusiasm to spend my first real Valentine's Day in bar with a bunch of arrogant investment bankers. It was really hard.

"Got the V-Day shaft, huh?"

I looked over to see Amelia looking at me with something akin to amusement, pity, and disdain on her face.

"Excuse me?" I said, forcing an expression of superiority on my face. "I don't know to what you're referring."

"Oh, come on," Amelia replied. "That was classic. You should have given him more crap than you did. I would have."

"Yes, well, I'm a supportive girlfriend," I said, not wanting to admit that I'd actually considered going her route.

"Or you're a pushover," she said, giving me a significant glance as she turned back to her computer. "Remember, next time, you are allowed to say no."

I turned back to my own screen, mulling over her words. I didn't actually think I'd made a mistake by agreeing to change our plans. It was, after all, a big day for Damian. But it made me think. How often did I roll over and do whatever Damian wanted, just because I was afraid to lose him? The answer to that question troubled me.

- - - - -

I walked into Uptown6 around quarter after eight and immediately spotted Damian and his friends. They were the loudest in the place, gathered around a group of three small circular tables in the corner of the bar. I stood and watched them for a moment, feeling distaste sweep over me. They were rowdy and aggressive patrons, and I noticed many people eyeing them with annoyance.

I watched Damian, noticing how he interacted with the others, feeling like I was seeing a completely different person. He seemed almost jubilant. I'd never seen him like that before. This deal must have been weighing on him a great deal over the past several months, because the conclusion of it seemed to have freed the beast.

I walked toward the group, finally catching Damian's eye when I was about halfway across the room.

"Ryder!" he called loudly. Very loudly. He moved toward me, and I noticed that his step was different. Instead of the smooth, confident movements I was used to seeing, he shuffled, almost stumbled across the space between us.

"Hi," I said uncertainly as he reached me.

"Hey, gorgeous," he said with a smile, leaning forward to press his mouth to mine. I was immediately overwhelmed by the smell of alcohol on his breath. He had obviously been drinking.

"Damian," I said, pushing him back and looking up into his face. He grinned at me carelessly, those perfect teeth gleaming in the dim light of the bar. He hadn't only been drinking—he was totally soused. Disappointment welled up inside me. "Why are you drinking? And how long have you been here, exactly?" I asked him. Given his current condition, he must have been there for quite a while.

"Couple hours," he replied, ignoring my first question. Throwing his arm around my shoulders, he practically dragged me toward his group of friends.

"Well, if it isn't the little Utah staff accountant!" Trip crowed, holding up his glass. I had no idea what was in it, but it certainly wasn't beer. Given his current state of vociferousness, it was undoubtedly something much harder. Wonderful. A group of drunk investment bankers and me.

Not sure how to handle the situation, I sat quietly in the corner and considered. I wondered if Damian would even notice if I got up and left. It wasn't as though he needed my company, and I didn't much like the sight of him at the moment anyway.

Deciding to just go ahead with the cut-and-run plan, I stood. But my movement caught the attention of several of the drunk businessmen. They turned to face me and seemed delighted at the materialization of a female in their vicinity.

"Hey baby," one of them crooned with a stupid look on his face. I rolled my eyes as I yanked my purse up on my shoulder.

"Aw, don't be like that," Pierce slobbered from my left. "Your face is too pretty to have an expression like that on it."

"Save it for Tricia," I said to him, wrenching my arm away as he trailed his hand down it.

"Ha! Tricia's long gone," said Dennis, as he closed in to my right. "Dumped him hard a few months ago."

If I'm being honest, I wasn't at all surprised to hear that. Tricia always seemed far too classy for Pierce anyway.

"Shut up, Dennis," Pierce said in a scathing tone, swinging a heavy, uncoordinated fist in his direction. He nearly hit me, and I jumped out of the way.

"Aw, relax," Dennis said with a laugh. "Maybe this one's got some potential." He gestured to me with his head, and they both turned back to me. I felt like their looks were almost predatory.

"Trust me, there's no potential here," I said, warning bells going off in my head. These guys were jerks stone cold sober. What happened to them when their scanty judgment was impaired by alcohol?

"Why not let us decide?" Pierce said with a leer. He took a step forward. Thankfully, he had slow response time, so I managed to sidestep him and immediately headed for the door. But I was impeded by a strong hand grasping my upper arm.

"Where are you off to?"

It was Damian. He'd been laughing with Trip since I'd arrived, so I didn't think he'd even look in my direction as I walked by, but I'd miscalculated.

"Home," I said, trying to keep the disgust out of my voice as his alcohol-laced breath brushed my face.

He leaned close and nuzzled his face into my neck. "It's kind of early for that, isn't it?" he purred, his lips grazing just below my ear. Usually such attention made my breath quicken and goose bumps rise on my arms, resulting in me pulling him closer. Tonight I just wanted him away from me.

"No, I don't think it is," I said, backing up and attempting to pull my arm away. "I have no interest in watching you drink yourself into a stupor, Damian."

Damian held fast to my arm and pulled me roughly back in close to him. "Oh, come on, Ryder. Don't be so self-righteous. Maybe you should have a drink to loosen up."

"No thanks," I said, glaring at him. His handsome face looked weak under the effect of the alcohol in his system. Normally he was so in control of himself, but not tonight. "Call me when you've sobered up. Then maybe we'll talk."

"But I don't want you to go," Damian said, almost conversationally. The change in his tone was so marked that for a moment, I wondered if he'd been sober all the time and just playing the part of a drunk. "I think you should stay. I want to be with you." He showed no sign of intending to loosen his hold on me.

"But I don't want to be with *you* right now," I said firmly, trying to extricate myself. "Let go of me, Damian."

"No," he said calmly, staring at me with those ice blue eyes. "I don't think I will."

"Damian, let me go," I insisted, trying, almost desperately now, to get out of his grasp. His hold tightened to an almost painful degree.

"No," he said again. "I don't want you to leave. I like having you with me."

I stared at him incredulously, opening my mouth to demand my freedom one more time, just because I didn't know what else to do. Suddenly Damian stumbled, falling backward. He released me as he fell, and I quickly backed up to keep from becoming entangled in his legs. I looked around to see what had caused his fall, and saw Amelia Applewhite standing there, looking down at him with disgust.

"So that's the boyfriend, huh?" she said, wrinkling her nose. "Not terribly impressed, to be honest."

"What are you doing here?" I demanded breathlessly.

She began pulling me away as Damian started to get to his feet, swearing vehemently. Apparently alcohol brought out his inner sailor.

"Oh, just passing by," she replied, towing me quickly across the bar and out the door, looking over her shoulder at Damian and his group. I seriously doubted this, but decided not to question her further as she said, somewhat urgently, "No offense, but can you move faster? Chances are he's not going to be any more enthusiastic about you leaving after his little accident than he was before it."

"So how exactly did you knock him over?" I asked, following her lead and high-stepping it down the sidewalk.

"Drunks are notoriously uncoordinated," Amelia informed me with an air of ease. "I just kicked him in the back of the knee."

I couldn't help myself. I laughed.

"Thanks for the save," I finally said when I caught my breath. "I promise, he's never like that. I've actually never even seen him drink before. He's usually a perfect gentleman."

"Oh yeah, he's a real winner," Amelia said with considerable sarcasm.

I didn't bother contradicting her.

"So . . ." I began, and then paused, wondering if it was wise to ask.

"What?" Amelia asked, glancing at me.

"Why did you help me, anyway?" I questioned, deciding to just go for it. "I never got the impression you liked me all that much. So . . . why bother?"

Amelia was quiet for a moment before answering. "Well, I never much liked the guys who refused to take no for an answer. And . . . I figured you'd probably do the same for me."

"I would," I said without stopping to think about it.

We walked along in silence for a bit before I noticed Amelia watching me contemplatively. "How did you do it?" she finally asked.

I scrunched my eyebrows in confusion. "How did I do what?"

"Get Jim and Bryan to like you so much," she answered. "I heard them talking in the hall today. I'd just gotten off the elevator and they didn't know I was there." She didn't look at me, and I couldn't help noticing how defeated she appeared. I'd never seen her like that before.

"Jim told Bryan that the partner group is talking about early promoting you to Senior because of the good job you've done on Feldman's refiling."

"Really?" I said, feeling my heart beat a little bit faster. An early promotion? Those didn't happen very often, I was told.

Amelia suddenly stopped and turned to face me. "I don't get it," she said, raising her hands in a gesture of frustration. "I put in more hours and more effort than anyone on the team. I work harder and faster. I'm good at my job. When they brought me onto Feldman, I thought they had brought me on specifically to work on that big M&A transaction they have going, but no, they just chucked me sideways onto the cash team. I'm fearless, Ryder!" she demanded, her eyes alight with fervor. "I could be really good at a role like that. I'm smart and competent and I don't take crap from anyone."

"I think that might be part of your problem," I said gently. "Look, Amelia, I don't have all the answers. But I think your issue might be your method of address. You can be the smartest person in the room, but if you don't have people skills, if you can't make people like you, you'll never get anywhere." I reached out and laid a soft hand on her shoulder, giving her a look that I hoped conveyed my sincerity. "Think how unstoppable you'd be if you were as fast and as accurate as you are now and still managed to be likable? You'd rise to the top so fast it'd almost be scary." I smiled at her.

She looked into my face silently for a minute before giving me a small smile back. And just like that, we were friends.

- - - - -

"Well, I hate to say I told you so, but—"

"Then don't," I gave Lily a scathing look, but she ignored it.

"I totally told you so."

I didn't have the energy to fight her on this, so I just let it pass.

"So what are you going to do?" Lily asked. "Dump him?"

I glanced at her, considering. "No," I finally said, looking away.

"What?" she demanded, all traces of her smile gone. "Why on earth not?"

"Look, Damian hasn't always lived like me," I defended. "I grew up a certain way, being taught certain things consistently. No alcohol, no drugs, no smoking, no, uh, intimate relations."

The corners of Lily's mouth twitched.

"Damian didn't. Not really," I continued. "Sure, he joined the Church at age eight, like me, but I have a feeling his dad didn't raise him like my parents raised me. And then Damian left the Church when he was a teenager and didn't go back until a couple of years ago. I'm actually surprised it's taken me six months to see this side of him."

Lily shook her head at me in disbelief.

"Plus," I couldn't seem to stop myself, "It was a really big day for him. He was celebrating. Maybe that's the only way he knows how. I've known him for over six months now and he's never done anything like that before. Do you honestly think it would be fair for me to dump him now, over one stupid night? I mean, after all the months of perfect ones?"

Surprisingly, I seemed to be persuading Lily. She looked less certain than before, anyway. "I guess not," she said. "People make mistakes. But this was one giant mistake, Ryder. I hope you at least make him pay for it somehow."

I nodded at her, but inside I was still undecided. I had no idea how this would play out. Part of me was completely disgusted with this new side of Damian, but another part really believed what I'd told Lily. Until I heard from him, I wouldn't make any hard and fast decisions.

- - - - -

"Baby, I'm *so sorry*."

Luckily for Damian, the next day was a Saturday. He had called me first thing in the morning. Well, as early as his unbelievable hangover would allow, no doubt.

"Really," I replied, finding it difficult to find my inclination toward forgiveness now that I was actually talking to him again.

"I've always been an idiot when I drink," Damian said, having the good grace to sound embarrassed.

"Huh, maybe that's why, as Mormons, we don't drink," I said pointedly.

"And I don't!" Damian replied, his tone emphatic. "Or at least I haven't. Not for the past couple of years. But then, last night, the guys kept pressuring me to have a drink, and I thought, 'Hey, it's a special occasion, why not?' And then I just fell into my old pattern." He sighed. "You know I never would have treated you like that if I'd been in my right mind, right? You know that."

I gave him a sigh of my own. "Yes," I finally admitted. "But that doesn't mean you're off the hook."

"I know," Damian said, his voice full of contrition. "And as soon as I'm able to get over this hangover and off my couch, I'm coming straight over there to show you how sorry I am."

"Yeah, well, take your time," I replied, letting a little of my irritation eke into my voice again. "I need to get over a few things myself."

After we hung up, I lay sprawled out on my bed for a long time, mulling the last twenty-four hours over in my head. I was still mulling when Hunter stuck his head through the curtain in my doorway. His eyes were closed.

"Are you decent?" he asked.

I chuckled and replied, "Come on in."

Hunter opened his eyes and walked into the room, coming to sit next to me on the bed. "Lily just told me."

"Of course she did," I said with an air of resignation. "And what do you have to say?"

"That I strongly encourage you to end things with Damian Wolfe," Hunter replied, his voice deadly serious. "Please. I don't want to see you get hurt, and he's the kind of man who will hurt you."

I studied him, for the first time really considering the words he said. But I couldn't end things with Damian. I was too invested. And, as I'd told Lily the day before, one night of stupidity didn't erase six prior months of bliss, now, did it?

"I can't," I told him.

He closed his eyes in frustration, his hand clenched on the side of my bed. "Ryder, why can't you see it?" He asked, his voice soft, but exasperated. "Everyone else can see him for what he is. Why can't you?"

"I care about him," I said. "I've seen a side of him that you haven't, and I know he's a good man. A good man who makes mistakes, but don't we all? I truly care about him and I—"

"Ryder Redmond, you are without a doubt the most pig-headed, blind, self-destructive person I have ever met!" Hunter suddenly roared, causing me to nearly jump right out of my skin.

"What the?" I gasped, holding a hand to my heart.

"I've had it," Hunter said, getting to his feet and shaking his head. "I'm sick of trying to step in and protect you and save you from yourself. I'm out. If you're so determined to crash and burn then you can go right ahead and do it. But excuse me if I don't stick around to watch." And he stalked out of the room as I stared, bewildered, after him.

Nineteen

"Hel—" I attempted to say into my phone but I was almost immediately cut off.

"I'm getting married!" Kara's voice assaulted my ears at an unholy volume. "I'm engaged, Ryder! Can you believe it?" I could practically see her dancing around her bedroom as she shouted into the phone.

"Really?" I cried. "Oh, I'm so happy for you, Kara! When's the big day?"

"May 20," she replied in a tone that simply glowed. "And you'd better be coming back here for it, because I want you to be my maid of honor."

"I'd love to!" I said happily. "But you realize that this means you've got to come out and see me before you consign yourself to wedded bliss, right?"

"I know! I've been thinking the same thing," she gushed. "And I've come up with the perfect plan. It will be in place of my bachelorette party! I'll come out and stay with you for a few days and we'll celebrate!"

"Sounds perfect."

We chatted for a few minutes about her hopes and dreams for her wedding before hanging up. The thought of my best buddy getting hitched was news good enough almost to make me forget that I was still feeling iffy about Damian, despite his continued and endless apologies, and that Hunter still wasn't speaking to me.

It had been nearly two weeks since Hunter had shouted at me and left, and although I'd seen him since then, he hadn't really acknowledged me. I had finally attempted to confront him about it the day before, and it had gone something like this:

"Are you really going to give me the silent treatment?" I had demanded from the doorway of his office. "Don't you realize how childish that is?"

Hunter had looked up from his computer screen and stared at me. "This isn't a protest, Ryder. This is a coping mechanism. It's easier for me to not worry about you and to not try to step in and curb your stupidity when I have no idea what's going on in your life. Will you please shut the door on your way out?" He looked back at his computer screen and continued on in his life without me.

And I was just beginning to realize how much I hated it.

- - - - -

I sat at my desk at the D&T offices one day in late March, thinking about how, if things were normal, as they hadn't been for over a month now, Hunter would probably be over here laughing and chatting with me, when Dave Parks stopped by my cubicle.

"Hey Ryder," he said cheerfully.

"Greetings, manager," I said glumly, staring at my computer screen.

"What's your problem?"

"Oh, nothing," I said, turning to face him and plastering a smile on my face. "What's up?"

"Jim wants to see you," Dave replied. "He's in his office."

"Right now?" I asked, raising an eyebrow.

"Yep," Dave said. "Hey, I hope you cheer up soon. I'm not used to seeing you with a frown, but I feel like it's happened a lot lately."

"It's just a phase," I assured him, but I knew I was lying. Hunter hadn't spoken to me in weeks and weeks, and he was giving no indication of changing his behavior patterns. Couple that with the still semi-awkward status of my relationship with Damian, and you had the reason for my current mood.

I walked to Jim's office, taking a deep breath to clear my cloudy disposition before knocking on the door. Jim spotted me through the glass panel beside the darkly wooded door and waved me inside. He was just wrapping up a phone call, and he gestured me to the seat in front of his desk as he said good-bye and hung up.

"Well, Ryder," Jim said with a smile. "Thanks for coming to see me. I appreciate it."

"Sure," I responded.

"I wanted to personally commend you on the fine job you've done on Feldman's refiling these past few months," Jim congratulated. "You've been with the firm, what? About a year now?"

"Nine months," I corrected, nodding. "Thank you. I enjoyed it, even though it was hard work."

"I'm glad to hear that," Jim said. "It was all very well done. In fact, we were so impressed with your work that we've decided to do something a little unorthodox."

"Oh really?" I asked, pretending like I had no idea what he was talking about. Thanks to Amelia's heads-up the month before, I had a pretty good guess.

"We've been a bit shorthanded this past year. We've experienced higher than usual turnover, particularly amongst our Seniors," Jim smiled again, a glint in his eye. "Given the quality of your work on Feldman thus far, we've decided to promote you to the Senior level. This will allow you to essentially skip a year in the hierarchy of the firm and start supervising audit work yourself." Jim sat back and let me soak that in.

"Wow," I responded, attempting to look surprised. Thankfully I didn't have to fake the gratification—that was wholly genuine. "That's very kind of you. Are you sure I'm ready for that?"

"The promotion will not be finalized until July 1," Jim replied. "We'll make sure to get you all the training you need before that time. Congratulations, Miss Redmond. This is a great accomplishment."

"Thank you very much," I said, getting to my feet. "I won't let you down."

I left the office, feeling lighter than I had in weeks, and I immediately wanted to share my good news with someone. Hunter was the first person who came to mind, given his proximity and his knowledge of the firm and the industry. But obviously that wouldn't work.

Next on my list was Damian, but things were still a little weird between us. We'd kept seeing each other, but things felt more hesitant than intense these days, although he hadn't messed up again. In fact, he had been the model boyfriend for the past month, almost to the point of being overattentive. But, honestly, I didn't feel like talking to him right now.

Next was Amelia. That idea actually really appealed to me. I started walking toward her cubicle, which was near mine. She and I had become relatively good friends in the past month and a half. I would never be as close to her as I was to Kara or to Lily—her personality wouldn't allow that—but we were definitely on warm terms these days.

"Hey," I said, walking into her cube and sitting down in the chair pushed into the corner.

"Hi," she greeted, turning to face me with a pencil twirling between her fingers. "What's up?"

"I just left Jim's office," I said, a little hesitantly. I hoped she wouldn't see this as gloating.

"Ah," she sighed, and I saw a brief shadow pass over her face. It cleared quickly, however. "Congratulations. It took them long enough."

"Thanks," I replied. "I'm glad you gave me a heads up. Otherwise I think I would have made a total idiot of myself—it would have been very unexpected."

"No problem," Amelia said, and her mouth turned up slightly at the corners. "So what's going on with you and Hunter Payne?"

"Sorry?" I asked, surprised at her sudden change of subject.

"You guys are usually thick as thieves when we're working in the office, but I haven't seen him over here once today. Actually, I haven't seen him for weeks. Are you guys fighting?"

"Well, kind of," I said. "He found out about Damian . . . you know."

Amelia smirked and nodded.

"Well, he demanded that I break up with Damian and I refused. And he said he was sick of trying to protect me and he was over it. And he hasn't talked to me since."

"Not a big Damian fan, is he?"

"Nope."

"Well, he's a smart guy," Amelia said, giving me a significant look. "I'd say he's got a good point. I still don't understand why you didn't break up with him."

"Apparently nobody does," I replied. "Look, while I'm definitely more wary of him than I was before, I am sincerely attached to him too. I haven't broken up with him because I don't *want* to. Why can nobody understand that?"

Amelia held her hands up in self-defense. "Hey, far be it from me to tell you how to live your life. Ultimately it's nobody's choice but yours."

I nodded resolutely at her. She was right. And nobody was going to make that choice but me. So . . . why was it that I felt the need for everyone's approval?

- - - - -

"How was your day?" Damian asked as we sat on the cushy black leather couch in his upscale Tribeca apartment. I'd never felt totally comfortable there. Everything was luxurious in a purely masculine sense, but it didn't really feel lived in. That probably was because Damian likely spent less than a quarter of his time there, given his hours at work and on the road.

"It was fine," I said cautiously to him. I felt like I said everything cautiously these days.

"And?" Damian pressed.

"And nothing," I responded with a shrug. "My day was fine."

Damian sighed and collapsed against the couch. "Okay, it was fine."

"How was yours?" I asked politely.

"It sucked," Damian said, and I turned to look at him. His face was mournful, but with a hard edge to it.

"What's going on with you?" I asked.

"You haven't forgiven me," Damian said, watching me with a knowing expression. "You say you have, but you're still mad about Valentine's Day."

That made it sound like I was upset that I'd had to spend the holiday in a bar instead of in a flowery, upscale restaurant. And that *so* didn't cover it.

"Not mad, exactly," I said. "I'm just trying to get to know you again with this added perspective."

"What added perspective?" Damian demanded. "I'm the same person I was before. I just made a mistake. Haven't you ever made a mistake, Ryder? Or are you perfect?" He looked at me pointedly. When he saw that his attempt to make me feel guilty for still being disturbed about that night wasn't going to work, he softened.

"I'm sorry," he apologized. "You don't deserve that. You didn't mess up—I did." He sat forward again, bracing his forearms on his knees. Leaning slightly toward me to put his face close to mine, he looked directly into my eyes and then reached out to brush his fingers softly across my cheek. I felt the familiar reaction to his touch and that hypnotizing gaze as my skin began to prickle with goose bumps. "Don't shut me out, Ryder," he whispered, close to my face. "Please forgive me."

I looked into those blue eyes and felt myself relax at the sincerity I saw there. The goose bumps didn't fade. In fact, they intensified as Damian turned fully to face me, taking me into his arms, one hand braced against my face. He kissed me, pressing his lips into mine over and over, finally trailing them down my jawline and onto my neck. He did that a lot, as though he was drawn to that part of my body, and I wasn't complaining. My hands clenched into fists on my trembling legs as I attempted to keep from grabbing him and showing him just how much I liked the sensation.

I felt my control slipping, soaring away as Damian's fingers stroked up and down my back. Just then, my cell phone began to vibrate in my pocket, shaking me from my stupor. I backed away from Damian, who groaned in frustration. I didn't blame him. I pulled my phone from my pocket and saw that it was my mom.

"Hello?" I answered, standing up and moving away from the couch as though my presence there would translate through the phone line.

"Hi, honey," Mom said. "How are you doing?"

"I'm good, Mom, how are you?"

"Are you sure?" she pressed, ignoring my question. She sounded concerned. "I really felt like I needed to call you. Is everything okay? Where are you?"

Yikes. If she had called in response to some kind of prompting, I must have been dangerously close to some kind of precipice. "I'm totally fine, Mom," I replied in a placating tone. "I'm over at Damian's."

"I see," Mom said, and it sounded like she'd had her question answered. "And how is Damian?"

"He's good," I said. "Would you like to say hello?"

"I'd love to talk to him," she replied, surprising me. I handed the phone over to Damian, who looked as startled as I did, but he covered it well.

"Hi, Emma," he said smoothly into the receiver. "How are things out your way?"

They spoke for a few minutes, with Damian updating her on the status of his M&A deal and the health and well-being of his parents before he finally finished with, "It's been great talking to you." He paused for a moment, listening to the voice on the other end of the line. His lips pursed fleetingly. "I understand, Emma. I'll do my very best. Talk to you soon." He handed the phone back to me.

"All good?" I asked Mom, putting the phone back to my ear.

"I certainly hope so," she said, attempting a joke that fell flat. "So what's going on with you? Anything exciting?"

"Yes, actually," I said, suddenly remembering. "I found out yesterday that I'm being early promoted to Senior in the firm. It's essentially jumping me forward a year."

"Oh, honey, that's fantastic!" Mom exclaimed. "I'm so proud of you!"

"Thanks, Mom," I said, smiling at the warmth in her voice. "I'm pretty excited about it. It's kind of a big deal. It doesn't happen very often."

"I can't wait to tell your dad," she gushed. "Or, wait, would you like to? He's just upstairs. I can go grab him."

"No, that's okay," I said quickly. I hadn't really spoken to my dad—at least not the way we used to—since Christmas, and I wasn't feeling up to a reconciliation right now. "You can tell him. It's getting late here anyway, and I need to be getting home to bed. I'm glad you called, Mom."

"I am too, honey. I love you."

"Love you too," I said, suddenly feeling choked up, for reasons I couldn't determine. I hung up and moved toward the entry hall table, where I'd left my purse.

"I'd better be getting home," I said over my shoulder to Damian, who sat watching me on the couch. "I really need to get to bed. I haven't been sleeping well lately."

"Sure," he said, still eyeing me speculatively. "When will I see you next?"

"I'm not sure," I said, stowing my phone in my purse and still studiously not looking at him.

"Later this week?" Damian asked. "I'm heading out to Asia for a few weeks after that, so this will be our last chance for a while."

"Yeah, okay, later this week then." I opened the door, glancing behind me. "See you."

"Why didn't you tell me about your promotion?" Damian asked suddenly, halting my departure. His eyes were still fixed on me. "If it's a big deal, like you said, then why wouldn't you share something like that with me?"

I didn't look at him, choosing instead to focus on my purse strap as I straightened it on my shoulder. "Um, I'm not sure," I said. "I guess I just wasn't thinking. I'll see you later, Damian."

He silently watched as I left the apartment, shutting the door softly behind me.

- - - - -

Damian's trip to Asia was something of a tender mercy for me. It gave me a chance to come to terms with things in a way I hadn't been able to since Valentine's Day, without him breathing down my neck. I spent time with Lily and Amelia, and I realized how much I'd missed girl chats. I still missed Hunter, but I was coming to terms with his absence as it showed no sign of ending anytime soon.

By the time Damian returned to New York in late April, I felt like I had my head back on straight and I was even happy to see him.

"Hey," I greeted him warmly when he showed up at Feldman one Thursday to take me to lunch. "Glad you're back."

"Are you?" he asked, seeming surprised. I felt a subtle pang of guilt, knowing that I had neglected him while he'd been gone, but I truly thought the time apart had done us good.

"I am," I said sincerely, and reached up to hug him and kiss his cheek. He returned the embrace fervently and I felt another pang of guilt. Had my silence really concerned him that much?

Neither of us had much time for lunch, so we headed to a small gourmet deli just down the street. We sat in a booth by the door and spoke enthusiastically—more enthusiastically than we had in months—about his trip and about the things I'd done while he'd been gone. The M&A deal was still pending the approval of government regulators, but Damian wasn't concerned.

"This can go on for months," he said, waving a hand through the air. "Especially when the two companies concerned are large. I won't start worrying until it takes upwards of a year for them to come back with their approval."

"But you think you'll get it?" I asked. "You're not concerned at all?"

"Not at all," he said carelessly.

Just then, the door behind him opened and Hunter Payne walked in. I stared up at him, and he stared down at me. The unexpected sight of me seemed to have startled him from his determined indifference toward me, and for once, he actually seemed about to say something. I hoped and prayed that he would. But then, he looked to his left and saw my lunch companion. The stone cold demeanor snapped back into place. He walked past us without a further glance, ordering his lunch to go. Once it was in hand, he quickly left the restaurant.

Twenty

"Aaaaargh!" Kara's scream was completely unnecessary as she raced toward me across the airport terminal and threw her arms around me. "I'm so happy to see you!" she cried.

I hugged her back fiercely, swearing to her that I could actually *smell* home on her.

"I'm going to pretend you didn't say that," Kara said, pulling back. "That's slightly creepy."

I laughed and grabbed at her left hand, wanting to get a better look at the ring sparkling there. It was perfectly Kara, a heavy looking, white gold and diamond concoction that was far too elaborate and had likely been far too expensive.

"Can you believe I'm getting married in a week?" Kara cried. "It's seemed like it would never come, and here it is, practically upon us."

I leaned down and grabbed the handle of her carry-on size suitcase, wheeling it toward the door. "Are you ready? Did you ever work out that issue with the florist?"

"Oh yeah," Kara said airily. "She's an angel and is totally working with us, bless her. But who knew that flowers could be so crazy expensive?"

Talk of the wedding carried us through the car ride back to the apartment. We burst into the apartment in whirl of laughter and noise, startling Lily. She jumped up from the couch ready for a fight, but relaxed when she saw who it was. Instead, she sauntered toward us, studying Kara with a calculating look on her face.

Kara turned toward her with much the same expression. If I were being honest, I'd been slightly nervous about this meeting. My two best girlfriends in the whole world, coming face-to-face with each other.

Both of them with strong, overbearing personalities and a tendency to speak their minds too freely.

"You must be Lily," Kara finally said. "You look nothing like I thought you would."

"Yeah, well Ryder's not known for her accurate physical descriptions," Lily replied. "She only got your hair color right."

I sputtered indignantly, but they ignored me. Of course they'd turn this situation into an opportunity to bash on me.

Kara looked around the apartment, noting the bright colors and eclectic furniture. "Did you decorate this place?" she asked Lily.

"Yeah," Lily answered, almost aggressively. As though she were daring Kara to criticize it. I hoped, for Kara's own safety, that she wouldn't.

"I like it," Kara said simply, nodding. "It's got a funky feel, but it all still works within the room. It's like I'm looking right at your personality."

Lily's face relaxed as she appraised her blonde counterpart. "Thanks," she finally said. "I like your outfit. I've been looking for a jacket like that. Where did you get it?"

And from that moment on, they were buds. The three of us did everything together over the next few days. Lily took Kara to all her favorite furniture and jewelry shops and I showed her all of the best restaurants and hangout spots. The numerous parks, while still chilly, were starting to bloom, and I told Kara all about the odd weekends here and there that I'd spent relaxing on one bench or another and watching humanity waltz by.

"You've really grown to feel at home here, haven't you?" Kara asked me as we sat in Bryant Park the day before she was supposed to leave. "I've watched you these past couple of days, as we've gone all over the city. You love it here."

"I really do," I replied, taking a deep breath and looking around at the leaves budding on the trees. "It took a little bit, but it all feels so familiar to me now."

Kara nodded, and her expression struck me as being half-pleased, half-dejected. "I always kind of hoped that you'd hate it and come back home," she admitted. "But now, having seen you here, I don't think you will. I'm happy that you're happy, though."

Damian came over the last night Kara was in town, just to say hi and congratulate her on her upcoming wedding.

"I'm happy for you, kiddo," he said with a grin. "Jordan's a great guy."

"He is, isn't he?" Kara said. She smiled back at him, but I noticed that her expression looked uncertain. I wondered if she was feeling awkward about my relationship with him, knowing how my parents felt about it. I'd have to ask her about that. "So, um, are you coming with Ryder to the wedding?" she asked him.

"Can't, unfortunately," Damian replied. He put on a really good show of mourning, but I knew he was relieved. The last thing he wanted was to go toe-to-toe with my dad again. "I'm heading to California the day before for client meetings, and I'll be gone the whole weekend."

"Aw, that's too bad," Kara replied, but knowing her as I did, I could tell she was just as relieved as he was that he wasn't coming. I couldn't exactly blame her. I wouldn't want to risk a brawl between the maid of honor's father and her boyfriend at my wedding, either.

Damian hung around for about a half hour chatting pleasantly with us before leaving us to our "girl talk," as he put it. He rose from his lounging position on the couch, kissed me quickly on the forehead, and told me he'd call me later. Smiling and nodding at Kara, he let himself out.

Kara watched him go, that same strange expression of uncertainty on her face. "So, um, how are things going with you two?" she asked after he left. She turned to face me, tucking her feet beneath her on the couch.

"Pretty good," I replied, smiling at her tentative expression. "We went through a rough patch a few months ago, but I think we've worked it out for the most part."

"What happened?" Kara asked curiously.

And although I didn't really want to give her a reason to dislike Damian, I told her about Valentine's Day. Her expression became steadily graver as I told the story, and I found myself really wishing that I'd decided against it.

"But everything's okay now," I insisted after I finished. "It took me a while, but really, it was just an isolated incident. He hasn't done anything like that since. And he's been so sweet to me, trying to make it all up."

Kara didn't look convinced. She chewed on her lip determinedly, playing with a stray thread on the couch.

"Really!" I said, feeling almost desperate. Here I was, despite my insistence that this was my choice to make, trying to convince someone else that Damian was a good person. Why did it always come back to this?

"Ryder, I need to tell you something," Kara finally said, looking up at me. "I've needed to for a while, but . . . well, I just didn't know how. Plus, I didn't really know what happened or what caused it, and I didn't want to hurt you, so . . ." she trailed off.

"What?" I demanded, feeling a strange sinking feeling in my middle for some reason I couldn't identify.

"So you remember the day after Christmas? When your dad and Damian had that fight?" Kara asked, giving me a careful glance.

I nodded. How on earth could I forget it?

"Well, that night, Jordan and I were downtown looking at the lights at Temple Square. They turn them off at New Year's, you know, and we hadn't seen them yet. Anyway, we were walking down Main Street toward the plaza when I happened to glance into the window of a bar we were passing. And I saw Damian in there."

"Okay . . ." I said. So far nothing terribly alarming. Damian spent a lot of time in bars, but other than that one time, it had never caused a problem before.

"I stopped, just because it was so surprising to see him there, you know, all of a sudden," Kara continued. "And I watched him for a minute. I saw that you weren't with him, so I figured he must have taken a taxi or something. I almost went in to say hi, but Jordan said he looked like he wanted to be alone, so we just kept walking."

She looked up at me again, gauging my reaction. I could tell she wasn't finished, so I just nodded at her again.

"Well, on our way back, a couple of hours later, I made sure to look through the window of the same bar, just to see if he was still there. He was," Kara wasn't looking at me again. I had a feeling that the bad part was coming. "He wasn't alone anymore, though. He was sitting with this blonde girl, pretty scantily clad for December, if you ask me. They were talking and laughing, and as we watched, he leaned over and kissed her. Like, inappropriately in public kissed her."

I felt my heart stutter a bit. Damian had been kissing random girls in bars the night he'd stormed out of my parents' house? *That* was how he had chosen to deal with the situation?

But Kara still wasn't finished.

"I watched him for a second, wondering if I should go in and tear him a new one for it, you know," she said with an indignant look. "When the blonde girl stood and grabbed his hand. She leaned down and whispered something in his ear, and he smiled. And then, they . . . well, they left together."

"What?" I asked, attempting to keep my voice calm and measured.

"They left together," Kara replied. "They walked out of the bar. I thought he would see me and Jordan standing there, but they turned the opposite direction. Jordan didn't want to, but I made him come with me as I followed them. They ended up in that big apartment complex over on First South. You know, the one between Main and State? Anyway, she pulled him inside, and he just went, grinning all the way. And . . . didn't you say that he didn't come home that night?"

I stared at her, blinking silently. I knew what had happened. No, I had no proof of how far things had gone after my boyfriend had disappeared into another girl's apartment for an entire evening, but it really didn't matter. I could feel it in my bones. It was as though everything I had heard from everyone I knew about the kind of person Damian was, and the things I myself had observed in him that I had willfully ignored were crowding in around me, smothering me.

I knew what Damian had done. And that knowledge changed absolutely everything.

- - - - -

I spent much of the next couple of days processing what Kara had told me. I was less than fabulous company for the last twenty-four hours of her visit, but she seemed to understand. When I walked her out to the car we'd called to take her to the airport, she turned and threw her arms around me before getting into the backseat.

"I'm so sorry," she said, and she actually had tears in her eyes. "I know you're hurting. I'm sorry I didn't tell you sooner. Maybe you wouldn't be hurting so much if I had. But if I'm being honest, I really didn't think your relationship with Damian would last as long as it has. You guys had so much going against you, I thought it might end without my help. I know it sounds terrible. But I think it's time you knew what you were up against. You're worth more than this, and you deserve better."

"Thanks," I said with a weak smile. "Love you, Kare-Bear."

She returned my smile halfheartedly. "Love you, too." She hugged me again and then disappeared into the car. I watched her drive away, feeling more alone than I had in a long time.

Finally though, I determined on a course of action. As attached to Damian as I had always felt myself to be, I knew that our relationship wouldn't come back from this one. And honestly, I didn't want it to. I was disgusted. I was angry. And I would never be able to trust him again.

The day before I was supposed to leave for Utah to attend Kara's wedding, I called Damian. I hadn't spoken to him since he'd left my apartment the weekend before, and I'd ignored all of his texts and calls. I was actually quite surprised that he hadn't shown up on my doorstep demanding answers. He'd been so attentive lately that such a reaction would have been totally expected.

"Ryder!" Damian said by way of greeting. "Where have you been? I've been worried sick! Why haven't you responded to my texts?"

"Sorry, I've been busy," I replied benignly. "I got some news that I've been mulling over, and it's kind of kept me preoccupied."

"Are you okay?" he asked solicitously. Why was it that those silky tones now sounded so oily?

"I'm fine, now that I've had time to think it all over," I answered. "Anyway, I wondered if you'd mind coming over tonight."

"Of course," Damian agreed readily. "How about nine-ish? I'll be at the office a little late."

"That works for me," I replied. "Lily's working a late shift tonight so we'll have the place to ourselves."

"That's just how I like it," Damian teased.

I couldn't suppress a shudder.

- - - - -

I got home from Feldman at about eight p.m. that evening, and I spent a solid hour fidgeting anxiously on the couch. I thought about getting some dinner for myself, but I suspected my nerves might compel me to throw it up later.

Lily left for work around 8:30, and she actually hugged me before she left, telling me she was proud of me for what I was doing. She told me to call her if I needed her and even promised to blow off work to come home and be with me if things went poorly. What a gem.

Damian arrived shortly after nine, charismatic grin draped casually on his face.

"Hey, beautiful," he said, leaning forward to kiss me as he walked into the apartment. I pretended not to see and turned my head so his lips brushed my cheek instead. "I'm glad you called," he continued, looking at me carefully. "I've been worried about you."

"Oh, I'm fine," I replied, attempting to match his tone of nonchalance. "Have a seat."

He studied me again, reaching out to grasp my shoulders so he could get a good look at my face. "What's wrong?" he asked.

"I'm getting to that," I insisted, pulling away and gesturing to the couch. "But first, could we please sit down?"

"Sure," Damian said, eyebrows raised in surprise at my aggressive tone.

Once we were seated side-by-side, Damian reached out for my hand, and I let him take it, even though his touch made me want to immediately go shower. Maybe if we maintained some physical contact, it would make it easier for him to accept what I had to say.

I turned to face him, folding one of my legs underneath me. "Damian, I have something I need to say to you," I said, taking a deep breath. I'd debated how to begin this conversation, but now, confronted with his presence, I decided not to beat around the bush. "I know what happened over Christmas," I said.

He looked at me in confusion, a line forming between his eyebrows. "I don't know what that means," he said.

"The night you walked out of my parents' house, when you fought with my dad," I clarified. "I know where you went. I know what happened."

Damian's handsome face maintained its expression of bewilderment, but I saw something shift in those blue eyes. The creases between his eyebrows smoothed ever so slightly. "What are you talking about?" he asked innocently.

"Kara and Jordan saw you," I informed him. "Downtown. They saw you leave the bar with that girl and they followed you. I know you spent the night with her." I shook my head and looked away from him, unable to stomach the feigned look of pained blamelessness on his face. "Really, Damian? Some random girl you picked up in a bar?"

I felt his hand clench almost convulsively over mine. I glanced back at his face to see his features smooth into a look of careless ease. It was as though, in that moment, he'd decided the entire charade was no longer worth it. He'd been caught. The jig was up. And either he couldn't talk his way out of it, or he decided it wasn't worth the effort.

"Honestly, Ryder, you are such a hopeless prude," he said, his voice returning to its normal state of silkiness. "Haven't I given you everything you wanted? Haven't I been a good little boy? I've faithfully chased you and only you for the past almost entire year. I've kept my distance to not tarnish your precious virtue, I've taken you to nice places, I've paid you endless compliments, and what have I gotten in return?" He snorted derisively and rose to his feet. "Nothing. Nothing but infuriating teasing from you and constant insults from your family and friends. And while you may think your company is worth all the fuss and inconvenience, I can assure you that it is not."

I stared at him, simultaneously shocked and outraged at this foreign individual standing before me. Was this who'd he'd been the entire time? Why hadn't I sensed it? Was I really so blind?

"I don't understand," I stuttered. I felt utterly cold inside. "Were you . . . was any of it real?"

Damian watched me, his face an unfamiliar mask of cruel amusement. "Some of it," he said carelessly. "Even you have your moments, gorgeous."

He was insane. He had to be. I couldn't comprehend any other explanation for why he would spend nearly a year pursuing me and pretending to be something completely different than what he was. What had he been expecting to gain from the charade?

"I . . . I'm sorry," I said, putting a hand to my forehead. "I don't even . . . this makes absolutely no sense to me." I looked up at him, shaking my head. "Why would you do this?"

"Because it's *fun*." His face twisted into a wolfish grin.

I stared at him in disbelief. "Get out," I hissed. "I never want to see you again."

Damian snorted. "I don't think so," he replied, and his voice had softened considerably. It was a hideous, slimy thing. An evil thing.

Suddenly I was afraid.

"I'm not the kind of person who likes paying for something I never received," he slithered in the same dangerous tone.

"Get out," I repeated, pointing at the door.

But Damian moved toward me, seating himself again on the couch next to me, but closer than he had been before. Much, much too close. I attempted to back up, but I was already pinned between him and the high armrest of the couch. Damian's hand shot out, grasping my arm in a painful grip.

"Damian, don't do this," I pleaded, desperately trying to yank my arm away. I attempted to stand, to get away from those icy blue eyes that were now focused intently on my mouth.

"Don't worry, Ryder," he reassured in a voice that was calculated to calm me, but had the exact opposite effect. I redoubled my efforts to pull away. He smiled at me, holding me fast, his perfect teeth gleaming. His expression was strangely agreeable. "I promise you'll enjoy this."

And suddenly he was upon me. His lips were demanding and intense on mine, his body weight pressing me into the back of the couch as he attempted to force me horizontal. But I was not going to make this easy on him.

I pushed and fought, tried to push his face away from mine. He was far too strong. He caught my hands and trapped them in one of his, pressing them above my head against the couch cushion as he yanked me into position. His other hand grappled at my waist, searching for the hem of my shirt. I felt his fingers brush across the skin of my stomach, and something inside me broke.

I screamed as loudly as I could, despite his mouth on mine, and brought my knee up hard. I didn't connect with the part of his anatomy I had been aiming for, but I was close enough that I managed to incapacitate him momentarily. His mouth freed mine as he swore in pain. With that, he renewed his efforts to subdue me, pressing me hard into the couch with his full weight.

"Don't do that again," he breathed into my ear. "Or I'll forget about trying to make this pleasant for you."

Pleasant? Was he so arrogant as to think that I would consider him assaulting me as some kind of privilege?

I cried out again, and Damian pressed a hand to my mouth, his blue eyes blazing into mine. I tried to bite his hand, but I couldn't even get my mouth open under the force he was exerting on my face.

"I mean it, Ryder," he growled. "Don't test me."

Was he serious? Did he honestly think I was just going to stop fighting and let him have his way?

He removed his hand from my mouth, and I immediately shrieked again, writhing as I tried desperately to get out from under him. My ears rang with panic as his hand closed again over my mouth and his lips began moving down my throat toward my collarbone. I screamed again and again against his hand, attempting to shake off its weight.

Then, suddenly, he was gone. I scrambled upright, just in time to see Damian crash against the far wall of the living room, just below the TV screen mounted on the wall. It shook precariously with the force of the blow.

Damian groaned and stirred as the tall, broad-shouldered form of Hunter Payne reached down to grasp the front of Damian's shirt. He hauled him up from the floor and slammed him hard against the wall, holding him there. I looked across the apartment and saw the door standing wide open, the lock obviously broken.

Hunter had heard me screaming from the hallway and had kicked in the door to come to my rescue. I stared at him in astonishment, just as my body began to shake with the shock of what I'd just experienced.

"How dare you!" Hunter was seething in Damian's face. "How *dare* you touch her? You sick, evil, depraved mass of slime, how dare you force yourself on her like that!" He rammed Damian against the wall again with incredible force.

Damian grunted in pain and narrowed his eyes, glaring at the taller man. The corner of his mouth curled in a sneer as he looked up at him. "I always knew you had a thing for her, Payne. Must have killed you, seeing her hanging all over me for all those months, knowing she wanted me more than she wanted you."

Hunter threw Damian to the floor with a growl. He looked ready to give him a stiff kick in the ribs, but managed to hold himself back. "Get out," he barked, calling Damian a filthy name. "You come near Ryder again, you contact her, you so much as *look* at her, you're dead. And if you think I'm joking, you just test me."

Damian picked himself up off the floor, glaring all the while at Hunter. "Doesn't matter," he said with a sneer. "I was done with her anyway." He stumbled toward the door, but stopped when he heard my voice.

"Your father would be ashamed of you," I croaked at Damian's back.

It was almost a whisper, but he stiffened momentarily. He even looked as though he might glance back at me. But, finally, he just walked away.

- - - - -

I sat huddled on the couch, shaking with the trauma of the experience for a long time afterward. Hunter sat next to me, his arm warm around my shoulders. He stroked my back as I alternated between crying and fuming, comforting me when he could and agreeing with me when I raged at Damian.

"I'm sorry," I finally said, a couple of hours later when I'd managed to calm down. We still sat side by side on the couch, shoulders touching.

"Pardon?" Hunter said, as though his thoughts had been elsewhere.

"I'm sorry," I repeated.

"For what?" he asked, confusion evident on his face.

"You were right. You were always right," I sighed. "I should have listened to you."

Hunter shook his head. "It doesn't matter now. It's over."

"How did you know I needed you?" I asked, gesturing to the broken door.

"I didn't," Hunter replied. "Well, not really. I'd been feeling all day like I needed to talk to you. To air things out between us." He gave me a self-deprecating smile. "Then, finally, around nine, I couldn't ignore it anymore. Seriously, it nearly pushed me out the door. So, I figured I'd just stop by and see if I could convince you to talk to me. I was standing in the hall, trying to come up with a persuasive argument." He took a deep breath and brushed a slightly trembling hand over his face. "And then I heard you scream."

He didn't continue, and I didn't need him to. I knew what had happened after that.

"Thank you," I said fervently, reaching out to squeeze his hand. "I don't know what would have happened if you hadn't come."

"I do," Hunter said, and his voice shook as his hand tightened on mine. "I know exactly what would have happened." Without another word, he pulled me against his chest, his hand resting on my head as I listened to the beating of his heart.

Twenty-One

Hunter tried to convince me to immediately call my parents and tell them what had happened, but I refused. I was going to see them the next day anyway, once I arrived in Salt Lake for Kara's wedding, so what was the point of needlessly alarming them now? Hunter wasn't happy about it, but he eventually agreed.

He refused to leave me that night, insisting that he would stay with me until I was safely on the plane to Salt Lake, especially given the state of the front door and its lack of seemly protection. We sat together on the couch and talked far into the night, until Lily arrived home around three a.m.

"What the crap are you doing here?" she asked him in shock as she stood in the doorway. "And what happened to the door?"

"We had an eventful night," Hunter replied with a smile. "Come on in and we'll tell you about it."

By the time Hunter had finished the story, I thought we might have to lock Lily in her bedroom so she couldn't march over to Damian's apartment and throttle him.

"I knew it," she seethed. "I just *knew* it! I knew he was a no-good, scummy, underhanded dirtbag. See, this is why you should always listen to me." She insisted, pointing at me.

"I know, Lil," I sighed. "I screwed up big time on this one. But of the two of us, I'm the one that paid the price, so at least there's that."

"I didn't *want* you to have to pay the price!" Lily cried, and I was shocked to see tears in her eyes. She shook her head and stood, pacing around the living room as she wiped at her eyes.

"Lil?" I asked tentatively.

"Ohh," she groaned in frustration and came over to sit by me, wrapping her arms around me tightly. "This is why it sucks to care about people," she whined. "Don't ever do something like this again, okay? My heart can't take it."

"Promise," I vowed, hugging her tightly.

None of us appeared to want to go to bed that night. We sat in the living room talking until the sun rose, and neither Lily nor Hunter seemed willing to let go of me, each of them holding fast to one of my hands.

Despite this being one of the worst nights of my life, I had never felt more loved.

- - - - -

My flight to Salt Lake was in the early afternoon and I had yet to pack. Hunter watched TV in the living room while Lily helped me stuff my suitcase with anything and everything I might conceivably need for a wedding in Salt Lake.

"So, Hunter really turned out to be your knight in shining armor, didn't he?" Lily said, folding shirts and stuffing them into my suitcase. She didn't look at me.

"Lil," I started, my heart sinking. I'd hoped she'd be so preoccupied with hating Damian that she wouldn't notice how Hunter's protectiveness had manifested itself physically over the past several hours.

"Don't worry about it," Lily assured me, finally looking up. "I've known for a while now that things probably weren't going to work out between him and me."

"You have?" I asked in surprise. I was ashamed to think how wrapped up I'd been in my own problems that I hadn't even bothered to notice Lily going through that particular disappointment. "Why do you say that?"

Lily shrugged. "Oh, just little things here and there," she commented, looking around for shoes to throw into the case. "He never was as affectionate with me as he is with you. And while he was always sweet to me, he was never protective. And he seems to *live* to protect you." She shook her head in amazement. "So, do you think you'll give him a chance? He obviously wants you to."

I blinked at her for a minute, a little shaken by the turn the conversation had suddenly taken. "Well, I'm not so sure I'm ready for anything like that right now," I replied as I tucked a couple of pairs of jeans into my bag. "I just got out of a relationship with a pretty profound scumbag like, literally, twelve hours ago. I think I might need a little bit of a break from romance."

Lily chuckled as she flipped the lid of my suitcase closed and zipped it up. "Well, I'm pretty sure he'll wait." She nudged me playfully and left the room.

- - - - -

Kara's wedding day was cold and blustery, but she didn't seem to care in the slightest. As we all stood huddled in groups around the temple grounds while she and her handsome groom had their picture taken in a variety of corny poses, I vowed I would be married in the heart of summer to spare my wedding party the same dreadful fate.

My mood had improved by the reception, however. I sat in a chair at one of the large circular tables at the reception center and watched with a smile on my face as Kara beamed and chatted and waltzed around the room with her new husband. She was virtually glowing with happiness. It was nice to see what the result of a successful dating experiment could be, even if I'd never experienced one.

I had been pretty good at staving off thoughts of Damian over the past twenty-four hours, and I found it got easier and easier by the minute. If it had been a painful breakup, that would have been one thing, but all I could feel was relief that Damian had finally dropped his act and that I'd been so disgusted by it that any former feelings for him had immediately evaporated. And especially that Hunter had been there to save me when I needed him most. He was good like that.

"Hey, Red," came the familiar voice from behind me. My dad reached out to tweak my earlobe and took the chair next to me. "You look beautiful. It was thoughtful of Kara to choose a color that didn't clash with your hair." He winked at me, and I laughed as I looked down at the bright red dress.

"Could be worse," I commented with a grin. "Could be orange."

Dad gave me a significant nod and looked out over the crowd with me, taking in the general joyfulness of the gathering. "Nice day, wasn't it?" he said. "One of those days that makes you glad you're alive to see such a beautiful thing." He gestured to Kara and Jordan, who were swaying amongst the throng of dancing couples in the middle of the room.

"I know," I agreed fervently. "Dad," I said, turning to him with a sudden sense of urgency. "I'm sorry I've been so awful to you these past several months. I'm sorry I didn't take anything you said about Damian seriously."

Dad looked at me severely and the smile fell immediately off his face. "What happened, Ryder?"

I gulped, not wanting to ruin the glowing warmth I'd been feeling all day, surrounded by the people I loved. But I knew my dad deserved to know what had happened, especially since I suspected he'd foreseen something like it.

"I just found out some things about Damian," I told him, my face pained. "Things that required me to break off our relationship. He . . . he didn't take it well."

"What did he do?" Dad pressed, leaning forward to grasp my arm. "What happened?"

"I'm fine, Dad," I assured him. "He got a little bit physical with me, but Hunter arrived in time to pull him off and he threatened him to within an inch of his life. Damian is definitely a cool customer, but I don't think he wants to tangle with Hunter."

My dad's countenance was downright frightening as he attempted to control his temper. "He attacked you?" He demanded, his eyes fixed on my face.

"No, not really," I said. I reached out a hand, attempting to placate him. "I think he was just frustrated that he'd been denied certain, uh, physical attention for the months we dated, so he wanted to settle the account."

"*What?*" Dad shouted, rising to his feet.

"Dad," I scolded. People were staring. "Calm down. I told you, nothing happened. Hunter got there in time to prevent him from getting what he wanted."

"Did you report him?"

"Hunter said he would take care of it," I told him. "I was leaving for Salt Lake that day and honestly, I just wanted to get away from the whole thing. I didn't even really think about it."

Dad appeared to be actively trying to calm himself. He sat back down, but he reached out to grasp my hand tightly in his. "I'm so glad you're okay," he said fervently, his voice shaking slightly.

"Me too," I replied with a smile. "I really owe it all to Hunter. Things wouldn't have turned out so well if not for him."

"He's a good man," my dad agreed, and I laughed.

"You haven't even met him," I pointed out.

"He protected you from a despicable person who was trying to hurt you," Dad replied with a significant look. "That's all I need to know about him. Besides, your mom filled me in. She likes him too. We both approve. You know, in case you were wondering."

"Good to know," I said, my lips ticking up at the corners. "You realize that he's not a member, right? Since when do you encourage me in a relationship with someone outside the Church?"

Dad smiled, not looking at me. "Hey, I never said a thing about marrying him," he said offhandedly. He stood, winked at me, and walked away into the crowd.

- - - - -

The weekend at home with my parents was just what I needed. It was like old times, but better, because my relationship with my mom was completely different. Somehow in the past year, the feeling that she was trying to make me into Emma, Version 2.0, had faded. And the vanishing of that barrier opened the doors to a full and happy relationship with her. We talked and laughed together, cried together (particularly when I told her about Damian), and prayed together. And it wasn't even over a meal or before bedtime. That was a first.

I knew my parents were worried about me going back to New York by myself after what had happened, but I assured them that I was perfectly safe. Especially with watchdog Hunter looking out for me. I hugged them both tightly when they dropped me off at the airport and promised to call when I landed.

"And every night after work," my dad insisted.

"Every night?" I repeated. "You'll get sick of me. I won't have anything to report."

"That's fine," he said. "Even if you just call and say 'nothing to report,' that will ease my mind greatly."

"Okay," I said, capitulating. "If that makes you feel better."

I kissed them both and headed toward the terminal, turning to wave again at the last minute. They both still stood there, watching me go with affection written all over their faces. I loved them for it.

Hunter picked me up from JFK, even though I could have easily made it back to my apartment on my own.

"Lily wanted to come too, but she had rehearsal," Hunter informed me as we waited on the curb for our ride.

"I didn't need an escort," I pointed out. "I know the way back to my apartment perfectly well, thank you."

He gave me a slightly frustrated look as he retorted, "Look, Damian knew all about your travel schedule. He could have been waiting here at the airport for you. He got home from California yesterday, you know."

"Yes, I know," I said, eyeing him. "But how do *you* know? Are the police watching him or something?"

"No, nothing like that," Hunter assured me. "Lily told me."

I didn't remember telling Lily about Damian's travel schedule for his client trip, but it wouldn't be the first time I'd forgotten something like that. "You realize Damian is not some mob boss, right? Why on earth would he want to kidnap me from an airport? I got the sense he was glad to be rid of me."

Hunter grabbed my bag and carried it to the trunk of the black car that had just pulled up to the curb. "You never know with someone as criminal as he is. He's unpredictable. I don't like it."

"You are such a drama queen," I sighed, collapsing into the backseat of the car.

"I'm happy to take on that role if it keeps you safe," Hunter replied as he stepped into the car from the other side. "Has he attempted to contact you at all?"

"No," I said, picking at a stray cuticle. "Nor do I expect him to. Besides, if he'd tried, I'm pretty sure my dad would have called his New York FBI contacts and had him hauled in for questioning."

"You told your dad?" Hunter said, a look of relief on his face. "That's good."

"I guess," I conceded. I bit the inside of my lip as I remembered the conversation. "He almost had a coronary over it, though."

Hunter smiled to himself. "I'll bet he did." He glanced at my stormy expression and wiped the smile off his face. "I mean, I would too, if you were my daughter. Cut the guy a break."

"So how have things been here?" I asked him. "Any progress on the M&A transaction?" Hunter had been doing some of the legal review for the transaction, so he was up to speed on the status of the project.

"Not really," Hunter said with a shrug. "You only missed a couple of days, you know. Still, Feldman and Collins Weiss heard back from the regulators on Friday. They expect to have a response back on the transaction, whether it's an approval or not I don't know, by the end of next month."

"Well, that's good news," I said. I leaned back against the seat, trying not think about who might have sat there last and what their state of personal hygiene might have been. "This deal has been running everyone ragged."

"Including Damian," Hunter commented offhandedly.

"Can we go thirty seconds without discussing him, please?" I requested. I felt a headache coming on, and I pinched the bridge of my nose sharply to head it off.

"Sorry."

The rest of the car ride passed in silence and I even managed to fall asleep for a few minutes before the fervent honking of the driver next to us jarred me awake.

Hunter carried my bag up to my apartment and deposited it in my bedroom. I noticed that the front door had been repaired and three new locks had been added.

"Three?" I said, gesturing to the shiny new locks. "Man, you don't do things by halves, do you? What on earth do you think he's going to do? Burst in here, guns blazing?"

Hunter ignored me and settled himself on the couch, TV remote in hand.

"You hanging out for a while?" I assumed, watching him.

"I'm on the day shift," he answered nonchalantly. "Lily takes the night shift."

"Guard duty? Really?"

"Hey, I'm not charging you." Hunter held up his hands defensively. "You can't fire someone you're not paying."

"Whatever," I said, settling myself next to him on the couch. It was kind of nice having him there, anyway. I'd really missed him over the past several months.

Hunter seemed to be thinking the same thing. He looked over at me, his adorable freckled face splitting with a contented smile as we lounged next to each other on the couch and watched the news together. And then, without a word, he reached over and took my hand in his.

- - - - -

Life settled into a predictable pattern over the next month. Hunter spent most of his evenings with me until Lily arrived home from her rehearsals. Since he was working on the Feldman M&A deal, he'd been working at the Feldman offices every day instead of in his D&T office, so it provided plenty of opportunity for him to keep tabs on me.

Hunter showed up at my apartment at seven thirty on the dot each morning to escort me to Feldman. He left with me at the end of every day, regardless of the time, and shepherded me back to the apartment. I started to make dinner for him every night (as unsolicited payment for his guard services—it was generally something like cold cereal or my famous instant mac and cheese), and then we hung out and talked or watched old movies until Lily got home. Sometimes I felt like we were an old, married couple, set in our daily routine. And I didn't mind at all.

Lily had stopped her outrageous flirting with Hunter, and by the time I realized it, I couldn't actually remember the last time I'd seen her do it. She must have given up a long time ago, and I'd been so inwardly focused that I hadn't noticed.

Instead, Lily appeared to have switched tactics and was now shamelessly pushing Hunter and me together as much as possible. She encouraged Hunter to stay later and later each night to the point that I felt compelled to lie and tell her that her lack of sleep was impacting her complexion—just to get her to go to bed early so I could sneak Hunter out of the apartment. We were now seeing so much of each other, I was surprised he wasn't getting thoroughly sick of me.

However, one morning in mid-June, Hunter never arrived to usher me to work. At first I wondered if it was simply because he didn't plan to work at the Feldman offices that day. The regulator approval for the M&A transaction had come through a couple of days before, and it had been announced publicly in the news that morning, so the work was definitely wrapping up. But I wouldn't have expected Hunter's legal responsibilities at Feldman to end so abruptly. And it would be unlike him to simply decide not to pick me up, just because he wasn't needed at Feldman that day. I doubted his inner bodyguard would allow that kind of behavior.

I waited until almost eight before calling his cell. The call went to voicemail and I left a quick message to tell him that I was heading to the office and I hoped he was okay. I asked him to call me when he got the message, and then hung up.

A text arrived from him ten minutes later as I sat on the train.

So sorry I couldn't make it this morning, it said. *I'm fine, but something came up. Call me if you need anything.*

I quickly responded with an *okay*, wondered briefly what could have come up, and continued on my way. It wasn't until almost three that afternoon that I realized that Hunter had never shown up to Feldman at all. It was unusual for me to see him around the audit room, given that he spent much of his time with the legal team, but usually he stopped by at least a couple of times a day to check on me.

Around four-thirty, Jie collapsed into the chair next to me, a hand to her chest. Amelia and I both looked up, startled at her winded approach.

"Are you okay?" Jie asked me breathlessly, concern written all over her face.

"Huh?" I asked, bewildered.

"I just saw in the news about Damian," she panted. "It was on the television downstairs in the break room. I immediately came to see how you were holding up. I even took the stairs," she claimed, nodding in solidarity.

I blinked at her. "What are you talking about?" I asked, a strange churning in my stomach. "What about Damian and the news?"

"Don't you know?" she gasped, her eyes wide. "Didn't you see it?"

She grabbed my computer and typed a leading news site in the browser. Amelia and I crowded around the screen as the page loaded. The headline suddenly flashed in huge letters: "Collins Weiss rising star arrested for insider trading." A large photo of Damian being led from the Collins Weiss offices, hands restrained behind him, dominated the screen.

My eyes skated over the photograph, and my breath lodged painfully in my chest. Not at the sight of Damian being arrested—I wasn't as surprised by that as you would think. But my gaze locked on the face directly behind Damian's—the face of the man escorting Damian from the building in handcuffs, an FBI badge shining prominently on his belt.

It was Hunter.

Twenty-Two

I sat and stared at the photo for a long time, wondering if my eyes were actually seeing what I thought they were seeing. I looked over at Amelia, noting that her eyes were narrowed in concentration as she studied it as well.

"Did you know Hunter Payne was FBI?" she whispered to me.

Thankful that I wasn't losing my mind and seeing things that weren't actually there, I shook my head. "No idea," I replied.

My emotional state was a mixed bag at that point. As the daughter of a former FBI agent, I couldn't be upset that Hunter hadn't told me about his real job—he'd undoubtedly been undercover. But suddenly it forced me to look at the past year of conversations and experiences and fights with him in a whole new light.

No wonder he'd been so against my relationship with Damian from the start. No wonder he'd tried to intimidate him at their first meeting. And no wonder his physical prowess had been so unduly impressive when he'd rescued me from Damian's clutches the month before. The man had serious skills.

"Are you okay, Ryder?" Jie asked anxiously, studying my face. "I know you and Damian are dating—did you have any idea about this?"

I pulled out of my stupor and turned to look at her, my face breaking into a reassuring expression. "Oh, I'm fine, Jie, thanks," I comforted. "You don't need to worry about me. Damian and I broke up over a month ago and we haven't spoken since. Quite frankly, I'm not surprised he's guilty of insider trading."

I quickly skimmed over the news story, finding that Damian had been using third parties to buy up the stock of the target company in the Feldman/Collins Weiss M&A deal he had been managing.

Knowing that the stock price would immediately increase to include purchase premiums upon the completion of the deal, he stood to make a tidy sum. According to the article, he had been suspected of insider trading in other deals he had worked on, but the FBI hadn't been able to tie him directly to anything. This time, the article said, they had sent in an undercover agent to track the transaction from the inside as well as to monitor Damian's trading activities to find linkages.

I had barely finished my perusal of the news story when my cell phone rang. I picked it up without looking at the caller ID.

"Hello?"

"Hey Red, it's me." It was my dad. "Just saw the news. How you doing?"

"Did you know?" I asked him. "Did you know Damian was under investigation?" I wasn't sure how he could have possibly known, but the fact that he was former FBI and still kept in contact with the Bureau made it seem almost likely in my muddled head.

"I did," he answered, and I collapsed back against my chair.

"How?" I demanded.

He was quiet for a moment, but finally replied, "Hunter."

"What?" I screeched. Amelia and Jie were staring at me, so I got to my feet and headed for the door to the audit room to avoid an audience. "But you've never even met him!"

"Hunter is a former student of mine," Dad revealed in a placating tone of voice. "I trained him at the academy several years ago. We were—are—friends. Good friends."

I remembered the "mentor" that Hunter had mentioned to me several times. The one that had shared his religious beliefs freely and impressed Hunter with his integrity. I knew immediately who he had been talking about.

"Does he know I'm your daughter?" I asked.

"Of course he does," Dad said. "He's been looking in on you for me. I mean, he wanted to, of course. He's that kind of person, but—"

"Start at the beginning," I commanded him.

"Okay," he responded, and to my annoyance, it sounded like he was smiling. "I met Hunter about seven years ago, in my last year training for the Bureau. He was just a young sucker, then, barely over twenty-three. But gifted. His dad had been British secret service, and I think he wanted to follow in his footsteps in some sense. He'd just lost him a few years earlier.

"He was a mouthy kid when he started, but I got him whipped into shape in short order," Dad said with a chuckle. "He resented me at first, and I thought he was an arrogant sap, but the more we got to know each other, the more we respected each other. By the end of his training, we were good friends." Dad's voice warmed as he spoke. "We kept in contact over the years and even met up regularly every time I went to New York. He came out to Salt Lake on a few jobs and got to know your mom pretty well."

"Mom knows him too?" I wailed, feeling horribly thick. How had I not suspected that sense of camaraderie between them when she'd been visiting for Thanksgiving hinted at a past acquaintance?

"She does," Dad replied. "Actually, you've met him before as well. He came out to Salt Lake when you were about eighteen and stopped by the house for an hour. But you weren't terribly interested in one of your dad's old FBI buddies, and beyond an obligatory 'hello,' you never looked up from the book you were reading."

"He must think I'm such an idiot," I muttered.

"I can assure you, he does not," Dad laughed. "Anyway, I called him when you moved out to New York, just to ask him to look in on you now and then. When I told him you were going to work for D&T, he informed me that he'd just been given an undercover assignment that involved D&T. He was worried that you'd recognize him and blow everything, but I told him not to worry about that. Was I right or was I right?"

"Shut up," I muttered, and he laughed again.

"So he's been keeping his cover safe for the past year while he's been gathering intel on Wolfe and a few others at Collins Weiss who were suspected as well. Now do you understand why all of us were so worried about your relationship with Damian?"

"I got it, I got it," I said, not wanting to rehash my stupidity all over again. "So what now?" I asked.

"Well, now that Wolfe has been arrested, Hunter will leave D&T and start work on another case. At least until he's called to testify against Damian, which he almost certainly will be."

I frowned. Hunter would be leaving D&T. I hated the thought.

"Look, honey, don't blame him for any of this. He was just doing his job," my dad persuaded.

"I don't blame him," I assured him. "And I don't blame you. I know you secretive FBI types. I just feel stupid about being so out of the loop all this time. You guys were probably constantly shaking your heads at me for the past year."

"Only sometimes," Dad teased.

I groaned.

"Well, I have a feeling Hunter will be stopping by sometime soon to tell his side of the story," Dad hinted with a smile in his voice. "Just let him explain, okay? It will do you both good."

"Yeah," I agreed with a sigh. "Talk to you later, Dad."

I hung up and collapsed against the wall behind me, my head back. The conversation with Hunter had the potential to be very uncomfortable indeed.

- - - - -

My dad was right. Hunter showed up at my apartment around eight thirty that night, looking mildly sheepish.

"Well hello, special agent," I said, opening the door wider to let him in. "Nice of you stop by."

He nodded uncertainly. Was he nervous? Tongue-tied? Did he think I was going to go ballistic on him?

I watched him shifting uneasily, not sure how to approach the elephant in the room. He looked back at me with silent trepidation for several moments before opening his mouth.

"Are you upset with me, Ryder?" he asked. Only it sounded more like "Ah you upset with me, Rydah?" My eyes flew open wide in surprise. The guy wasn't nervous or tongue-tied at all . . . he was British!

I blinked at him. "Has that accent always been there or is this a recent acquisition?" I choked.

"It's always been there," he replied in his new voice, chuckling. "Just not lately."

"You're British?" I exclaimed.

"I told you I'd spent a lot of time in the UK," he defended with a shrug. "I just didn't mention that it was virtually my entire childhood."

"I don't know you at all, do I?" I said weakly, dropping into a kitchen chair.

Hunter smiled kindly at me and walked over to lay a comforting hand on my shoulder. "Well, why don't we start over, then?" he suggested. He held out his hand to me. "Ryder Redmond, it's a pleasure to meet you . . . again." He smirked, and I knew he'd spoken to my dad recently. They must have had a good laugh about my not remembering him from when I was a teenager. "My name is William. William Hunter," he introduced himself.

"What?" I wailed. "I didn't even know your real name?"

He laughed. "Undercover is undercover, darling," he said. The smooth tones of that accent were doing funny things to my spine. He reached out and pulled me to my feet, rubbing his hands up and down my arms, looking carefully into my face. "I'm sorry I couldn't tell you from the beginning."

I sighed and shook my head. "I understand. It comes with the gig."

"Well, let me make it up to you," he said, leading me to the couch and seating himself beside me. "As I said, my name is William Hunter. My mum used to call me Billy. Please don't call me Billy." He grinned cheekily at me. "I prefer to go by Will. My mum was American. My dad was a dual citizen, British and American. I was born in Los Angeles, but my parents moved to London when I was only a few months old and I grew up there until I was eighteen. My mum died of cancer that year, and my dad was heartbroken. He needed a change of scenery and moved us to Chicago. He'd been British secret service in London, so law enforcement came naturally to him. He joined the Chicago police force and was killed in the line of duty a year later."

I winced at the brief expression of pain on his face. "Yeesh," I said. "How awful. I'm so sorry."

Will gave me a grateful smile and continued. "At that point, I was the one that needed a change of scenery, so I withdrew from school at Northwestern and transferred to NYU. I was in law school when a recruiter from the FBI came and spoke to my class. Something inside me lit up and I knew that was what I wanted to do." His eyes seemed to light with fervor as he spoke, remembering his early days with the Bureau. I'd seen my dad with the exact same expression time and again. It made me smile.

"I made it through university relatively quickly given my need to distract myself from my grief," he continued. "So I graduated soon after my twenty-third birthday, having put in my application to the Bureau months before. I passed all the tests and physical examinations and eventually made it into the FBI academy. I went to Quantico the summer after I graduated from NYU. While I was there, I met this tough, loud, wonderful veteran trainer named George Redmond." He smiled at me and I couldn't help smiling back. I'd never heard stories of my dad told from the trainee perspective before.

"He challenged me. He pushed me far beyond what I thought I could accomplish. And while I loved the results, I hated the process and we were regularly at each other's throats," Will said, chuckling. "Eventually though, we gained a grudging respect for each other that, by the end of my twenty weeks of training, had become a close friendship. After I left Quantico, we stayed in contact and later, I even met his wife and his beautiful teenage daughter." He smiled adoringly into my face and reached out to squeeze my hand.

"I thought she was the loveliest thing I'd ever seen, but she barely looked twice at me," he said, feigning incredulity. He then gave me a teasing smile as he continued. "Being a somewhat arrogant twenty-four-year-old, I figured that was that. It was unlikely I'd ever see her again anyway. But, who would have guessed that five years later our paths would cross under very unusual circumstances?" Will's voice had taken on the cadence of a dedicated storyteller, and despite my determination to maintain a certain attitude of lighthearted irony toward him, I found that I was secretly enthralled by his tale.

"In those five years, I flatter myself that I had grown and matured quite a bit. My mentor's example and integrity had inspired me to look for answers to the questions I struggled with in places I had never even considered before. I had found new faith that brought me unbelievable comfort and happiness."

"Wait a second," I broke in, holding up a hand. "You joined the Church? When?"

"About four years ago," Will replied with a smile.

"Why didn't you just tell me you were a member?" I demanded of him, eyes narrowed. "Here I was, thinking I was the world's best ward missionary and everything."

"I would have, but . . . well, I was undercover." He looked at me pointedly. "Which brings me to my reintroduction to my mentor's lovely daughter. I had been assigned to go undercover at a large accounting firm that had agreed to help us facilitate our investigation into some suspected cases of insider trading," Will informed me. "I'd been investigating some illegal trades, all related to deals led by Collins Weiss, for over a year by then, but my team still hadn't been able to identify which bankers were behind them. As I dug into the documentation fed to the Bureau by the accounting firm and by certain third party traders who were working with us, I was able to identify the primary culprit as one Damian Wolfe . . . who just happened to be dating the beautiful daughter of my friend and mentor." Will heaved a belabored sigh as he shook his head at me.

I couldn't help it. I laughed.

"Ah, but it was no laughing matter," Will said, pointing at me and still shaking his head in exasperation. "Suddenly I was stuck between the proverbial rock and hard place, trying to get my mentor's daughter away from the rubbish she was regularly snogging, all while attempting to keep myself in her good graces so I could continue to watch over her, as her father had requested . . . and so I could continue to spend time with her." His eyes warmed as he said it. "Because, believe it or not, she had become very important to me."

The smile fell off my face quite suddenly as Will looked very earnestly into my eyes. I felt a slow burn begin somewhere in my middle.

"I turned out to be very inept at that particular responsibility," Will continued, breaking our tingle-charged gaze. "I couldn't convince the stubborn girl to break up with her boyfriend and instead ended up driving a wedge between us. We spent months apart, not speaking. While this was painful for me on many levels, it allowed me to refocus all my energy on the investigation and we made several breakthroughs." His tone suddenly became almost businesslike as he went into investigation briefing mode. "We were finally able to tie specific trades to individual bankers, which would allow us to make arrests. However, the M&A deal that was associated with this insider trading was actually legitimate. We allowed the deal to go through and be announced publicly before making our arrests. All of which took place this very morning." He looked very pleased with himself at this announcement.

"But," he continued conspiratorially, "I managed to get a bit of a bonus. You see, the beautiful daughter found out what a horrible person her boyfriend actually was, although in an unfortunate and tragic manner," Will added as a significant aside, glancing at me sympathetically. "And suddenly she and I were friends again. I spent almost every day with her the month after her tragedy, and I found that at no other time in my life had I ever felt a fraction of that level of happiness. The end." He sat back against the couch.

"Well," I said, mulling over his words. "That's . . . quite an adventure you've had."

"And it's not over yet," Will claimed, holding up a finger. "You see, more than anything, I want to show my mentor's lovely daughter just how much she means to me and how happy I know I can make her. But I have a problem."

I cleared my throat carefully before answering. "Oh, is that so?" I asked. "And what might that be?"

"I can't actually be with her right now."

Whatever I thought he was going to say, that was not it.

"What? Why not?" I demanded.

Will's face turned somber, his expression pained. "Because Damian Wolfe happens to know how I feel about her, and you can bet he's going to use it. He and his lawyers are going to do their best to make it look like I'm a non-credible witness in his trial because I'm involved with his ex-girlfriend, with whom he has an unpleasant history. They'll attempt to show it as a conflict of interest."

I stared at him, the sense of what he said sinking deep into me, pushing the hopes I hadn't even realized I was nursing down into my shoes. "So what do we do?" I asked.

Will smiled, reaching out to brush his fingers down my cheek. "We wait," he said. "Wolfe likely won't go to trial for three months at least, and the trial itself could last for much longer than that—possibly up to a year or more."

"A *year*?" I cried in dismay. What was wrong with our criminal justice system that it took a full year to prosecute and imprison a slimy investment banker caught red-handed?

"Trust me, I'm worth the wait," Will teased with a wink. But his ribbing smile abandoned his face almost immediately and was replaced by a look of intense longing as he studied my features, his eyes searching over them hungrily. "I don't want to wait any more than you do. I've been chasing you for nearly a year now, Red, and quite frankly, I'm exhausted. I'd like nothing better than to be with you now, today, but this trial . . . it's just too important. It's the culmination of all that my team has worked for for the past couple of years. Can you understand why us being apart is necessary?"

I really didn't want to, but I nodded. "I understand."

He smiled at me, but sadly. "We can't see each other, Ryder. Not at all," he warned me. "I have no doubt we'll both be watched, and we can't give the defense anything to use to help Wolfe. My testimony is the one that will convict him."

I took a deep breath, steeling myself, and nodded. "I understand," I said again. Something inside me was wilting, realizing that this was the last time I would see this man—this incredible, wonderful, sweet, good man—for a very long time.

He stood and pulled me up with him, moving in close to gather me in his arms. "As soon as this whole thing is over," he whispered into my ear. "The minute Damian Wolfe is put away, I promise, I will be right back here to you."

I closed my eyes, my cheek resting against his solid chest. He pressed a hand against my head and lowered his face to bury it in my hair. His other hand gently stroked my back over and over.

"I'll be right here," I promised him in return, savoring the feeling of the man I hadn't known I wanted holding me one last time before he left.

William pressed his lips into my hair, again and again, clasping me tightly for a long moment. And then, without a backward glance, he turned and walked away, neither one of us knowing when we would see the other again.

Twenty-Three

FIFTEEN MONTHS LATER

Lily and I sat at a small circular table in Bryant Park on 42nd Street, watching a mass yoga class as they stretched and posed on the lawn. It was early September and it was my absolute favorite time of year in New York. The small sliver of time between summer and fall where the trees were still leafy green and full, but the temperatures had dropped into a comfortable, breezy coolness.

"Why would anybody do something like that in public?" Lily wondered, watching two hundred yoga enthusiasts simultaneously raise their rear ends to the heavens.

"It's supposed to be relaxing, I think," I replied, shaking my head in bewilderment. "Not really my thing, though."

"No," Lily agreed emphatically. "So have you heard from Kara yet? Do they know?"

"Yep!" I replied with enthusiasm. "It's a girl! And it's a darn good thing, because I think Kara would be in a helpless huddle on the floor if it were a boy."

"Is Jordan okay with it?"

"Jordan's happy as long as Kara's happy," I assured her.

"Smart man," Lily determined. She pulled out her phone and glanced at the screen. "Have you heard from your dad lately?" she asked distractedly.

"Not lately," I replied in a mournful tone. Over the past year and change, random FBI buddies had been contacting my dad with somewhat cryptic messages. They all seemed very concerned with giving him status updates on Damian Wolfe's trial, even though my dad said he was fairly certain that none of them had been assigned to that case. I knew it was Will, attempting to keep us informed. And each update felt like a little nod from that adorable, freckled, gingery head of his. I had dated here and there throughout the past year, but I missed Will constantly through it all—every day there was a tangible ache in my middle, confirming to me that something vital was missing from my life.

"Damian's trial is about wrapped up, isn't it?" Lily asked, halting her texting for a split second to look up at me.

"I think so," I said, shrugging. "There hasn't been much coverage in the news. My dad thinks Damian's mom is leaning on people to make sure the story isn't covered in the big newspapers. Apparently she's very well connected in those circles. I guess I don't blame her, really."

"Must be rough, having a felon for a son," Lily said with a nod, going back to her typing with a satisfied smile on her face. "You think he's going to be convicted? Get a nice long prison sentence?" Her tone was hopeful.

"Sounds like it," I said. I gazed over the green park, watching the scores of people strolling along the pathways in the perfect weather. "The last report we got from our mysterious informant was that the trial was going well and Damian's defense hadn't been able to pull together anything concrete to help him counter the charges. I think they're expecting a conviction."

"Best news I've heard all year," Lily declared, dropping her phone back in her purse. "Well, I need to head over to the theater."

"Why?" I asked in confusion. "I thought you didn't have to be there until five."

"I don't, but I need to talk to the sound people. Last night my microphone was all fuzzy and I want to make sure I get one of the good ones tonight. It's my first real lead role. The last thing I want is to be unintelligible. You never know who's going to be in the audience." She winked at me and jumped to her feet. "You should hang out around here for a bit longer. It's a nice day and you never know how many of those we'll have left. Besides, someone interesting might walk by."

She gave a significant look to the table behind me, and I shook my head in disbelief. She was constantly checking out the good-looking male specimens in our vicinity and sometimes it got downright embarrassing.

"Really," she whispered as she walked past me. "You should take a look at this one."

I suppressed a smile as I watched her go. Then, truly curious, I took a quick glance over my shoulder at the guy sitting behind me. In a split second, I took in his dark wash jeans and gray T-shirt with a camel-colored jacket. As my eyes rose to study his face and his longish, somewhat disheveled hair, my mouth fell open. I turned to stare.

"Hello, there," he said in that exquisite British cadence, his freckled face breaking into a smile so familiar I almost teared up at the sight. He rose to his feet and came to sit at my side in Lily's vacated chair. His eyes crinkled at the corner as he held out a hand. "William Hunter, Special Agent, FBI. It's lovely to meet you . . . again."

I felt my mouth tremble as I blinked rapidly, trying to accept the sight of him, there, in front of me. At last.

"Is it over?" I asked, my voice quivering slightly.

"It's over," he confirmed, leaning forward and bracing his elbows on his knees. He took my hand in his, studying it for a moment, and then raised it to his lips. His eyes closed as he held it to his face, seeming to breathe in my scent. And then he kissed it again and again. I felt him take a deep, shuddering breath of release into my skin. "It's over," he said again.

And without warning, he stood and pulled me into his arms, crushing me to him. I inhaled deeply, drawing in his presence, my cheek finding that familiar spot against his chest.

"I missed you terribly," he said, lowering his lips into my hair. "Every day."

I nodded, not trusting myself to speak, and I clutched the front of his shirt tightly in my fist, attempting to pull him closer.

We stood like that for several minutes, Will's hand sliding up and down my back, over my shoulder and down my arm. The warmth in my chest that had been missing since he left over a year ago was back, pulsing brightly. I could breathe again, but I still felt dazed. Light-headed.

"How did you know where I was?" I asked, looking up at him.

"I texted Lily," Will answered with a smile. "She told me where to find you and then graciously departed to give us some time alone."

I nodded as I numbly took in the answer. "What happened?" I finally pressed. "When did the trial end?"

"This morning," he replied. He picked up my purse from where it lay on the ground by my chair and handed it to me. Then, his arm around my shoulders, he began to lead me toward the sidewalk. "Guilty. Wolfe was sentenced to fifteen years in prison and a two-million-dollar fine."

"Is that what you wanted?" I asked curiously.

"It will do," Will replied, smiling down at me. We walked down 42nd Street toward the New York Public Library, the crowds blurring around us. We only saw each other.

When we got to the corner of 42nd and 5th, Will halted, pulling me to a stop beside him. He slid his arm down to grasp my hand, but didn't meet my eyes as he mulled over the words he wanted to say.

"I'm sorry. I told myself I would wait, but I need to know," he finally asked, somewhat hesitantly. He seemed to be afraid to look at me, choosing instead to study the sidewalk, one hand in his pocket. "Has it been too long? Have you moved on?"

I watched the uncertainty flit across his face and my heart warmed even further at this betrayal of vulnerability. "William Hunter," I said, and he looked up at me, eyes wide. "You said once that you'd been chasing me steadily for an entire year and you were exhausted." I smiled wider at the memory. He smiled in unison and nodded slowly. "Well, you should know that I consider myself completely and thoroughly caught," I informed him. "I'm all yours, no more chasing necessary."

And with that, I reached up and ran my fingers through the thick strands of his hair, something I had always wanted to do. Sliding my fingers softly down the side of his face, I brushed my thumb across his lips. His eyes closed and I felt his breathing accelerate under my fingertip.

And there, with New York pulsing its steady beat around us, I pulled him close, never intending to let go.

The End

Acknowledgments

It really took a village to write this book. I'm so grateful to everyone who helped in my research . . . it was a huge undertaking.

Specifically, I'd like to thank my fabulous and oh-so-handsome Wall Street investment banker cousins, James and Jordan, my incredible New York colleagues who answered my endless questions about the city (I'm lookin' at you, Ivan, Brooke, Maura, Shanta, and Ben), the lovely ladies of the Taylorsville Fourth Ward who inspired me with their amazing imaginations, and of course, my usual little band of supporters (which consists of all my sweet family and in-laws, but special mentions go to Ali, Emily, Lauren, Mom, Dad, and my favorite person in the entire world and the reason I manage to hang on to my sanity—Bryan).

Thank you all so much for your continued enabling of my writing habit. I would be forever lost without all of you.

About the Author

Lauren Winder Farnsworth was born and raised in Salt Lake City, Utah. She is an avid reader, a chocolate enthusiast, and a CPA with a slight alternative music obsession and dreams of one day becoming a gourmet chef.

She obtained bachelor's and master's degrees in accounting from the University of Utah, went to work as a financial statement auditor, and then decided that since creative accounting wasn't an option, creative writing would have to do. As a nice compromise, accountants tend to crop up in her stories (as she firmly believes they're underutilized in literature anyway).

Having obtained two degrees from the same institution has made Lauren somewhat of a compound collegiate fan, and the only entity that holds more of her heart than the University of Utah is her hunky husband, Bryan. Lauren currently lives in South Jordan, Utah, where she spends entirely too much time watching *Gilmore Girls* and looking for excuses not to clean.

Lauren loves to hear from her readers! You can reach her at www.laurenwinderfarnsworth.com.

SCAN TO VISIT

LAURENWINDERFARNSWORTH.COM